PRAISE

CAROLINE B. COONEY

PRAISE FOR *BEFORE SHE WAS HELEN*

"[M]ore Columbo than Miss Marple... A fine mystery."
—*Booklist*

"Caroline B. Cooney is a master of taking a small, common moment—seeing a face on a milk carton, posting a harmless photo—and turning that moment into a thrilling story. In this mystery, Cooney gives us Clemmie, a senior citizen living a long deception, who fights back with intelligence and courage against dangerous foes, both present and past. *Before She Was Helen* is an emotionally rich page-turner about the lives we want—and the lives we make."
—Jeff Abbott, *New York Times* bestselling author of *Never Ask Me*

"As *Before She Was Helen* opens, readers are drawn into what appears to be a light, retirement-community caper. But author Caroline B. Cooney quickly flips expectations upside down in this deceptively dark mystery. Between old crimes and fresh murders, septuagenarian protagonist Clemmie faces an unspeakable fear that will keep readers hooked in this twisty whodunit."
—Julie Hyzy, *New York Times* bestselling author

"Caroline B. Cooney has a genius for skewering culture, crime, and society. As once she demonstrated to the world a pressing level of danger we needed to understand, now she whips millennial angst, recreational drug use, and one feisty, heroic retiree into a thrilling, toxic brew that will leave readers cheering by the end. Retirement villages never seemed so mysterious and exciting! Under Cooney's

deft hand, hidden dangers emerge, and the ties that bind us, young and old, just may save us in the end."
—Jenny Milchman, *USA Today* bestselling author of *Cover of Snow* and *Wicked River*

"Caroline B. Cooney's *Before She Was Helen* is a clever whodunit featuring an immensely likable septuagenarian heroine with a tragic past. Cooney is deft at weaving together the mysteries of a fifty-year-old cold case murder and a still-warm body at a retirement community, slowly unveiling a slew of possible motives and suspects for both crimes. Loaded with action, fast-paced, and offering a series of emotional punches, this book will leave mystery lovers wanting more."
—Carter Wilson, *USA Today* bestselling author of *The Dead Girl in 2A* and *Mister Tender's Girl*

PRAISE FOR *THE FACE ON THE MILK CARTON*

"Absorbing and convincing. Strong characterizations and suspenseful, impeccably paced action add to this novel's appeal."
—*Publishers Weekly*

"A real page-turner."
—*Kirkus Reviews*

"It's a gripper. You can't put it down until you've gone through the whole trauma with Janie Johnson, from that first moment of horrified recognition to the thoroughly satisfying conclusion."
—*Entertainment Weekly*

PRAISE FOR *THE RANSOM OF MERCY CARTER*

"Gripping and thought provoking."

—Publishers Weekly

PRAISE FOR *WHATEVER HAPPENED TO JANIE?*

"The power and nature of love is wrenchingly illustrated through-out this provocative novel... The emotions of its characters remain excruciatingly real."

—Publishers Weekly, Starred Review

"The gut-wrenching circumstances in which the characters find themselves are honestly conveyed."

—Booklist

PRAISE FOR *THE VOICE ON THE RADIO*

"Cooney's outstanding command of emotional tension has taken this novel to extraordinary heights."

—School Library Journal, Starred Review

PRAISE FOR *TWINS*

"[A] thriller master."

—Publishers Weekly

PRAISE FOR *NO SUCH PERSON*

"Full of twists and turns...has all the elements that keep young mystery lovers coming back for more."

—School Library Journal

"No one writes suspense like Cooney. Haunting, harrowing...hard to put down."

—*Kirkus Reviews*

"Cleverly plotted...rooted in suspense...fully satisfying. Mystery fans will be delighted."

—*Booklist*

"Jangling suspense juxtaposed with cozy details of family life keeps thriller master Cooney's latest zooming along."

—*Publishers Weekly*, Starred Review

"Cooney has hit it out of the ballpark yet again. A must read."

—*VOYA*

PRAISE FOR *DRIVER'S ED*

"As convincing as it is believable."

—*Publishers Weekly*, Starred Review

PRAISE FOR *DIAMONDS IN THE SHADOW*

"Crackling language and nail-biting cliffhangers provide an easy way into the novel's big ideas, transforming topics that can often seem distant and abstract into a grippingly immediate reading experience."

—*Publishers Weekly*, Starred Review

PRAISE FOR *HIT THE ROAD*

"Cooney masterfully combines nonstop, cleverly plotted action with heartfelt emotion."

—*Booklist*, Starred Review

"An unexpected, touching, and effective sojourn from the always entertaining Cooney."

—*Kirkus Reviews*

PRAISE FOR *REAR-VIEW MIRROR*

"So tightly written, so fast-moving, that it's easy not to realize until the last paragraph is over that one hasn't been breathing all the while."

—*Washington Post*

PRAISE FOR *A FRIEND AT MIDNIGHT*

"Brimming with realistic characters, unexpected twists, and heart-warming redemptions, this is a superior read!"

—Melody Carlson, award-winning author

"Wrathful, courageous, resourceful, loving, and even occasionally light-hearted..."

—*Publishers Weekly*, Starred Review

PRAISE FOR *FAMILY REUNION*:

"Cooney's gifts for humor and characterization are well blended here."

—*Kirkus Reviews*

PRAISE FOR *IF THE WITNESS LIED*

"...a nerve-jangling, disquieting read."

—*LA Times*

Also by Caroline B. Cooney

THE GRANDMOTHER PLOT

CAROLINE B. COONEY

Poisoned Pen
PRESS

Published by Poisoned Pen Press, an imprint of Sourcebooks
P.O. Box 4410, Naperville, Illinois 60567-4410
(630) 961-3900
sourcebooks.com

Library of Congress Cataloging-in-Publication Data

Names: Cooney, Caroline B., author.
Title: The grandmother plot / Caroline B Cooney.
Description: Naperville, Illinois : Poisoned Pen Press, 2021. | Summary:
  "Freddy leads a life of little responsibility, following his own
  meandering path. His only real attachment is to his memory-challenged
  grandmother, whose nursing home he regularly visits. His far-flung
  sisters may belittle his artistic ambitions, and his grandmother only
  occasionally knows who he is, but he can go with the flow. When another
  nursing home resident is murdered, though, Freddy panics. He can't take
  care of his grandmother alone, and a hiccup in his less-than-legal side
  business is causing extra complications-complications that could be
  deadly. To stay safe, he'll have to straighten up and face the music"--
  Provided by publisher.
Identifiers: LCCN 2020033191 (print) | LCCN 2020033192
  (ebook) | (trade paperback) | (epub) | (pdf)
Subjects: GSAFD: Mystery fiction
Classification: LCC PS3553.O578 G73 2021 (print) | LCC PS3553.O578
  (ebook) | DDC 813/.54--dc23
LC record available at https://lccn.loc.gov/2020033191
LC ebook record available at https://lccn.loc.gov/2020033192

Printed and bound in the United States of America.
VP 10 9 8 7 6 5 4 3 2 1

for my own Freddy,
and in honor of my mother,
Martha Bruce,
who faced her fate so bravely,
and with her beautiful smile

TUESDAY

ONE

Freddy rode his bike instead of taking his grandmother's old Avalon or his grandfather's old pickup. He raced happily up narrow back roads wrapped in old stone walls and took the sharp curves at high speed. For nine miles, orange and red leaves drifted down on his shoulders and spun under the tires. Great trip. The destination—not so much. He was headed to Middletown Memory Care, an institution that was not in fact caring for memories. They were caring for people who had once had memories and would never find them again.

In a vehicle, he'd arrive at MMC from Route 9, but bikes weren't allowed on the divided highway. He ended up west of MMC in a neighborhood of tiny old houses, cramped lots, and street parking on short one-way roads. The houses favored fencing, and there were chain link and white picket, bamboo and cast iron—everybody safely tucked into their little kingdom. Each garage was a separate little building in the backyard. Freddy entertained himself by planning how to convert the garages into glassblowing studios.

Ahead of him was a four-way stop. Freddy was pretty casual about stop signs, on the theory that they didn't apply to bikes, but he did slow down.

Coming from the right, braking for the stop sign, was a white Toyota Corolla. The driver's window was down and his elbow halfway out of the car. He was looking straight ahead and had not glanced in Freddy's direction.

The profile was unmistakable.

It was Doc.

Doc?

He was supposed to be in Vegas. What was he doing in a plain little city in Connecticut?

He's not going to kneecap me, Freddy told himself. It's not as if I owe money. I just push paper.

Still.

Freddy swerved into the first driveway on his right, hoping for a fence-free escape route. The house sat close to the street, and almost immediately, it protected him from view. There was fencing, but just six-foot chain link to keep a dog in. The dog raced back and forth, barking. Freddy rode between shrubs into the yard directly behind. Here, a vegetable garden was fenced but not the driveway, so he zipped down it and came safely out on the parallel street.

He turned left to emerge behind the Toyota and get a second look at the driver.

The intersection was empty.

Either Freddy had conjured Doc out of thin air or Doc had driven on.

Freddy zigzagged uphill to the low brick buildings of MMC. He locked his bike behind the stinking dumpster and the row of massive, never-pruned rhododendrons, where it couldn't be seen from the road or the parking lot. He did this a lot because he liked alleys but now on the remote chance that Doc really was out there. Doc was not a guy you wanted in your life. He'd been in medical school years ago and got caught with marijuana in his book bag, back when possession was a crime and not a recreational puff. He ended up with a jail sentence instead of an MD.

Doc was furious and bitter every hour of every day. Society had screwed him because of a handful of dried-up flowers, turned him into a felon with a record because back, then the world didn't rank marijuana the same as coffee or cigarettes. Doc's hobby these days was mixed martial arts, a violent, full-combat sport popular in certain pipe circles. It had not siphoned off his anger.

Freddy went in through the employees' entrance, which was supposed to be locked. In good weather, though, they propped it open for fresh air, which was in short supply in a place that smelled of cleaning fluids and old bodies. He preferred to skip the front desk, because they liked you to sign in, and Freddy was opposed to any kind of regimentation.

Two aides were heading for the staff room.

"Hey, Grace," he said. "Hey, Mary Lou." Grace was short and squat, wore her hair in a crew cut, and today sported filigree earrings dangling to her shoulders. Mary Lou was slender and pretty but always smiled carefully, embarrassed by missing teeth. She was saving up for dental work. They both had circles under their eyes.

He told them how beautiful they were, because it boggled Freddy's mind that anybody would actually do this for a living, and the women *were* beautiful in his eyes, no matter how overweight or underweight, no matter how tired or bedraggled. They didn't yell at him for coming through the employees' entrance because he was the only young man who visited and they loved him for it.

Grace and Mary Lou were on break or they wouldn't be in this part of the building. Listen, if he worked here, Freddy would be "on break" the whole shift. He headed to the locked door that led to the residence wings and tapped in the code that opened the door.

He walked through the big common room full of aides, dining tables, sitting areas, visitors, and residents. He didn't see Mrs. Maple, who generally visited her aunt Polly the same time he was visiting Grandma. That was too bad, because Mrs. Maple was his first line of defense against the horror of dementia visits.

In Grandma's wing, Jade was working. She was a few years older than Freddy, and why she didn't get a restaurant job or a grocery-store job or anything at all except taking care of his incontinent grandmother, Freddy didn't know. He asked once and she was surprised. "I like this," she said and didn't seem to be lying.

"Hi, Jade," said Freddy.

"Miss Cordelia doin' well today," said Jade.

"Hey! Great news," said Freddy. Except that Grandma doing well simply meant she'd had lunch.

Freddy found his grandmother in her little room, where the single shelf held photographs of the husband she no longer remembered. Jade had dressed her with care in a pale-yellow sweater, a soft gray skirt, and a necklace of Freddy's glass beads that his ex-girlfriend, Cynthia, had strung together. The color range was apricot apple, using an early swirl technique that Freddy would execute a lot better if he were making it today.

"Hey, Grandma," said Freddy. He knelt down in front of her so she'd see who was talking.

Her face lit up, which meant she knew him, and Freddy felt his own face going happy. She said, "Arthur!" in that eager, breathy voice.

Freddy took her hand. It was frighteningly thin, toothpick bones draped in saggy skin. She no longer had any grip, so it was like a piece of paper resting inside his own callused, burned, hard palm. Right up until last week, his grandmother could remember his name, and then last week, she said, "Arthur, dear, did you have a good lunch?" Arthur was Grandma's son. Died in Vietnam, so long ago Freddy couldn't even remember the decade, but Arthur's death was burned in Grandma's soul.

Freddy didn't mind being Arthur. At least she knew he was family.

The activity director scurried up. Heidi's amazing enthusiasm penetrated even the most comatose dementia patients. "Freddy! Yay! Marvelous to see you! We're playing ball! Let's you two join us!"

Playing ball when you were deep in dementia involved using a foam noodle, like for a swimming pool, as a bat. You whacked at a heavy-duty balloon, generally bright red, so that even a really vague person could spot it. Half the residents were too vague even for that and just sat there. Half really got into it, whapping the balloon across the room to another patient, who would not notice or else swing hard but miss. Heidi would cheer, "Go, Edna! Yes, Herbert! Thatta girl, Betty!"

Respectively, Edna, Herbert, and Betty had been a history teacher, a civil engineer, and a bank executive. What had Grandma been, exactly? She had never held a job, never had that thing called a career. The list of her achievements was homely: typing up the stencil for the church bulletin and running the mimeograph machine; chair of the church fair for decades, every year stitching up a couple dozen aprons to sell, each with pockets and bibs and matching pot holders. She'd been on the library board for half a century, writing the newsletter and running the summer reading clubs. She had played pinochle and euchre and cherished her perennial garden.

She didn't remember any of it.

"Thanks, Heidi," said Freddy, suppressing a shudder at the thought of dementia ball. "You're awesome, but I think we'll go for a spin." He pushed Grandma's wheelchair through the common room to the locked exit, tapped in the code, and out they went.

At first, Grandma had asked about that code. "Where do you get it, Freddy?"

"I'll find out for you," Freddy would say. "Now let's put this scarf on because it's chilly. You look great in that scarf, Grandma." And they would be through the door and she would have forgotten about codes.

Middletown Memory Care was a lockup because a large fraction of its residents spent all day trying to leave. The deep anxiety that ruled so many dementia patients meant they wanted only one thing: out. They didn't know much, but they always knew this wasn't the life they used to lead.

A large fraction of families never took their loved one on a drive or out for dinner because they'd never be able to shovel them back in.

Freddy and Grandma arrived in the sunshine. Since his grand-mother always forgot that the outside even existed, it thrilled her. "It's so nice out!" she cried.

Listen, it was nice to be outside Memory Care no matter what the weather was.

Freddy sucked in fresh, uncaged air and said hi to Kenneth Yardley, who was just arriving. Mr. Yardley visited his wife, Maude, a lot. He fed her lunch, brushed her teeth, put her down for a nap, read out loud to her. If Maude knew her husband was around, she didn't show it.

It's strange to love somebody who is not all there, which was Freddy's lot.

It's strange to love somebody who does not know you, which was true for a good percentage of MMC residents.

It is strangest of all to love somebody who will not know or care if you ever show up again, and that was Kenneth Yardley's situation.

Mr. Yardley gave Freddy a distracted, desperate smile. He fumbled around trying to find the doorknob. This was not a good sign, because the street door was normal. Freddy had a bad feeling Maude was going to get a roommate in here before long. He waited till Mr. Yardley found his way in and then pushed Grandma down the sidewalk to a gate in the big iron fence.

"I don't like him," said his grandmother. "He's a meany beany."

Freddy was startled. Grandma's lifelong rule was to like every-body, and if she didn't like the person, she certainly never said so out loud. "Mr. Yardley?" he asked.

"I don't know who he is," said Grandma, who did not recognize her own daily aides. "But that little girl? He's mean to her."

Freddy pondered this information. There were no little girls around here. Maude was the same size as Grandma, though: down to maybe a hundred pounds with a lot of white hair that was no longer possible to brush or comb but just did its weird electric-outlet thing. Maybe Maude looked like an elementary school child to a ninety-three-year-old. Or maybe Grandma had some other little girl in mind, was thinking of all the little girls she had known over nine decades.

"He's a good guy," said Freddy. "He comes most days."

"Who does?" asked his grandmother.

"Mr. Yardley."

"Is that a friend of yours, Arthur?"

Freddy decided not to pursue this conversation. He lifted the gate bolt, too high up and too stiff for a resident to manage, even if the resident escaped the unit. They followed a paved sidewalk that wound slowly downhill toward the same neighborhood he'd just ridden through.

Sometimes he pointed out dogs and bikes and flowers to his grandmother, and after much direction, she might actually spot them. She loved airplanes and cried out with pleasure if she followed his pointing finger and actually saw a little silver streak in the sky. Once, she confided to him, "It must really be bigger than that."

Now she asked, "Where is Alice?"

Alice was Freddy's mother. She'd been killed in an accident last year. "Alice is in France," Freddy lied. Grandma had attended her daughter's funeral, but she had forgotten. Freddy usually went with the France excuse, and because his mother had loved France, visiting some region every year, he could pretend it was true. He certainly wished it was true. "You lived in France once, Grandma."

Grandma was puzzled. Freddy didn't know if she couldn't remember taking her year abroad in France or couldn't remember France in general.

Now they were among the little old homes wrapped in old-fashioned shrubs like lilac next to old-fashioned front porches. Freddy was currently camping in Grandma's house, which was seriously old-fashioned, like a history museum for a curator who was never coming back. He'd turned the entire lower level into a glass studio. Everything he was doing in his life was a trespass on his grandparents, but especially smoking weed in the room where his anti-alcohol, anti-tobacco, anti-swearing grandpa had watched baseball and worked on his model trains.

Grandma said in a panicky voice, "Arthur?"

He circled the chair and stooped beside her again. "It's me, Freddy," he said softly. "Everything's okay, Grandma."

He often made this ridiculous claim. Sometimes Grandma called him on it. "What's okay, Freddy?" she would ask, as if she expected a list, since certainly *she* didn't know of anything okay. But today his answer soothed her.

He picked up an especially bright-red leaf and gave it to her. She took it wonderingly, as if it held secrets.

There at the corner, maybe twenty or thirty yards away, sat the white Toyota Corolla, as if it had never moved but had been waiting patiently, knowing that Freddy, with his stoner brain and lousy short-term memory, would be back.

No, Freddy told himself, white sedans are generic. It's a different one. It can't be Doc. I need it not to be Doc.

It was going the opposite direction from before, so now the passenger side was closer to Freddy. The front-seat passenger rolled down his window and leaned out. He was young, probably not out of his teens, and skinny, with pale hair pulled into a ponytail dry as dead grass.

"Hey, Freddy," he shouted, his voice a playground taunt. *Gotcha!* Freddy had never seen him before.

The driver shoved the kid out of his way and thrust his immense torso toward the window. Doc.

Freddy had a well-developed sense of fear, but since moving to Connecticut to take care of his grandmother, he had shelved it, convinced of his invisibility. After all, he had the same cell phone number from when he lived in Evanston, so no one in glass could know that he had moved across the country to his grandmother's house. Grandpa had been dead for ten years, but bills and taxes were still in Vincent Chase's name, while Freddy's last name was Bell. Freddy had a Facebook site and Instagram and hundreds of followers, but he talked only of glass. He certainly never mentioned his grandmother.

Even after the Leper's last phone call—Freddy still saying no when the only answer the Lep accepted from anybody was yes— Freddy had not been worried, let alone afraid. The Lep even texted him a photograph of Doc, stripped from the waist up, all muscle, tattoo, and scar.

He's coming, said the caption.

Freddy just laughed. They couldn't find him.

But here was Doc. Not just in Connecticut but in Middletown, where Freddy *didn't* live, and nobody could have suspected his presence in this neighborhood.

"Arthur?" said Grandma anxiously.

He really had to cut back on weed. He was not thinking at all today, never mind thinking straight. He had been caught with the most vulnerable person in his life. The person he loved most, even though most of the person had evaporated, and the most dangerous man he knew was looking straight at her.

Bad enough Doc had seen Freddy pushing a wheelchair. He couldn't let Doc figure out that it was his own helpless grandmother, living a quarter mile away.

Freddy mentally mapped the maze of short one-way streets. The Toyota could not turn down the street where he and Grandma had paused. At least not legally. But Freddy didn't care about stuff like that. Why would Doc?

One good thing. The intersection had now filled with other cars who were getting impatient. Freddy could go down a one-way street where Doc couldn't follow, but he could push a wheelchair only so fast. The sidewalks weren't great. There were dips and cracks. The slightest jolt could tip his grandmother out. She might even fall face-first because among all the other essential skills lost in dementia was the ability to protect yourself from a fall. And bizarrely, wheelchairs had no seat belts, because in the institutional world, they were considered cruel restraints.

Freddy's glass specialty—lampwork—involved holding rods in front of his body for hours at a time, so Freddy was very strong. He could easily lower and lift the wheelchair at curbs. But what he couldn't do was gather speed.

He could carry Grandma, abandoning the wheelchair, and cut through yards the way he had with the bike. But then he'd really be helpless, both arms holding a very fragile package. And the wheelchair had Grandma's name and room number on the back. He couldn't leave it for Doc to read up on Cordelia Chase.

The car behind Doc honked.

"Stay put, Freddy," yelled Doc. He drove through the intersection, presumably planning to go around the block and come up next to Freddy.

The basic white Corolla had to be a rental because no model could be less suitable for Doc's personality. Freddy was kind of amazed it fit Doc's body. He couldn't fathom that the Leper, who was in Vegas, would fly Doc and some other guy to Connecticut and send them to little old Middletown, of all places, to drive around on the off chance they'd spot Freddy.

The Toyota's passenger window was still down. The skinny teenager mimed a gunshot with his thumb and first finger.

What was that about? This was weed they were talking about, not coke.

Doc wouldn't be armed, because guys who got into mixed martial arts prided themselves on doing violence without a weapon. But the kid? What was with the hand gesture? Did *he* have a gun?

On the other hand, this *was* about money. Lots of money.

The weed world had changed dramatically when many states legalized it. You mostly didn't face jail for smoking weed now, but vast amounts of money were still changing hands, and everybody

wanted some. States that had legalized weed strutted around claim-
ing they now had control over growers, because only a select handful
were allowed a permit. They were all proud that instead of dealers,
their state had distributors.

Like a different vocabulary was going to change anything.

What did they think all the growers who *didn't* get a permit
would do? Become dental hygienists?

Every one of them was still growing and still dealing, and for
them, it was still criminal, still lucrative, and still roped in stupid
guys like Freddy. None of them paid taxes. Their own personal mil-
lions were still kept away from the IRS and out of sight.

Freddy had just dramatically failed the "out of sight" test.

He had to get Grandma to safety. He hustled down the street
Doc had just left, turned up yet another one-way street because it
was his only option, and there was Mrs. Maple in her fire-engine-
red Cadillac SRX, headed for Middletown Memory Care.

Freddy waved wildly.

She stopped and put her window down. "Mapes!" he yelled.
"We need a ride back!" He bumped the wheelchair down the curb,
she clicked the door locks, and Freddy ripped open the passenger
door. "Hey, Mapes. Emergency. Gotta be quick here."

"Shall I call 911?" she asked, enunciating so carefully Freddy
could practically see the punctuation hanging in the air.

Freddy could not get Grandma and the wheelchair into the car
in two seconds, plus take advantage of Mapes thinking this was a
medical emergency and also come up with a lie that kept it an emergency but prevented her from calling 911. "Not that serious."

Once you were dealing with dementia, any activity was kind of
like getting a two-year-old into a snowsuit, which he had witnessed
the winter he visited his sister Kara and her kids in South Dakota.
They can't find the armholes, and you finally get them zipped and
into their boots and mittens and hats and out the door and then they
have to come back inside and go potty.

Grandma had to have instructions every single time she got in or out of a vehicle, so Freddy skipped that, picked her up, lifted her into the front seat, and slammed the door.

Mrs. Maple popped the trunk. Freddy removed the wheelchair footrests, tossed them into the trunk, folded the wheelchair, lifted it in, pressed the close button on the hatch, waved thank you to the courteously stopped traffic, leaped into the back seat, and slumped down. "You're a champ, Mapes."

Had the Toyota caught up? Had Doc guessed the correct turns and made them fast enough? Had Doc seen him load Grandma into this car?

Freddy wouldn't know the answers unless he looked, but if he looked, they might spot him. So he didn't look. Ignorance could be dangerous but it was always restful.

"Is she having trouble breathing?" demanded Mrs. Maple.

"No, no. She's having diarrhea."

"On my front seat?" wailed Mrs. Maple. "Oh well, it's leather. We can clean it up. I don't smell anything, though, Freddy."

"Awesome. False alarm."

Two

All morning, Laura Maple had been dancing with excitement. After years of daydreaming, she was finally getting her own practice pipe organ.

It was the height of self-indulgence, since the Congregational church and its fine organ were just a few blocks away. Laura could stroll over anytime. In fact, she could practice in lots of churches, because she'd subbed as organist all over the shoreline. She always requested a key to the church because every organ was different, and you wanted to prepare on the actual instrument you'd play on Sunday. They always gave her a key and never asked for it back. Should she ever be in need of ecclesiastical silver, Laura could anonymously enter any church anytime.

But she wanted her own organ so she could learn all six Bach Trio Sonatas at last. It would take years, because her fingers and feet weren't as limber as they had been, not to mention her brain.

Howard, the organ tech, looked around the sprawling high-ceilinged great room next to the kitchen and grimaced. "I need a little guidance on what to do with your stuff."

The pipe organ would join two grand pianos, a harpsichord, a Victorian parlor pump organ, a keyboard, and a collection of smashed brass. One grand was an old mahogany Steinway, and in its curve was parked her beloved Chickering. The harpsichord Laura had built from a kit in the 1970s when musicians did that kind of thing, even though everybody despises harpsichords because they have to be tuned every five minutes. The parlor pump organ was walnut, with high, elaborate shelves and ornate molding. Laura sometimes played it for exercise on rainy days because pumping with her feet was a true workout.

"Just shove them into corners," said Laura.

"There's a limit to what we can accomplish, shoving-wise. Maybe you could trade in the grand pianos and get uprights," Howard suggested.

Laura did not dignify this with a response.

No one else in her four-hand club or even her two-piano club had two pianos. They met here. The rule was, you could never practice; you had to sight-read. Since much of the music was difficult, even for Laura, there was a lot of faking, blaming, and laughter. They had agreed that nobody could die or move away, because they had no replacements.

Upright pianos had no cachet.

Not that her grands currently had any cachet. They had been shrink-wrapped to protect them from the dust of organ installation, and they looked silly. The organ console wasn't here yet, but the room was filled with pipe crates, massive as coffins and one of them big enough for a yeti. Even a small organ needed a lot of pipes. Luckily, her great room had a soaring ceiling.

Laura's house was set up so that the front door was usually ignored; it was the back door with its decorative portico over the driveway that drew people in. The back hall was quite lovely, connected to the great room with a wide arch. "Let's roll the pianos over and block the arch opening," said Laura. "I can go back and forth through the kitchen."

"But if there's a fire, you'd have only one way out," said Marco, Howard's assistant, "and plus, you don't want your musician buddies traipsing through the kitchen every time they come. You're going to have a grand room and you want a grand entrance."

Laura loved the idea of a grand room, although more likely, it would just look eccentric. She reminded herself that she didn't care what other people thought, although nobody *really* felt that way; everybody really cared a lot.

Marco said, "How about we move the parlor organ into the parlor and put the harpsichord in your upstairs hall?"

Laura did have a small front living room, which was handy because there was no seating in the great room unless you liked piano benches. But if she moved the pump organ into the parlor, the sofa might have to go. The house needed some semblance of normalcy.

"We can try," she said doubtfully.

Howard and Marco had the harpsichord relocated in a minute and, after unscrewing the taller finials, effortlessly moved the pump organ on sliders. They shifted Laura's little sofa under the window, giving the inside wall to the pump organ, where its intricate walnut carvings rose dramatically against the white paint.

Laura clapped. "It really *is* a parlor now!"

In the great room, they shifted one grand under her shelf of smashed brass. Laura had found her first smashed bugle many years ago in an antique shop, looking as if an elephant had stepped on it. Not long after that, she found a trombone bent in half. She'd spent decades with her eyes peeled for ruined brass instruments.

The other grand blocked the arch for now, but once the pipe crates were gone, the two pianos could return to their original position. Everybody was happy.

Laura left Howard and Marco to do their thing and set out for Middletown. She loved Route 9, which sliced through Connecticut River Valley hills, its rock cuts weathered to great jagged slabs of brown jewelry. White steeples peeked out from trees hot with fall color.

But there was nothing like a visit to Middletown Memory Care to make the heart sink. Her aunt Polly's memories were few. It was Laura saddled with memory.

The pipe organ was just another time filler, just another, albeit very expensive, way to think about anything except what mattered.

She hoped Freddy would also be at MMC. Such a sweet boy, and so attentive to his grandmother.

He never called her Laura and had only once called her Mrs. Maple. He usually said "Mapes" or "Tree Lady." The silly, affectionate nicknames felt like junior high to Laura, but Freddy didn't even know what junior high was, because they were middle schools by the time he was old enough to attend, and anyway, she was pretty sure he used the nicknames for distance rather than closeness.

When she got off Route 9, Laura wandered among teeny houses shaded by huge trees, pretending she lived in one and her life was perfect. Clapboard siding on a house, hanging baskets on a porch, a child and a puppy behind the white picket fence—these people had no problems. These people had always done the right thing.

Laura's biggest sin was no secret, and yet nobody ever commented. Maybe it didn't seem like a sin to them. Maybe Laura herself was so insignificant that her actions, right or wrong, failed to register. Or maybe time diluted sin, and what had once been deeply wrong was now just background.

She turned up the volume on the classical music station so she could drown in chords instead of heartache, and suddenly there was Freddy on the side of the street, flagging her down.

Sometimes Laura thought that things were "meant" and some power guided you to be in the right place at the right time, like now. But more often, you were in the wrong place at the wrong time. So what did that mean?

Almost before Laura knew what was happening, Freddy popped his grandmother into the front seat where the poor, sweet old lady looked around in panic. *What's this chair? Who's this stranger?*

"Mrs. Chase, how pretty you look," said Laura, knowing that Cordelia Chase would not recognize her although they'd said hello a hundred times. She smoothed Cordelia's snow-white hair and fastened the seat belt carefully around her. Dementia having taken Cordelia's appetite as well as her mind, she was a wisp of a person now. "You and Freddy went for a walk, didn't you, Mrs. Chase? Such a nice fall day."

Cordelia Chase regarded her uncertainly. "Alice?"

Laura was tempted to say yes. There were so few gifts you could give a dementia patient. If she said, *Yes, I'm Alice*, Cordelia would be comforted, because what was better than your daughter visiting you? But even Laura, who had done her fair share of lying, could not pretend to be somebody's dead daughter.

Freddy leaped into the back seat and slouched down. Children these days had dreadful posture and Freddy led the pack. Or didn't lead, actually. If she'd ever dealt with a nonleader, it was Freddy. "Freddy, did you make this necklace your grandmother is wearing? It's just lovely."

"I make the beads," he reminded her. "Somebody else makes the necklaces."

THREE

Freddy had been selling those beads at the Milwaukee show where he first agreed to work for the Leper. Freddy had been in the game only a few years and was still astonished that it wasn't enough to *make* the glass; you had to *sell* it. He could lampwork around the clock and often did, but retail was crushing. You sold beads singly or in threes or fives or sevens, because odd numbers always looked better. Twenty dollars here, eleven dollars there, fifty dollars now and then. It added up so slowly.

His booth was one of hundreds filling a convention hall the size of an airport hangar and about as attractive. Everybody had a little square, marked off with aluminum poles, curtains, and skirts. Freddy couldn't believe he participated in anything requiring a skirt, let alone that the tablecloth had to be wrinkle-free. He now had a tablecloth *collection*, which somebody could blackmail him about.

It had been almost 10:00 a.m. that day, just prior to the opening bell. The last forklifts were trundling away and the final carpet sweeping was over. Food-booth smell was starting to kick in: Mexican, doughnuts, Chinese, popcorn.

Freddy had worked four months to produce enough beads for this show, and with luck, a third of it would sell. His beads were arranged in shallow velvet-lined boxes, which themselves were arranged in tiers and aisles, with Freddy's tiny cute signage for color and design. He wished the display didn't look so trinkety. He wanted it to be glamorous. More representative of the time, skill, and hope invested in it.

The five-minute warning came over the PA system, complete

with recorded trumpets and crazed applause. Jason, who sold kilns, torches, and safety glasses, had the adjacent booth. "Brace yourself, Freddy," he said. "Five thousand middle-aged overweight white ladies are about to charge."

That wasn't a completely fair demographic for beading, but close. Freddy loved these women, though, because they loved his glass, and glass was the core of his life. Freddy loved the torch, loved the techniques of each task. He especially loved anybody who wanted his glass enough to pay for it.

The doors opened.

Hundreds of women tromped in, intense and happy, like a victorious army or maybe gamblers, sure that this throw would win it all. Freddy had an excellent booth position, close to the entry so that almost everybody had to walk past.

That, of course, was the problem. Almost everybody did walk past. They wanted cheap beads: beads from China or India. For what Freddy charged for a single bead, they could buy a dozen strands from the third world. But it was a numbers game and Freddy just needed the cream: women who would *really* spend, for whom beading was not a hobby but a calling, or women who owned bead shops and wanted product to make their customers swoon.

The convention hall was even more of an airport now, people swirling and scurrying and meeting and buying and eating and looking for someplace, anyplace, to sit.

Time after time, a woman Freddy did not recognize hurried up to him, beaming, sure he would remember her from a fifteen-minute purchase last year. He would lope out from behind the exhibit. "Heyyyyyy," he'd say, stretching the greeting until he was close enough to read the name tag. "Sonya! Lookin' grand."

Some of the ladies wore necklaces of great drama and beauty. If the centerpiece was one of Freddy's beads, he'd photograph the woman on his cell and put the picture on Instagram and Facebook.

Women who loved beading really loved it. They made tons of

necklaces. Freddy always wondered what they did with them all. They only had one neck. Necklaces followed styles: one year, they were all glitter, and the next year, they would feature ropes of tiny beads, and the following spring, they would be more like collars.

He had a few customers who kicked ass and took names all day, and they wanted jewelry to match: bold, stern, and striking. These women invariably shopped the first morning of the convention and marched around stroking beads, looking for a personality match.

But no matter how intriguing the customer, the instant they left the booth, he forgot them because he had to fuss over the next set.

Freddy had been at a low point at that Milwaukee Bead and Button. He was straddling two glass worlds: beads because he wanted to be an artist and pipes for smoking weed because he wanted an income. There weren't enough hours to do both, he couldn't hone the technical skill for both, and he had to choose.

Cynthia, his girlfriend, who ought to have known all along that he had convention girlfriends, had expressed rage and hatred upon discovering that Freddy did not, in fact, save motel money by spending the night on the floor under his booth hidden by the table skirt but by sharing rooms with various bead ladies. Cynthia had wrecked enough of his studio back in Evanston that he had to earn serious money to replace it, and Freddy did not earn serious money.

He had found himself too broke to pay the fees for this very important show. Shows were hideously expensive. It took twelve, fourteen hours a day to create enough beads for three shows a year, but after he packed everything and had to pay a bag fee plus leave it with TSA baggage handlers and pray the airline didn't break all his product, shell out for plane fare, hotel, meals, and convention fees (which would make anybody homicidal—extra fees for electricity just so he could have a light bulb and the customer could actually *see* the beads?), he ended up with barely enough to buy a burrito.

He joked about this on the Instagram site where he sold pipes and within hours had a message from Gary Leperov offering to cover his costs. All the Lep asked in return was that both their names were on record for the booth.

Freddy was in awe of the Leper. They were the same age, and yet the Lep had accomplished a hundred times more. His marijuana rigs were collectible sculptures, astounding grotesque creations way beyond Freddy's skill set. Since his real name was Leperov, he chose the Leper as his glass name. Leprosy being a disease that involved the loss of toes, nose, or fingers, the Leper was famous for pendants that were dead, sloughed-off digits, ridiculously expensive for your basic stoner. He sold them on a hemp string to the hippie crowd and on a silver chain to the rich dudes. A pendant on a chain was a weed world statement.

The Leper's signature was that each glass pipe had small mangled feet. It was brilliant work, and also horrifying. People paid tons of money for a Leper pipe.

But Milwaukee was a bead show, not a pipe show, and there was no place for Gary Leperov's work, brilliant or not. So why would the Lep want his name on Freddy's booth?

But Freddy had forgotten he even had an agreement with the guy—because forgetting stuff came naturally to Freddy—until the second afternoon, when traffic was slower and Jason was covering Freddy's booth so he could grab a late lunch.

Freddy bumped into the Lep in the hall outside the show.

The Lep was wearing skateboard clothes: Toro cap on backward, a custom T-shirt from Sherbet, a glass pendant from Salt. It didn't tell the bead ladies anything, but it told Freddy everything. The Leper was not showing off his own stuff, but he was showing off. Freddy, comfortable in jeans and his favorite lucky sweatshirt, probably looked homeless and maybe even desperate next to Gary Leperov. He suddenly worried that his bead ladies were buying from pity.

The Lep nodded toward an up escalator and Freddy followed him to a level not currently in use, where they sat at a small table overlooking the chaos below. The Lep handed Freddy a paper bag that held an excellent lunch, way more delicious than Freddy could afford: a thick sourdough sandwich with hummus, ham, avocado, bacon, and tomatoes. He felt kind of important because the Leper had remembered Freddy's taste in sandwiches from back at the Vegas show, which was all pipes and no beads.

He wanted to eat slowly and enjoy every bite, but he couldn't make Jason watch his booth for too long, so he scarfed the sandwich down.

The Leper set a sheaf of papers on the table. "Sales receipts," he said, smiling.

"Huh?" said Freddy.

"I filled everything out. You just sign 'em."

Freddy was not fond of official forms. "What are they for?"

"Bead sales. You are some salesman, Freddy. You sold fifty thousand dollars' worth of my beads."

Freddy stared blankly. He would be lucky to sell a tenth of that. Besides, the Leper had not given him any beads to sell.

"This is a cash business, Freddy. You especially. You don't take credit cards, debit cards, or checks. You point your customers to the ATM outside the hall. And who's to say whether a bead sells for fifteen dollars or five hundred?"

Freddy couldn't chew, let alone swallow.

"This," said the Leper, adding a thick envelope to the pile of sales receipts, "is cash. You'll take the cash to the sales tax booth, because everything you do here is nice and legal, so of course you're paying sales tax on the beads you and your booth partner sold."

Freddy's mind crawled slowly toward understanding. Gary Leperov would now have fifty thousand dollars to declare as regular old taxable income from beads.

Sounded iffy, but the Lep had paid for Freddy's booth and his lunch, and Freddy couldn't see how this would hurt him or the world at large, and he couldn't leave Jason hanging much longer, so he agreed to fake a few sales for Gary Leperov.

FOUR

Laura let Freddy, the wheelchair, and Cordelia Chase out at the entrance, circled the visitor lot, and parked at the far edge where she was least likely to end up with a ding from some poorly parked vehicle. She loved her car. It was too large for her and over-the-top expensive, but she had seen that fire-engine red across the dealer lot, sparkling with a metallic finish, and she fell in love. Car love was a new experience for Laura. Usually she just thought of a car as wheels that sheltered her from the weather and could also play music. She loved to park her glittery scarlet SRX in her drive and admire her excellent taste from every window.

She walked across MMC's pretty little campus and into the big lobby, whose high ceiling reminded her of the pipe-organ installation in her own high-ceilinged room. She called Howard to be sure everything was going all right. Not that she really worried. If you couldn't trust a pipe-organ installer, who could you trust?

Then she signed in.

Freddy never signed in. Or out, for that matter. He said it offended his anarchist nature. Laura thought Freddy was pretty conformist, actually, but she would never have insulted him with that observation.

She caught up to him and bent over the wheelchair to tug his grandmother's skirt down. Cordelia Chase was the only female resident who did not wear pants, usually mail-order super-cheap double-knit elastic-waist pants that these women would not have been caught dead in when they were themselves but that easily went over their pull-ups. Cordelia had a fine wardrobe, all of it far too big now. She was still a lovely woman, though painfully frail. Her smile had remained intact, which was unusual. Dementia and Alzheimer's often collapsed normal facial expressions.

The locked entrance was problematic, because from the inside, Mr. Griffin was politely knocking, hoping to be let out, and they couldn't let that happen.

Mr. Griffin had been a patent attorney and he was dressed for work, because he was always, every hour of every day at Memory Care, on his way to the office. His adult children took his button-down collar shirts to the cleaner for heavy starch and endlessly scrubbed the jacket lapels on which he spilled every meal and even bought him new ties to wear and listened over and over to his worries about where he might have parked his car.

Mr. Griffin had not been allowed to drive for years.

Laura held Cordelia's wheelchair while Freddy unlocked the door and courteously took Mr. Griffin's arm. "Hey, Mr. Griffin. How are you today?"

"I'm very well, thank you," said Mr. Griffin. "I wonder if you could help me find my car keys. I've set them down somewhere and I can't locate them."

He and Freddy went down this path at least once a week. "Sure," said Freddy. He walked Mr. Griffin away from the door and down the interior hallway toward one of the other wings. It would take Mr. Griffin quite a while to navigate back to the exit. "The parking lot is that way," lied Freddy, patting the old man's shoulder.

"You're very kind," said Mr. Griffin gratefully.

Laura pushed Cordelia's wheelchair into the common room.

Nancy, daughter of Betty, came most afternoons and sat with Betty through wheelchair exercise or bingo for the no longer numerically literate. Today Betty was singing the same four measures over and over, "Don't sit under the apple tree with anybody else but me." Betty could no longer match pitch. Sometimes Laura thought the absolute worst part of Alzheimer's was that inborn abilities, like singing, came to a halt. It seemed so unfair that you could be musical from birth, but in your dotage, when you needed it most, it abandoned you.

Of course there were so many absolute worst parts to Alzheimer's that you couldn't really number them.

Big, broad-shouldered Philip, who usually swore steadily but quietly, was instead whacking his cane at the legs of passersby and shouting, "Get away from me! This is *my* desk!"

Anna-Rose, wife of poor Ned, whose mind had dissolved at fifty, was telling a new aide her husband's history. How Ned had once been an excellent tennis player, HR manager of a medium-sized corporation, and collector of antique tractors.

Will, husband of Irene, was watching his wife circle the room. Many residents were room-circlers. The only words Irene could still speak were numbers. "Fifty-six," she would tell Laura softly.

Kenneth Yardley swayed on the threshold of his wife's room. How many times had Laura watched Kenneth spoon pudding into his wife's mouth as Maude shuddered with palsy and failed to swallow? Today, poor Kenneth couldn't seem to go into Maude's room and couldn't seem to come out of it.

Aunt Polly was standing in the middle of this, unaware of anything, including Laura.

"It's a madhouse today," Laura said to Freddy.

"I think it's more like a séance. They're all trying to get in touch with their old selves."

Laura was very taken by that. She studied everyone again, but all she learned—by sniffing—was that Aunt Polly needed fresh underwear.

The first time Laura had to buy adult diapers for Polly, she drove to another town lest an acquaintance think she was buying those things for herself. Then she couldn't even find them at the store and had to ask for help. "We don't use the word 'diaper,'" said the clerk severely. "We stock maximum-absorbency underwear, tranquility pads, and protective briefs. Now, does she actually need diapers? Because they are an entirely different product from pull-ups."

Aunt Polly had been a gym teacher who loved sports, coached at a high school for decades, and passionately followed several pro teams. But Polly could no longer hold a fork, let alone a field hockey stick. Once, Laura went to considerable effort to take her to a softball game, since Polly had coached the girls for decades, and all Polly said was "I'm cold," so they went home.

Laura waved for help. She and Grace coaxed Polly into her bathroom. Laura played word games on her phone while poor Grace did the dirty work. Finally back in the common room with Polly, she was surprised to find Freddy still there. An hour was pretty much tops for Freddy, and he'd already taken his grandmother for a spin. Perhaps he needed to talk. Laura sat on a sofa, positioned Aunt Polly's wheelchair next to her, and patted the seat as an invitation to Freddy.

"I don't sit on anything upholstered," said Freddy. "You never know who was there before you or what bodily liquid might have soaked in." Freddy dragged over a metal and plastic chair from the dining room, gave it a careful inspection, and sat.

FIVE

Freddy had three older sisters, and people always asked why the sisters weren't caring for Grandma.

Sadly, the girls had good excuses.

Emma had married a forest ranger and lived in wonderful remote places Freddy loved to visit. Emma herself never visited anybody, because people came to her, and this was a good thing, because she would have gone berserk at the sight of her brother making drug paraphernalia in their grandmother's house. She and her husband had two kids Freddy adored, even after Emma told him to make something of himself so his niece and nephew could be proud of him.

Jenny had married an Australian, and they had a place in Sydney and a place in the Outback they referred to as their ranch, although it was only twenty acres and Freddy wasn't sure you could use the word "ranch" at the same time as the words "twenty acres." Freddy yearned to visit but had never gotten himself organized to buy a plane ticket, not to mention that he could hardly afford to fly to Albuquerque, let alone Sydney.

Kara was married to a UPS pilot based in South Dakota. Perhaps because her husband was always gone, Kara had many time-consuming and expensive hobbies. The big one was horses, and once you had a stable, you weren't going anywhere. Meanwhile, the kids were busy in 4-H, showing rabbits and horses and even chickens with feathers like ribbons, and Freddy would stare at their photographs on Facebook and wonder how Kara, brought up in suburban Connecticut, had even *thought* of this life, let alone created it.

With her daughters so far flung and too broke or too busy to show up in Connecticut, their mother had assigned *her* mother to Freddy. Every time Alice left the country, which was a lot, she'd call him. "Remember the deal, Freddy. If anything happens to me, you're responsible for your grandmother."

"Not to worry, Mom," he would say, paying no attention. Like, sure, whatever. Piece of cake.

Freddy loved his mother, but she was tiring and he was relieved when she was out of the country. Well, even *in* the country, he lived a thousand miles away from her, but he could feel her out there, disapproving of his lifestyle. That was what she called it, *lifestyle*, because discussing Freddy's actual profession was impossible for her, although you'd think a woman who went anywhere and did anything could say out loud what her son did for a living.

Not that Freddy usually said out loud what he did for a living either.

After Alice was killed in Peru, Freddy drove fourteen hours from Evanston every month to spend a long weekend with Grandma. He'd fix a screen door, repair the ancient dryer, have the old black-top driveway oiled, take her for a grocery run, whatever. Sunday mornings, of course, he took her to church.

The four Bell children had grown up going to church: Sunday school, youth group, helping in the nursery (his sisters), working dawn till dusk on Chore Saturday (Freddy). They had all lapsed. Freddy did not know what his sisters thought now about God or church except that the topics did not get featured on their Facebook profiles, which probably meant something.

Grandma, however, had sung in church choir from early child-hood: cherub choir, children's choir, and adult choir since her teens. She had rehearsed Wednesday nights for three-quarters of a cen-tury. It scared Freddy to think of doing *anything* that long, never mind choir rehearsal, but he loved that Grandma did it. Somebody ought to have that kind of life.

Sundays began to worry Freddy. He had low clothing standards and was comfortable in Salvation Army–store shirts he bought for twenty-five cents, but he had to make Grandma go back into her closet and choose something more suitable for church than a food-stained red T-shirt with a weird slogan. She was getting pretty loose around the edges, but Freddy shrugged, because he loved Grandma however nuts she was.

Then the minister, George Burnworth, sat Freddy down and said, "Cordelia can't live on her own anymore. She's too old and confused. She can't keep the house clean, and she can't keep herself clean. She can't prepare meals. She can't remember to turn the stove off. She can't remember how to pay her bills."

The theory was to put his grandmother in a thing called assisted living, but she would not go and it turned out you could not actually drag your grandmother into a building, slam the door, and leave her there. With his sisters' help and the minister's, Freddy got power of attorney. It turned out that even *with* a power of attorney, you could not drag your grandmother into a building, slam the door, and leave her there.

"You have no choice, Freddy," said his sisters. "You have to move in with her."

"How come *you* can't move in with her?"

They chuckled. Freddy—always so unrealistic.

His sisters did not think of what Freddy did as a career. Making glass beads was just silly. He had a perfectly good head on his shoulders. He should get a real job, pay taxes for a change, and stop being such an adolescent.

And they didn't even know about the pipes.

And Freddy had, after all, made a deal with his mother.

So Freddy dismantled his glass studio, one of the most painful things he had ever done, because he loved everything about it: the bench, the company of other glass artists, the sunlight, how he had everything stored and cached. He loved the graffiti wall and the sad old broom for sweeping up the daily mess.

And then he took a deep breath and moved across the country to stay with Grandma.

The very first week, he ran into Shawn Aminetti, a classmate of one of his sisters. Shawn had a glass studio right here on the shoreline and offered to share until Freddy got his own studio up and going. Of all things, Shawn was a constable. The villages up and down the shoreline didn't have police departments exactly, but constables under the supervision of a state trooper. Mainly Shawn drove around town looking for stuff that was different or wrong or walked up and down hallways at the middle school.

Since Shawn was also a stoner and made cheap, amateurish little pipes he sold by the dozen for almost nothing, Freddy thought it was a riot that the guy's main job was to patrol schools and streets. "I'm good at it," Shawn would protest. "I like what I do."

Normally Freddy both hated and feared cops, but Shawn was a partial cop who carried all the equipment but had half the power.

Living with Grandma was so much more awful than Freddy had expected that without George and Lily Burnworth to talk to, Freddy would have bailed. Literally. He would have run. Changed his name. Gone underground.

On the day he had to clean his grandmother's bottom—and front, which was the truly awful part—when she had a poop accident and couldn't get her feet out of her soiled panties, Freddy had fought tears for the first time since he was a toddler. Grandma seemed not to notice the hideous situation they were in, which Freddy supposed was a good thing, because in real life, Grandma would have preferred death to this humiliation with her only grandson. Dr. Burnworth used the adjective "undignified" when he talked about dementia, but this was so far beyond undignified that Freddy didn't even have a word for it. He couldn't even tell his sisters about it.

After weeks of George and Lily Burnworth searching for a place, his grandmother ended up in Memory Care, which was sort of assisted living for the completely confused. Assisted living for those beyond all personal embarrassment. Assisted living for people you love and cannot take care of anymore.

The first thing Freddy figured out was that every family of every person in Memory Care was riddled with guilt for foisting their loved one off on paid staff. "Loved one" was what the institution called it, which sounded like an ad for coffins.

And meanwhile, faking bead sales had become another nightmare. Extricating himself from the Leper was a lot harder than extricating himself from his grandmother's bowel care.

Freddy could make only enough product for three shows a year, but the Leper said that Freddy had to do six. He and Freddy would share booths at all of these.

"I can't make enough beads for three more shows," Freddy protested.

Gary Leperov replied, "I don't care if you look like an idiot, sitting behind an empty table. And you shouldn't care either because I'm fronting your plane tickets, your hotels, your meals, and your rental car. I'm even supplying Freddy T-shirts."

Freddy didn't have good judgment when all he was smoking was a cigarette, but when he was high, he felt pretty clever, and he chose a moment when he was higher than two kites to tell the Leper that one year of pretend sales receipts was enough and he wasn't doing it anymore. The Leper had not taken the news well. And now his muscle, Doc, was right here in Middletown.

Hippie Crime 101 had a rule, which Freddy knew well and had chosen not to think about: You bring a guy in, you keep an eye on him.

Yet another personal flaw to consider: failure to think. Sometimes Freddy imagined all his flaws stacked in a teetering pile, ready to collapse and smash him. As for virtues, he couldn't think of any right now. He looked at his wonderful grandmother, who was all virtue and didn't deserve this terrible fate (not that anybody did) and who trusted him to take care of her.

She didn't even *know* she was trusting him, which made the situation profoundly more awful. Freddy felt a sort of terror, the kind that MMC often evoked.

It was Doc he should be terrified of, but compared to dementia, Doc seemed more like an annoyance than a nightmare.

Freddy decided to kill some more time at MMC and maybe figure out how to escape his latest major error. "I finally remembered," he said to Mapes. "I've been promising you some of my beads for, like, decades now."

In fact, they had known each other about six months. In some ways, Freddy had never known another person so intimately. He and Mapes talked about death, the soul, God, bowel movements, music, and cars that were impossible to fit a wheelchair into the trunk of them.

He handed her a small, stapled plastic bag containing five one-inch-diameter beads.

The beads had the watercolor look of a garden in the morning mist: green and gold and vivid blue. The colors spilled differently on each one.

He didn't usually give away his good stuff because people had no idea what they were getting. They could not grasp the years of learning and experimenting and designing to master the skills of flamework; all they saw was a pretty little round thing.

"Freddy, they are breathtaking," whispered Mrs. Maple. "A feast for the eyes. Renoir in glass. I'm in love with them. Oh, Freddy, thank you so much! I will take up beading now and turn them into a necklace. Or maybe put them in a little glass bowl on my coffee table where they will catch the sun and make my friends jealous."

This was one bonus of dealing with the older ladies who were Freddy's basic customers: they knew how to give a compliment.

Mrs. Maple began another chapter in the book she was reading out loud to Polly, who gave no sign of listening. But Betty stopped singing and came over, entranced. Philip stopped whacking his cane and leaned forward to hear better.

The book was an ancient prairie romance called *A Lantern in Her Hand*, and Freddy wanted to give Philip a better choice, something manly, but Freddy was not much of a reader himself and had no idea what that book should be.

Heidi herded the residents who could walk back from balloon ball while Grace helped the rest maneuver their walkers and Mary Lou pushed a wheelchair. Half the allotted activity time was spent getting people there and then bringing them back, plus collecting people who wandered away or taking them to the bathroom.

Freddy was abruptly swamped with visit horror. He had to get out of here. He looked at his sweet, destroyed grandmother, thinking of all those after-school hours at Grandma and Grandpa's house before their mother got home from work and how somebody was always scraping a knee or an elbow, and Grandma would kiss it to make it better. There was no kiss, medicine, or treatment that made dementia better.

He kissed Grandma goodbye anyway, and she smiled in the wrong direction. She didn't seem to be sure who he was or why he was leaving or, for that matter, why he had come.

Freddy felt as if he had a hole in his heart and was sliding out of it.

Six

Freddy left by the employees' door and looked through rhododendron leaves. No white Toyota Corolla in the parking lot, which meant Doc didn't know about MMC. He didn't know about Grandma's house either, or he'd have cornered Freddy there. But he might be circling town, ready to snag Freddy.

The bike was a problem. He'd be exposed and slow. He wasn't sure how to get home under these circumstances. He couldn't use Uber because his credit card would be denied. Who might give him a free ride home and ask no questions?

Freddy never let anybody visit his grandmother's house, an ugly raised ranch with an obnoxious peaky entry. Aesthetics weren't what stopped him. He had built a glass shop in a neighborhood not zoned for business, never mind this one, and neighbors hardly ever like finding out that the guy next door is playing with fire.

On the main level, Grandma's furniture was old and clunky but not enough to be stylish. His sisters said to sell it and buy whatever he wanted instead, but aside from the fact that Freddy had no idea what he wanted instead, it seemed grotesque to remove all traces of his grandmother in her house when there was so little trace of her in her own body. Something had to stay.

Mrs. Maple would love to drive him home, but she was all questions. Plus she probably had grown kids like Freddy's sisters: driven, successful, articulate, well dressed, married—in other words, exhausting to a guy who had his eyes on some other ball entirely. Except when Freddy didn't have his eyes on anything because he was stoned.

Freddy postponed more thought by taking out his cell phone. He had to keep it silenced and in his back pocket when he was with Grandma, because the desire to escape the dementia situation was so strong, he'd have played games the whole time.

There was a text from the Leper.

> I don't know what '80s cop movie you think you're in, but get over it. Talk to Doc.

Freddy didn't have a handle on his glass future, but faking sales with Gary Leperov wasn't it. Of course if he refused to fake sales with Gary Leperov, he might not have a future at all.

It was entirely possible that Doc and his passenger in that Toyota did actual drugs. Depending on the drug of choice, neither one of them would necessarily be sane at any given moment, which did not bode well for negotiations. But Freddy didn't really believe Doc would be armed any more than he really believed that Alice Bell had died in Peru.

He realized suddenly that he didn't even know if she'd seen Machu Picchu. Had she been coming or going? Had she died without reaching her destination?

Freddy thought more about his mother now that she was dead than he had when she was alive, which was pretty awful. They had never really come to terms. And he was not on any terms to speak of with his sisters. It was only Grandma, with whom there were no terms, just affection.

He shook off a train of thought that could only lead to some dark dead-end of the heart and set out for Main Street.

There was a woman with a shop in Middletown who might drive him part way, although leaving the bike at MMC was a totally lousy option. Auburn lived down in Essex, which was close enough, and she could drop him, say, at the gas station in Haddam. Auburn would want to take him to his own front door, though, because she would want to see where he lived and, most of all, learn his last name.

Freddy focused on the walk instead of his problems. He liked swinging his legs and studying buildings. The works of man were more interesting to Freddy than the works of nature. He found architectural details and the geometry of brick, stone, and concrete endlessly pleasing.

Middletown had survived a lot of bad years and was gentrifying at a great rate, full of restaurants and shops Freddy could not afford. He walked past the police department, well disguised in a charming brick building, and kept going in the direction of the Himalayan gift shop and the Hispanic grocery.

Auburn ran a boutique that sold handmade jewelry hanging on chicken wire, thin cotton skirts from India, candles, incense, Freddy's beads in a locked glass-top case (where they looked, one customer said, as delicious as candy), and, once you got to know her, pipes.

Auburn considered herself beautiful, but she was way too thin for Freddy. Her hair was jet black, her complexion paper white, and she wore wide-rimmed hats with ribbons and scarves to prevent even the slightest tan. She liked to stand very close to people and flick her pierced tongue like a snake. She'd say, "Come on, Freddy. You can tell me. What's your actual factual name?"

"I'm planning ahead. I'm going to be very famous and need only one name."

"Me too," she told him once. "I'm going to control everybody I meet."

Freddy had never controlled anybody he met.

Cars were diagonally parked along Main Street, the color choices mainly white, gray, and black. Freddy's life was color, and he couldn't fathom choosing a noncolor for something as important as your vehicle. Of course white was anonymous, and Freddy himself was in an anonymous stage, so a plain white sedan—like the one parked in front of Auburn's—might do.

It was Doc's car.

Doc was standing in Auburn's doorway.

Freddy backed into a pizza palace, the last greasy survivor in the midst of yogurt shops and juice bars. Had Doc seen him? Freddy didn't think so. Doc had been talking to Auburn, not paying attention to approaching pedestrians. Still and all, Doc survived by paying attention.

Freddy slid into a booth. If he slumped against the window and pressed his nose against the glass like a kid, he could just make out Doc's front fender.

He ordered two pizzas, and when the waitress had left, it crossed his mind that Auburn put his beads on her website. On Etsy, she sold finished necklaces that featured his beads. One Etsy search, he thought, and the Lep finds my beads. One text message, and he finds out I bring Auburn my work in person. Meaning I can't live that far off. Meaning send Doc to Middletown.

A *hamster* could have found me in Middletown, he thought. A *rodent* is smarter than I am.

It was weird, though.

Airfare from Vegas to Hartford was relatively cheap, but a rental car? Hotel? Meals? All to have a conversation with Freddy? But then, Doc also marketed and delivered the Leper's glass, so maybe the actual reason he was here was selling to Auburn, in which case Freddy was a minor, coincidental side trip.

Freddy found this easy to believe. His whole life was a minor, coincidental side trip for people.

The rented Toyota backed out of its space. Doc and the skinny ponytail guy swung an illegal U-turn and disappeared.

Freddy was a very fast eater of pizza. There was something about the combination of grease, cheese, and tomato that required him to chow down as if he were in a contest. He paid, tipped, went out the back, and walked down the alley to Auburn's. He knocked on the heavy windowless door. It had a peephole. He stood in front of it. Auburn let him in.

"Hey, Aub," said Freddy, holding out a pizza box. "Hungry?"

"Freddy, I eat sushi, not pizza. But you may enter, because I have questions." She swept him in and locked the door after him. "Two men who represent the Leper were here asking after you, and five minutes later, you appear bearing gifts?"

"I'm kind of in a bind."

"I love men in binds," she said, leaning too close.

Freddy strolled into the shop to get some space and hardly recognized the place. Gone were the cheap skirts. In their place were supremely ugly handbags that Freddy guessed were also supremely expensive. Fabulous scarves. And where a month ago pathetic little trinkets had been, Leper pendants hung from a wire sculpture. Rotting fingers.

Auburn's college clientele could afford those?

It was actually good news. Doc *had* been here for sales and delivery.

"I'm looking for a more sophisticated customer," Auburn explained. "My taste and displays are changing. Now meet my good, good friend Danielle."

Danielle was a very chunky young woman who had nevertheless chosen to wear leggings and a closely fitted long-sleeved tee, making her a painful contrast to Auburn. Danielle knew it too. She had the bitter expression of a person who would always come in second. Or maybe twentieth.

Freddy was sympathetic. He had three sisters who always vied for first place and would certainly not have awarded Freddy second place. Ninetieth, maybe. On a good day.

"I like pizza," said Danielle. She locked the front door and put the Closed sign in the window. "What toppings did you choose? I hope no anchovies."

"Never anchovies," Freddy assured her. He kept his eyes on their cell phones. He didn't want them texting his location to Doc. They gathered around the tiny table in the tiny back room. There was one stool. Nobody took it.

"The Leper sent Doc and some loser," said Auburn. "You must be very important to be a two-man errand."

Freddy handed Danielle paper napkins. Danielle was giggling, like she knew a secret Freddy didn't. "You're not having pizza, Freddy?"

"I already had mine, thanks. So what did they want?"

"You," said Auburn. "I feel the same. Come on home with me."

Freddy was really glad he hadn't asked for a ride. He'd walk the nine miles first. In fact, now that he thought of it, he wanted to walk. What a great hike! "Thanks, Aub," he said, "but I have to feed my cat." Freddy had no pets.

"I love cats!" cried Danielle. "What's her name?"

"Vinaigrette," said Freddy, and the women laughed.

"You know why they call him the Leper, right?" asked Auburn.

Because he was Russian, and his real name was Leperov. But Freddy had learned long ago that girls like knowing more than you do, so he said, "No. Why?"

"Because you only get leprosy after you've been near it for years, Freddy, and then you die. That's the Leper's theme song. Play my way or die."

Die? They'd kill me just because I don't want to fake a bead show?

Now he *really* didn't want to talk to Doc. He didn't want to play a role in Auburn's melodrama either. Coming here was yet another check on today's list of stupid actions.

Auburn was tapping rhythmically on the table. On her fingernails were twisted-toe decals. Wow. The Leper thought of everything: not just your usual T-shirts and stickers but even fingernail art. Freddy had to salute the guy. Not only was Gary Leperov a drug kingpin, with hired muscle crossing the country to punish wayward bead dudes, but he manufactured sidelines and kept track of them and also made sculptural glass that sold for a fortune.

Or didn't sell.

It was entirely possible that the Lep faked the sales of *his own glass* in order to get clean money. How much money? Freddy wondered. If he was at three hundred thousand a year, were there other guys doing the same thing? Adding up to what?

Freddy couldn't imagine being organized enough to pull that off. On the same day he visited Grandma, Freddy could hardly manage to put gas in the car and also buy a taco.

"The Leper is not a cakewalk," said Auburn. "And his buddy, Doc? You're pissing him off, Freddy. What's going on?" Auburn opened a small cabinet on the wall, removed a slim gaudy purse, and unzipped it. She took out a small rectangular mirror and a single-edged razor blade.

It was the end of the day. Okay, she needed to relax, but she wasn't relaxing with weed. She was about to do a line of coke. To bring out her kit in front of him, Auburn must trust him something serious, but Freddy didn't trust her at all, and he never hung out with people who did coke.

"Guess what Danielle and I did the other night." Auburn peeled away the cardboard cover of the blade. "We met this guy at a party, and he said he'd give us a ride home, and Danielle wanted to ride with him because he was adorable, in a sort of L.L. Bean catalog way. And then what does he do? You will not believe what he does."

Somebody out there could shock Auburn? Against his will, Freddy got interested.

"It's my story, Auburn," said Danielle irritably. "I'll tell. So I'm the front-seat passenger and Auburn's in back and Br—"

"No names," said Auburn sharply.

Danielle blinked. "Okay, no names," she agreed, puzzled but shrugging. Freddy had a feeling Danielle could shrug about anything.

"Anyway, he's driving. He starts telling us how we have to shape *up* and get all middle *class* and finish our *bachelors'* degrees, and above all, stop *using*." She accented her words heavily, turning the run-on sentence into a mocking chant. "I mean, that's why I left home. I am so not into nagging. And he invites us to a mind and spirit group. It will be so *healthy* for us. We will realize the importance of our *souls* and not throw ourselves away on *chemicals*. So Auburn and me, we're looking at each over the seats. What are we doing with some uptight dude who doesn't like us just the way we are? Next thing he'll be preaching. And don't I spot a cop car in the lane behind us. So I grab the steering wheel and jerk it around, and now his car is all over the road, crossing the center lane, almost hitting another car, and he's yelling 'Stop it!' and he's trying to knock my hand off the wheel, and the cop, the good little boy cop, pulls us over."

Auburn and Danielle exchanged looks, like satisfied lionesses over a kill. Freddy could almost see the blood on their chops.

"Guess what Danielle did next," whispered Auburn.

From the look in their eyes, they could have dismembered the guy's body. Freddy had to get out of here.

"The cop makes him get out of the car, right?" said Danielle, giggling. "And he gets out? And he has to put his hands on the hood? I mean, it's a riot. So Auburn has a baggie of coke in her purse, and I put the baggie under the driver's seat, and when I was talking to the cop, I said, 'Oh no, look what just slipped out of its hiding place,' like we didn't realize what this guy is up to.'"

Freddy's lips were dry. His mouth and throat were dry. Even his brain was dry.

"And Br—well, the dude—is saying over and over, 'It isn't mine! I didn't have that! I don't know where it came from!'" Danielle imitated the panicked voice.

"And the cop is like, 'Yeah, right, I've heard that one before.' And the cop arrests him," said Auburn. A smile crawled over her face. She licked her smile.

Freddy thought, *She really is a snake.*

"He was so proud of himself, little Mister Virtue," Danielle said softly. "And now he's in jail."

"Wow," said Freddy. "What a story. Listen, I have to run. But thanks for the company."

Auburn let him out, laughing at him or Br.

Freddy normally enjoyed the secret, dark feel of an alley, but right now, he wanted light, not shadow. He cut over to the sidewalk, grateful for every pedestrian, his thoughts a shuddery jumble. That poor slob Br was behind bars; in Connecticut, depending on the judge, Br could walk tomorrow or end up with a serious sentence.

Neither of these two would go to a police department and take back their story. It would incriminate them and probably not set the guy free either. The cops would figure Auburn and Danielle were throwing themselves under the bus for love.

Why had they told Freddy? Was it a message? Something to do with the Leper?

Or did Auburn think he would be entertained?

Freddy walked back to Memory Care, too busy sorting out Auburn and Danielle to remember he ought to be thinking about Doc. By the time he reached his bike, Doc had become a distant cloudy event.

There were only two main roads going south. Route 9 was a divided highway and bikes were forbidden, plus it was pretty well patrolled and the last thing he wanted was a chat with a cop like the one Br had had. He took 154 instead, the old parallel route. The shoulder was potholed, the sun was setting, and the cars surging past could hardly see him.

Freddy didn't even notice. He kept thinking about Br, who had been pushy with his virtues and was now ruined.

THURSDAY

Seven

Glass poured out of Freddy, as if he himself were molten, but then he got cocky.

In his left hand, he was holding the hollow body of black-and-white tubing he'd made a few months ago. In his right, he gripped a short 5mm clear glass rod, which he dragged through the molten glass to stripe it. His pressure was too intense. The glass snapped and gouged his wrist. Since he was holding the striping rod like a pencil, his pencil finger was also cut. Immediately, his whole hand was sticky with blood.

Freddy kept a roll of bandage tape on a nail over the shop table so he could wrap a wound as fast as possible and not stop spinning, because molten glass drooped if he didn't keep the rotation going. He bandaged himself with practiced motions, keeping the hot glass in the fire and wiping the blood on his T-shirt.

He had been so sure of his focus, and just to prove you should never be sure of anything, glass had given him yet another lesson. Blood was everywhere and the morning was shot. He needed company. Shawn was his only pot-smoking, pipe-making buddy, the only dude around here he could really chill with and be himself. But Shawn was probably at work.

Freddy gave up, fixed himself more coffee, and even though he'd just been at Memory Care the day before yesterday, the curvy needle of visitation guilt poked his heart.

His grandmother was fine without him. She was warm, safe, fed, bathed, escorted to activities, and medicated. He did not need to visit today. He didn't need to visit tomorrow either.

But she was so happy to see him. Her face lit up and she held out her hands, and he would take her hands, even though she probably hadn't washed them after her last potty trip and thought he was Arthur.

Nonvisitation guilt was probably like malaria. You had a bout of suffering and then you improved and forgot you'd ever had it, and then you had another bout.

He decided to drive Grandma's dark-silver four-door Toyota Avalon, just the right car for an elderly woman off to her canasta game but not the right car for Freddy. On the other hand, it was free, comfortable, got good gas mileage, looked anonymous, and as a bonus, had a sweet name for the finish: *Phantom Gray*.

Of course, it would be better if Freddy had kept up the insurance payments, but oh well.

He got settled in the Avalon, all comfortable and centered, and then forced himself to listen to Gary Leperov's latest voicemail.

"Freddy," said a sharp, irritated voice. "This isn't middle school. You can't run down a different hall. I sent Doc to your stupid little state with all its stupid trees and guys who wear collared shirts and *you are wasting his time*! I've paid your fees at BABE. You let Doc know what airport you're flying out of, and he'll let you know how much product you're selling. He's got your paperwork. Where's the negative here, Freddy? Don't screw me up."

BABE. The Bay Area Bead Show in November. Freddy had a lot of customers there. They would expect bounty on his table, and he didn't have it.

He drove carefully to Middletown, saw nothing of Doc, and parked safely in the employee lot. It started to rain. He and Grandma would have to stay inside. He might even have to partake of an activity.

He couldn't make himself go in.

He lit up and breathed deep.

Laura arrived at the front desk as Freddy was ambling through the employees' door. "Tree Lady!" he said, grinning. She felt the rush of relief and happiness that Freddy's presence brought. She did not want to analyze this. Freddy was forty years younger than she was. More than.

Laura signed in. Freddy did not.

Constanza was on the desk. She did not remind Freddy to sign in. "Mrs. Yardley died yesterday," she announced.

This was breaking policy. Nobody here mentioned death. Even the hospice people, working at any given time with several residents, wore name tags that read Palliative Medicine Specialist, implying everything including death could be palliated.

When death did come, MMC moved bodies to funeral homes clandestinely, closing the empty bedroom door so nobody would even see the stripped and naked mattress.

Yet death was a constant at Memory Care. People lived here because their organs were collapsing. Brains had already partially failed, and one by one, heart, lungs, skin, kidney, and liver would also fail. Freddy's grandmother and Laura's aunt had been using every organ for over nine decades, and every organ was signing off.

Spend enough time in a facility like this, and you knew that longevity was overrated.

Grandma was sitting in her wheelchair, folded over and down, like a doll losing her stuffing. Freddy kissed his grandmother's cheek and she didn't know. Smoothed her hair and she didn't know. "Grandma?" he said softly. "It's me, Freddy. I'm sitting with you. I'm holding your hand. You hold mine back, okay?"

She squeezed his hand so lightly, he could be making it up to suit himself. But then she gave him her old pixie smile, the mischief and love still there, and it was all worth it, and he approved of longevity after all. He gave her the careful hug you had to use with somebody whose bones could break just sitting there. "Love you, Grandma," he told her.

She wouldn't know about Maude Yardley's death even though her room was next door. She wouldn't miss Maude, because she couldn't remember people. Perhaps she had never learned Maude's name.

"Uh-oh, Mapes," he said. "Your aunt Polly is sitting here next to us, but I'm facing her room, and somebody's in her bed. Hey, Jade!" he yelled.

Jade stared at him with dislike.

He who dealt with bead ladies should have known better than to shout. "Lookin' great, Jade," he added. "Love the lipstick." There was nothing else to compliment because Jade wore scrubs with pandas on them, which did nothing for a generous figure, and that was too bad, because she had potential.

"You in need, Freddy?" she said without moving. "You want I should do a taco run for you?"

He waved at the occupied bed of Polly Lambert.

"Oh, that. Probably Irene. She's always testing beds." Jade moved slowly into Polly's room, argued with Irene, and finally coaxed her out of Polly's bed. Muttering her numbers, Irene shuffled into the common room. Jade snapped the covers back, leaving no clue that a stranger with a diaper and shoes on had just crept under Polly's covers.

Freddy had low sheet standards. He could go for a long time without washing his. Still, it was good to be high right now. He could just let this little sheet thing waft away.

Jade struck a pose Freddy knew to be the prelude to gossip. She was ticked at him, but he and Mapes were the only visitors at the moment, so her choices were limited. "They're doing an autopsy on her at Yale."

"Autopsy on whom?" asked Mrs. Maple.

"Maude Yardley."

"Maude had TIAs for years," said Mrs. Maple, "so they know how she died. Is the autopsy part of some ongoing research project?"

Freddy wished he didn't know that TIA meant transient ischemic attacks, little bitty strokes, not noticeable at the time but adding up to the vascular dementia that Grandma had. Patches of useless brain tissue all over the place. Whereas Polly had Alzheimer's, which was plaques all over the place. The net outcome was equally lousy.

Freddy was comforted by the thought of Yale's involvement. The very word "Yale" projected authority. His sister Jenny had gone to Yale, as she ceaselessly informed everybody. Yale would learn something from the autopsy and add it to the million of other things they had learned. Someday, although not soon enough for Grandma, they would solve this.

"The night nurse," said Jade, "she thinks something's not quite right."

Duh, thought Freddy. That's our theme song.

"What sort of 'not quite right' does Vera have in mind?" asked Mrs. Maple.

Freddy had met Vera only a few times because he didn't visit during the night shift, but now and then, she worked days. Vera was a commanding presence. Her breasts were the size of watermelons, and she stacked her braided hair in a towering black sculpture. Her earrings looked heavy enough to use as anchors, and her magenta lipstick embraced big, square white teeth.

Jade shrugged. "That's why they're doing the autopsy."

Meds, probably, thought Freddy.

Some residents were on a stunning amount of medication, which in Freddy's opinion kept them alive past their sell-by date.

You probably couldn't overdose anybody, because every patient had a big, plastic zip bag, each day's medications put by the pharmaceutical supplier into tiny pockets, labeled by day and hour. The bags were locked in the medicine cart in a sort of fat file drawer. But even with so many controls in place, maybe the wrong meds could go to the wrong person.

Freddy had enough to worry about with his own drug errors. I have to call the Lep back, he thought. I have to deal with it.

But Freddy's modus operandi had always been postponement.

"Hey," said Jade. She was oddly still. Holding her breath. Not blinking.

Freddy followed her gaze out the big picture windows that faced the front gardens and the parking lots beyond.

Two police cars idled, their roof lights silently twirling.

EIGHT

Freddy was not a fan of the police, since he made a market in drug paraphernalia and hung out with stoners, and this was a state that often jailed you.

Like every state with a lot of gambling—Connecticut had Foxwoods and Mohegan Sun—the authorities hated drugs. They didn't want crime surfacing where suburbanites were happily throwing away their money at tables and slots. But casinos hated weed more than hard drugs. If you were high on weed, you didn't need to get high on gambling because you stayed home and mellowed out. Vegas regarded grass as the enemy, not because it was a drug but because users didn't frequent casinos as often.

What was up with cop cars at MMC?

Local emergency protocol required fire trucks as well as ambulances if, say, a resident took a bad fall, but Freddy had never seen cops.

Immediately, he felt guilty, figuring they were here for him. He *was* guilty. Failure to pay income tax, failure to pay insurance premiums, faking sales receipts for the Leper, and probably trickiest of all, failure to notify Social Security that Alice Bell was no longer alive and they should stop sending money every month.

He told himself to behave normally if the cops came in here. Although *he* wasn't the one who'd look weird. A hundred and thirty people were way ahead of him.

Grandma woke up. "Where is my machine, Freddy?"

"Machine" was Grandma's all-purpose word. She could be referring to her hearing aids or the sippy cup in which she took her fortified chocolate drink. But usually she meant walker. "Your walker's in your room, Grandma," he said. "Want me to get it for you?"

"Are we going somewhere?"

"No," said Freddy. "It's raining."

"I don't need it unless we're going somewhere," Grandma pointed out, sounding completely lucid.

"Do you want to go somewhere?"

She pointed toward the hall and the wide opening through which Kenneth Yardley was approaching. "I want you to make that meany beany go away."

Freddy didn't think she could actually see that far. This was some generalized statement, not an indictment of poor Kenneth.

Kenneth looked around vaguely, as if he'd never visited before. He stared one by one at each door. No patient's room was down a hall or out of sight; they encircled the common room. Very slowly, he walked toward his dead wife's room. "Tottered" was a better word. He was literally unbalanced.

"This place is full of meany beanies," said Freddy's grandmother darkly.

"What *is* a meany beany, Grandma?"

But she was already gone, having drifted back to her own world with the ease and speed Freddy found so unnerving.

Laura considered the sheet event in Aunt Polly's room. She could report Jade, deliver a lecture to Jade, or change the sheets herself.

Or ignore it. She had exactly the right amount of energy to ignore it.

Poor newly widowed Kenneth paused in front of Maude's door exactly as he had the other day. Not in, not out, just swaying.

How dreadful he must feel, thought Laura.

Kenneth would have named a funeral home prior to Maude

moving in, because they didn't give a new resident a bed until the death plans were made. Now, with her body gone, Kenneth stood at the edge of a grim task: clearing up the dregs of an institutionalized existence. He could not dillydally. There was a waiting list: families who needed the death of somebody else's loved one so their own loved one could move in.

That was all Maude was now. A vacancy.

Laura thought of the vacancy in her own heart. Many vacancies. Her heart was a motel of empty rooms. She walked over. Maude's door was taped shut, a peculiarity Laura hadn't seen before. "I'm sorry, Kenneth," she said softly. "You loved Maude so. You never let her down. You always came." It was her supreme compliment: he always came.

Kenneth tried and failed to smile.

"Would you like help planning the service?" she asked. "I'm a church organist. Very familiar with funerals. I could email or phone friends and family for you."

He stared at her, backed away, and circled the nurses' station rather than have a conversation.

Laura hoped that she would be as rattled when Polly died. The end of a life should provoke a deep reaction. She said a prayer for Maude, for Kenneth, for Aunt Polly, for Cordelia Chase, for Freddy. *And for me, Lord*, she thought. *Please help me.*

Two cops came into the common room, one in uniform, one not. Patients shuffled in slippers or orthopedic shoes and staff squeaked in colorful sneakers, but the hard-soled shoes of the cops smacked the tile like storm troopers. Freddy had a hard time being rational around cops. He loathed them on principle. He took Grandma's hand and drew enough comfort from her presence to glance at the uniformed guy.

Shawn, thrilled when shoreline constables got body cameras, had demonstrated for Freddy. The battery pack, added to the row of waist-line stuff, had been both obvious and invisible in all the clutter. The camera, about the size of a lighter, was attached to Shawn's collar, sitting on his shoulder. Shawn could watch his own video of his own actions on his own cell phone, and the video was also sent to headquarters. It wasn't a selfie. It was more of a life-ie, recording every act and word.

The uniformed cop wore a camera.

The guy not in uniform could be a detective, not that Freddy had ever met one, so he was going by TV, but he wore a suit and did not appear to have any equipment.

They've come for me, he thought. He couldn't swallow.

Jade was still frozen in place, still staring out the window instead of at the cops in her very own ward.

They've come for *her*, maybe? Cops love a perp walk. They're going to terrify Jade and humiliate her. Or me. But I don't think Social Security sends cops.

He remembered Br. *What if I got set up? Like Br?*

But who would set him up? Not the Lep and Doc; they needed him for the paper pushing. Auburn? Was this her new hobby?

He didn't think Auburn would bother to destroy somebody unless she could watch. And how could Auburn know about MMC?

Grandma heard the loud slam of shoes and looked around ner-vously. "Arthur?" she said, her voice high and trembling. "Arthur, let's go home now."

This was a favorite line, and several residents picked it up.

"I want to go home too," said Betty. "Is there a train?"

"Thirty-seven," called Irene. "Thirty-eight."

"Get away from my desk!" yelled Philip.

Staff converged to comfort patients and get them back to their chairs or their rooms and especially to offer snacks, because there was nothing like a short cylinder of Ritz crackers, half a banana, or a paper cup of Froot Loops to distract a person.

Mrs. Reilly, the chief administrator, was right behind the cops.

He had met Mrs. Reilly when they were signing Grandma up, but mostly George and Lily Burnworth had pushed through the paperwork. Freddy's job had been the literal physical transfer of his grandmother. Sometimes when he thought of the lies he told Grandma so she would go easily, he wanted to smash himself with a tire iron.

Kenneth, having just escaped Mrs. Maple, now eased out of the room behind Mrs. Reilly and the cops. He kept his head down. He was either grieving for Maude or just as unhappy about cops as Freddy.

Wait. Had he changed his bloody T-shirt?

He looked down, and yes, he had, but the sweatshirt he'd chosen featured a Salt design, with a single insane eye and dragon's teeth below bright-pink gums. But seriously, if that meant anything to the cops, then they were into pot too, and they'd just wish they had a cool sweatshirt like this.

Mrs. Reilly waved at them. "These are two of our most frequent visitors, Mr. Bell and Mrs. Maple. Mr. Bell's grandmother has the room next door to Maude Yardley. Mrs. Maple's aunt lives directly across the common room from Maude."

The cop in uniform went on to Maude's room. Mrs. Maple, looking elegant and competent, held out her hand to the cop in the suit. Cops don't shake hands, because they don't want you getting a grip on them first. But public-courtesy-wise, Mrs. Maple gave him no choice.

"Wayne Ames," said the suit. "I'm a detective with the Middletown police."

"I'm Laura Maple," she said, "and this is my aunt, Miss Lambert."

"Good morning," said Polly in the loud monotone that dementia had given her. It was actually afternoon, but it had been years since Polly had the slightest idea of time.

"Good morning," Wayne Ames said to Polly, and Freddy reluctantly gave him points for not correcting her.

"How are you today?" Polly asked. She was wearing a food-stained bib, holding a rag doll in one hand and a hearing aid in the other.

"Very well, thank you," said the detective uncertainly.

Freddy understood. It took a while to get comfortable with dementia. Like never.

"You look quite dashing," said Aunt Polly, and a stranger had no way of knowing that Polly said this to any man, even fellow residents in food-stained sweatpants, and that she had now reached the end of her patter.

"Thank you," said Wayne Ames, pleased and surprised.

So he was susceptible to flattery even from a dementia patient. This seemed a useful piece of knowledge.

The cop turned his attention to Freddy.

What if he was required to identify himself? He'd left his wallet in the car, and no way was he going to that car when there were cops here and he was high and there was another nub in the cup holder. Okay, they didn't usually prosecute grass anymore, but still. "Freddy Bell," he said. "My grandmother, Mrs. Chase."

Out the window, he saw Kenneth emerge from the building. Three cops converged on him. Which meant a total of *five* cops at MMC. Kenneth Yardley's stocky body was engulfed in dark uniforms and bulging accessories.

A pipe guy needed only one accessory, made of glass. Well, two, if you counted the lighter. But cops, they needed a gun and a stun gun and a flashlight and a radio and something to bludgeon you with, and even through the iron fence and the landscaping, Freddy could see Kenneth wilt.

The guy had just lost his wife. Whatever their issue was, it didn't take three cops to ask a question or two. But that was cops. Their actual weapon was to loom over you and threaten you.

"Where is my machine?" asked his grandmother.

The detective looked around for a machine.

"Her walker," explained Freddy. "We don't need it right now, Grandma," he said softly.

The detective pulled up a chair. "Did either of you know Maude Yardley? The patient who just died?" he asked.

In the beginning, Freddy couldn't tell anybody apart: the men looked alike and the women looked alike. They were old and gray, in body and in personality. Most of the men were thin and bent and tended to frown or else stare vacantly. They knew this wasn't the life they were supposed to lead, but they didn't know how to get back. Most of the women had been given the same haircut: short porcupine hair. Maude's hair had been white and sort of vertical, as if gravity no long applied, while Grandma's was a white puffball. Maude and Grandma even had similar bodies: thin and shapeless, as if they had caved in and just their clothes existed.

Sometimes, on the bedroom door, a family would tape a photograph of the resident as she had been in better years. It made Freddy pretty gloomy to see a color portrait of some stylish woman with a twinkle in her eyes and know that it matched the dull-eyed carcass pushing a cheap aluminum walker with tennis balls fitted over the legs.

"Kind of," said Freddy. "Maude and my grandmother sat at the same table for meals."

"We've got some questions about her death."

Freddy had already forgotten that Yale was doing an autopsy. He was suddenly terrified of how easily he forgot stuff. I'm barely twenty-six and I'm a candidate for memory care, he thought. Too much weed? Too much mental burden from Grandma and the house and the Leper and all?

He knew what his sisters would say. *Pull yourself together, Freddy. You don't have any burdens compared to everybody else. Behave like a grown-up for once.*

The autopsy had to be about drugs in Maude's system.

What if MMC gets into trouble for some medication doled out by mistake? he thought. What if they shut the place down? What if I have to move Grandma? What if we can't afford anyplace else? What if I have to bring her home again? How am I going to do that? Nothing in the house is safe. Stairs, gas stove, lots of doors, railroad tracks at the back of the yard. I'd have to hire aides, 24-7. They might have to live in. And a cleaning lady, because nobody's going to stay half an hour the way the house is right now.

"The forensic examiner thinks Mrs. Yardley was suffocated," said the cop.

Freddy had meant to be silent and uninvolved, but he moaned. "Suffocated! Just when you think you know the worst of this dementia crap, it gets even more worse. It can take away your ability to steer a pencil and recognize your own family, but I wouldn't have said it took away your ability to turn over and keep breathing. I mean, that comes from some cortex or something, doesn't it? Even if your thinking brain is full of holes, doesn't your breathing brain still work? Now I have to worry about my grandmother squashing her nose against her own pillow?" He was babbling, a sure sign of being high. The cop's eyes narrowed thoughtfully.

"Maude Yardley didn't suffocate from not turning over," said the detective. "Cloth was held over her face. Her mouth is full of lint. Her jaw and neck are bruised where she was held down."

NINE

Oh, Kenneth! thought Laura. Did you suffocate your wife? Because who else would? You should just have stopped visiting if you were that upset.

Her entire body shivered, inside and out. She imagined Kenneth in a flurry of desperation or frustration or rage just lunging at poor Maude. Perhaps his only thought at the time was that he would no longer have a wife who breathed, ate, and defecated but did not, in fact, live.

Laura was one of the lucky ones, because Aunt Polly was somewhat savvy on her good days. They could still sit with old family albums, and Polly could identify many of the photographs and tell the old stories. They could still play checkers, although Polly could never remember whether she was black or red, and sometimes couldn't even recognize black and red, and the game was apt to peter out from sheer confusion.

Whereas Philip cursed and whacked people with his cane.

Edna had not smiled in a year and generally stared at her lap all day long.

Although Polly would not be able to follow the detective's conversation, another resident might, so Laura said, "Let us not discuss this in the presence of my aunt and Mr. Bell's grandmother."

"Oh," said the detective. "I was sort of thinking they don't know what's going on."

Laura stood up. "It's unpredictable. We'll chat in the parlor off the lobby."

The detective was startled and annoyed. Probably liked to be in charge, but so did Laura. "I'm headed home now, Aunt Polly," she said, patting Polly's shoulder. "I'll see you later."

"It was nice of you to come," said her aunt. But that was just a remaining memorized phrase. Polly did not look into Laura's eyes nor register that Laura was leaving.

"What is your aunt even doing here?" the detective asked. "She seems fine to me."

Suffocated meaning *murdered*?

Freddy did swat mosquitos, but other than that, he was pretty much a no-kill kind of guy. And yet he loved violent movies, violent video games, and television series. The more gunshots, explosions, chases, knives, and broken jaws, the better. What did that say about his psyche?

Anyway, murder? Here in Memory Care? Where there wasn't even function, let alone violence? Who could possibly have done that to Maude? And why?

The utter helplessness of a person like Maude made it immensely more awful. Freddy had a nightmare vision of fingers closing on a thin, wrinkled sagging throat, gripping a towel and jamming it into the mouth, flattening the tongue, cutting off the oxygen. And what could Maude do? Nothing except die.

He'd never seen anybody but Kenneth visit Maude. Not that that meant anything. Freddy was here only three or four times a week and rarely stayed over an hour.

It would be easy enough for anybody to get into MMC, he thought. You just say you're visiting your great-aunt or whatever. It's not like they ask for proof. You sign in, the front desk clerk opens the inner door for you or gives you the door code, you find your way to the right area, you visit.

The aides were often so busy that there was no staff in the

common room. They were in bathrooms lowering people onto the toilet and cleaning them up; they had taken a patient to the shower/tub room; they were walking somebody in the back garden or doing a resident's laundry.

You wouldn't choose mealtime, when the staff gathered all residents and were busy mopping up spilled milk or spooning in mashed potatoes. No, you needed your victim alone in her room.

Freddy figured the best time was after lunch and before the shift change. Patients were exhausted, napping in their wheelchairs or their rooms, while the staff grabbed a bite to eat in the TV area. People with Alzheimer's and dementia did not watch television, because the speed of the action was too much to process, so the corner with the big TV, the two vinyl sofas (easier to mop up), and the little card table (as if anybody here still knew hearts from diamonds) were unused.

The aides kept an eye out, but they wouldn't know every visitor. Freddy didn't recognize half the visitors, and he'd been coming for months. Adult children of residents generally worked by day and visited evenings or weekends, which Freddy never did. And old friends—golf partners, bridge partners, neighbors—could have visited fifty times and never crossed paths with a particular aide.

Freddy didn't even recognize half the residents. There was high turnover. Elderly people going downhill always found death at the bottom. Or if the person needed medical nursing care, he had to go to some other facility. Or families ran out of money and found a less expensive place. Or felt too guilty and brought their loved one back home.

A stranger could fit in pretty easily if he had any idea what the routine was or was good at party crashing. Freddy had always thought that crashing parties would be a fun hobby, but he didn't have the clothes for it or the time.

Mrs. Maple marched out of the common room.

"Mr. Bell?" said the detective. "Mind coming along?"

Freddy minded a lot, but coming along would result in less attention than refusing. Mapes guided them into the little yellow sitting room on the public side of the locked doors, where the staff interviewed job applicants and families discussed fees. The sofas were very soft, presumably to cushion the blow of finding out how much memory care cost.

Freddy told himself that nobody in diapers ever sat here, but he kept standing. Mrs. Maple sat, adjusting pillows and sweater edges. The detective took the only hard chair and said to Freddy, "So you like this place? You're comfortable with the staff?"

"Sure."

"You feel your grandmother is safe here?"

"Of course. What are you saying? You think somebody on the *staff* hurt Maude?"

The detective was expressionless and silent.

"I totally promise you that the staff is... They... No! Never. They would never hurt a resident."

"Why are you so sure?" asked the detective, as if the only reason Freddy could be sure the staff hadn't murdered Maude was because he, Freddy, had done it.

Murder is a million miles from not changing a sheet, thought Freddy. If a staff member killed Maude, that person is insane. I know these people. They're poster women for sanity.

"The staff," said Mrs. Maple icily, "is above reproach," she added, enunciating so carefully the words all but spattered on the guy's jacket.

"How many employees do you actually know? Have you met the night staff?" asked the detective.

Freddy had never once been here after dinner or before breakfast. He did not know a single person on the night shift, except Vera because now and then, she worked days. "Listen, you're going in the wrong direction," he told Ames. "The residents sleep all the time. Half of them are always dozing in their wheelchairs or at the dining table. They sleep so hard you can't even wake them. Maybe Maude just fell asleep against her pillow. Like the way with newborn babies it can happen? I forget what they call it, but it's why babies have to sleep on their backs and their heads get all flat."

"The forensic people think there was more pressure than that."

Freddy remembered Grandma and her meany beanies. What was a meany beany anyway, and how mean was he? Was he a murderer? Had Grandma seen something?

But Cordelia Chase couldn't recognize a Christmas tree anymore, let alone spot that somebody was using a pillow to smush a patient.

And Grandma hadn't sounded scared. Some dementia patients were scared all the time, but Grandma was only occasionally scared, mostly when he was pushing the wheelchair, so she couldn't see him and she'd cry out, "Who's there?" He would circle the wheelchair, kneel, take her hands, and say comforting things until she felt better.

Freddy couldn't believe Maude had been murdered. There was no point in murdering anyone here. Every resident was already en route to death.

Out the single window of the yellow room, he saw Kenneth Yardley, now sitting alone on a bench. On TV cop shows, they always suspected the spouse first. Freddy could imagine a husband getting desperate; all the families got desperate. But there was a lot easier solution: just stop visiting.

But in sober fact—not that Freddy was sober—such a death could have been planned by both spouses. Back when she was herself, Maude and her husband might have discussed situations like this. Back when she could put on makeup, meet her girlfriends for lunch, and play golf, back when there was no such thing in their lives as cognitive decline, Maude might have said, "Promise you'll just knock me off if I ever get Alzheimer's. If you love me, take me out of this body and send me into the next world."

But talking about offing the person you love and doing it aren't the same. It's more of a pact: This is not happening to *us*. *We* are not getting Alzheimer's. *We* are going to die comfortably in our sleep on our incredibly expensive mattress.

"You know one of the things that happens to people with dementia?" Freddy said to the cop. "Or Alzheimer's? They revert to being very little kids, like a one-year-old. And they forget how to brace for a fall. And they can't balance to start with. So when they fall, they fall face-first. You're going to see people with black eyes and gashed chins. Nobody got rough with them. They tipped over and hit the floor without flinging their hands out. So probably the bruises on Maude are from a fall. Nobody held her down. And don't go after the staff. It'll ruin MMC, and we need this place, and besides, I don't believe it. It had to be somebody from the outside."

"And how would that work, exactly?" asked the cop. "Start with signing in at that front desk."

"You could write any old name on the sign-in sheet," said Freddy. He had a bad feeling this was going to backfire, because if the detective knew about the sign-in sheets, he'd already confiscated or copied them, and Freddy's name wouldn't be there. But what would it matter? He had nothing to do with Kenneth or Maude. "Or come in with a group, like that Suzuki violin class that shows up every month with doting parents and video cams. As for the door code, it isn't to keep visitors out; it's to keep residents in. If you don't know it, the desk clerk just gives it to you. But you'd just be a violin parent and slide right in."

People loved doing good deeds, and what better good deed than to brighten a day at MMC? There was constant traffic of puppeteers, accordion players, storytellers, high school madrigal choirs, finger painters, and whatever. Half the residents were too deaf or mentally groggy to follow any action, song, or skill. The other half did enjoy it, even if they didn't know what it was or left in the middle.

Freddy preferred to take Grandma out. There were others who

did the same: the woman who saved up all her errands so she could take her Alzheimer's sister along, the son who still took his father bowling. The dad just sat there smiling at nothing while the son bowled for both of them.

Freddy wondered how the outsider murderer would know which bedroom was Maude's. They weren't labeled. The staff would have to show him. They'd say to the patient, "Here's your nephew!" or whatever. They'd be glad Maude had somebody in her life besides Kenneth. You wouldn't suffocate somebody while the staff stood there, so you'd hang tight till they left.

There were usually three or four aides, one LPN in charge, and one housekeeper. And of course there were other wings, identical in layout, all opening to the activity center, all with their own staff. The residents wandered constantly from wing to wing, but it wouldn't be easy for a stranger to wander.

But okay, the guy gets into the common room and somehow knows where to go and nobody sees him. What's he going to do? Shut Maude's door, press down the pillow, walk out? What if Kenneth was around? What about the physical therapist or visiting folk singers or the guy who clips everybody's warped toenails?

If you did a daytime strangle, since Maude probably wore pull-ups, needed meds, and had to be coaxed to drink liquids, an aide would shortly check on her, find her dead. You, the killer, would just have left.

But maybe nobody would link those two events. They'd just be glad that the poor "nephew" didn't actually witness the death. And if a day or two later, an aide mentioned the nephew's visit to Kenneth Yardley, and Kenneth said, "What nephew?" the aide would figure that in all the confusion, she'd mixed people up.

Or maybe the killer would pretend to be visiting somebody else altogether, so there really *was* no connection with Maude.

It wouldn't get easier to murder Maude by night. There were the before- and after-supper visitors. Then residents got washed up, given meds, put into their nightclothes, and tucked in. They were checked on all night long. There was no deep closet in which a visitor could hide, waiting for an opportunity, because people with dementia often had sufficient paranoia to like hiding, so instead of a closet, rooms had built-in drawers.

And what about when the murderer left MMC? He'd have to remember the exit code and pass the front-desk clerk again. Doable. But visible.

On the other hand, there were a lot of exit doors.

Each wing had two exits to the outside in case of fire. From the back garden with its shrubbery and fencing, there was an emergency exit gate. The bolt was very high up. Too high for a resident and, in Freddy's opinion, too high for half the staff. What were they supposed to do in case of fire—bring step stools? Ask a ninety-three-year-old for a leg up?

Freddy had been here once during a fire drill. Talk about nightmare. The alarm was so loud it gave Freddy a heart attack, and not a single resident noticed it. The aides had to coax everybody to walk outside, or push their wheelchairs, or give them their walkers. Half the residents didn't want to go. Half were asleep in chairs or sprawled on their beds, and it took two aides to move them. Half were going to the bathroom. Then when everybody was finally congregated at the proper exit, the aides did a head count and one resident was missing.

Freddy had been pushing his grandmother and also holding Mr. Griffin's arm. Mr. Griffin appeared to notice nothing amiss, but his grandmother could tell they were taking a trip. "Freddy, where is my hat?" She wouldn't move until Freddy located a hat.

The missing resident turned up in another resident's bathroom. The aide had to wait for him to finish pooping.

Grandma's wing failed miserably to get all the residents out of the building in the time allotted. If it had really been a fire, they would also have had to open the emergency gate and push everybody out into the parking lot. Freddy couldn't imagine keeping track of this crowd while fire engines whipped onto the property.

It occurred to him that a person could get into Memory Care from the garden gate instead of the front door. They'd need a stepladder on the outside to reach over and down to the bolt.

Freddy found that he was telling the detective about the garden-entry possibility.

"The back exit doors are just open?" asked the detective. "But we checked those. They have a code both directions."

"It's the same code. Even nondementia people can't remember more than one. So if you've ever been here, you know the code." Which opened up hundreds of possibilities: every friend, relative, medical worker, volunteer, and entertainer.

"What I think is," he told the detective, "you need another opinion on that autopsy. Do you trust that pathologist or is he a jerk?"

"She. Not a jerk. But I will tell her about people falling all the time."

"Don't make that sound like the staff's fault either," Freddy directed him. "It just happens." Too late, Freddy remembered another rule from Hippie Crime 101—don't give cops instructions. Don't give them anything. Just stand there and be stupid and silent.

Mrs. Maple said, "I'm uncertain that I accept the pathologist's report. But if it's true, Freddy is right. You have a lot of people to look at. There are many outsiders."

The detective smiled indulgently at Mrs. Maple. "And what threatening outsider have you seen around here lately?"

TEN

A rushing sound filled Freddy's skull. His brain swayed, as if it had come unattached.

Doc. The ultimate threatening outsider.

Doc had seen Freddy with Grandma. Grandma lived next door to Maude. Maude Yardley and Grandma had the same white hair and the same tiny breakable bodies. Could Doc have come into MMC and murdered Maude, thinking she was Freddy's grandmother? All because he wouldn't fake bead sales for Gary Leperov?

Some poor, confused old woman suddenly felt a vise of fingers, a mouthful of towel, her face crushed, her body thrashing, her life ending—*and it was Freddy's fault?*

The inside of his head went dark and seemed to implode. Freddy had always wondered what a faint was. You're standing there and you fall over? Come on.

He lowered himself carefully onto a soft yellow chair and managed to focus on the yellow wallpaper and the bowl of wooden apples in the center of a pointless little table. Somehow he drew a breath and then another, and when he could look around, the cop was talking to Mrs. Maple, and neither of them seemed aware that Freddy was hot, humiliated, and shaky. His faint had been on the interior. There were no witnesses.

Wait.

If the Leper had told Doc to hurt Freddy, he'd hurt Freddy, not his grandmother. And Doc wouldn't use a pillow on Freddy. Not a bullet in the head either. Given his commitment to mixed martial arts, he'd beat Freddy to a pulp.

Besides, offing old ladies wasn't the Leper's master plan: paying taxes so he'd look legal was his master plan.

Plus, a guy like Doc, built like a refrigerator and wearing spiked rings on tattooed hands, wouldn't blend into the parking lot, never mind the common room.

And the Leper didn't know that Freddy even *had* a grandmother, let alone one at MMC. Yes, Doc and Skinny had seen him push the wheelchair, which was, like, a clue. But it wasn't a name or a place.

You don't kill somebody over beads, Freddy told himself.

Except that there were no beads. There was dirty money, and maybe you did kill somebody over dirty money.

"You don't sign in or out, Mr. Bell," said the cop, "so you could have been here Wednesday night."

Had he admitted that he never signed in? Had the cop already examined the sign-in sheets? Or was the cop guessing?

A flaw of being high was that listening closely was out of reach; you could only listen loosely and then you drifted.

"Where were you Wednesday night?" asked the cop in a kind and neighborly voice. *I'm just your friendly patrolman; you can tell me anything.*

I was in my shop, thought Freddy. Alone. Making bongs. Which I plan to sell to your college-age kid.

Whoa. Had he said that out loud?

Apparently not, because Mapes snapped at the detective, "I beg your pardon! What is going on here? Why are you asking foolish questions of *us*?"

The cop sighed. "Mrs. Maple, I'm not saying either of you guys clipped the old lady. I'm just trying to get information, and instead, you're giving me opinions and interrupting me. How about I ask the questions and you give the answers?"

Laura did not care for this man. She nodded out the window. "I am concerned about Kenneth. He looks ill." She left the sitting room and walked through the lobby and out the front door to join Kenneth Yardley on the bench. The rain had stopped but the sun had not come out. It was gloomy and funereal and cold.

Kenneth was knotting his fingers and then releasing them, staring at his joints the way Alzheimer's patients stared at things: with absolutely no idea what they were looking at. Was he sliding into dementia himself or remembering all too clearly that these very fingers had held a pillow or a towel on Wednesday night?

Supposedly a person being suffocated fought with every bit of strength he or she possessed. What did fighting back consist of when you were nine decades old and weak as tissue paper?

"You let us know when the funeral is, Kenneth," she said. "We'll want to go." Laura wasn't sure who *we* meant, since in fact she did not want to go and couldn't imagine that anybody else here did. But a life must be honored, and Laura believed in the power of a funeral to comfort the family and guide the soul.

"There won't be a service," said Kenneth drearily. "Maude didn't believe in anything. Neither do I."

People who didn't believe in anything still had funerals. It was hard to drive up to a hole in the ground, drop the coffin in, and walk away. Even committed proselytizing atheists sometimes arranged church services, hedging their bets, perhaps, or succumbing to a last-minute horror over the dark nothingness they preached. Laura had been organist for a few of these. Don't play sacred music, they would tell her. But she always did. If they wanted secular, they'd be at a funeral home.

Kenneth was wringing his hands. His nails had not turned yellow or gotten ugly ridges, nor was his skin covered with age spots. The fingers were young. And now that Laura paid attention, his white hair had a settled, stiff look, too lush for a man Kenneth's age. Was it a hairpiece? Did men going bald ever buy white wigs instead of brown?

How old was Kenneth anyway? Maude had been in her nineties. But Kenneth did not seem anything like that old. Maybe Maude had once been a sexy chick and married a much younger man. Had Kenneth tired of waiters asking what he and his mother would like for dinner? Had he decided on a white hairpiece to present himself as a better match for his elderly wife?

"I wasn't here Wednesday night when they say it happened," said Kenneth, his voice full of anguish, "but they're treating me as if I sneaked back in and did it myself."

"Kenneth, I'm so sorry," she said helplessly.

She prayed for Maude. *Dear Lord, forget that she's an atheist who believes in nothing. Take her anyway. Let Maude be joyous and beautiful. Let her laugh and run. Let her hug friends and read books. Forgive Kenneth.*

Forgive me.

Freddy was not happy being alone in a small room with a cop, but he was filled with admiration for Mapes, just walking out on a detective.

He wondered if an autopsy started more than a day late could establish much of a time of death. "Wednesday night" was a bunch of hours. Suppose Maude had been murdered Wednesday afternoon instead, when visitors and activity people were still around, and nobody noticed the murderer or the temporarily closed bedroom door. Visitors tended to leave by five, as the staff gathered everybody for dinner. Would they notice if Maude was dead?

Most residents slept a lot of the time and a few slept practically all the time. If an aide glanced in and thought Maude was sleeping, would they shake her awake for dinner? Fix her a plate and hold it for later? Let her skip the meal altogether, figuring she needed her sleep?

MMC, which had seemed a nice cocoon last week, seemed pretty penetrable today. Freddy suppressed a shudder but not well enough, because the cop said, "Your grandmother is safe."

Freddy had trouble believing that a cop wanted to deliver comfort, but the guy actually patted Freddy's shoulder. "I think of you, and all these families, as heroes."

If I led Doc here, I'm no hero. And if the Leper ordered that murder, he'll check the online banners of the local paper and the TV station. He'll find out that the wrong resident got offed. He'll be back.

Freddy would never tell a cop about Gary Leperov. But if Freddy *didn't* tell, and Doc came back a second time...

Cut it out, he told himself. It wasn't Doc. The Lep doesn't want me or anybody else dead; he wants me to exhibit at BABE and fake another fifty thousand. There is no threatening stranger. There's Kenneth.

"The administrator told me you take your grandmother for a walk three, four times a week so she can get fresh air and sunshine," said the detective. Now he sounded snarky. Freddy looked up and saw mild contempt. *You're a loser, kid,* the cop was saying. *You have to get wasted to make yourself come in the door.*

Freddy was saved from an inappropriate response by another cop stepping into the parlor and muttering urgently. Freddy headed for his car. Nobody paid attention.

It's fine to be a loser to a cop, he told himself. Respect doesn't matter. This is a good outcome. Drive away.

And that nub in the cup holder?

Smoke it.

Eleven

Laura got home to find that the organ crew was long gone and had locked up. It didn't look as if they had done a thing, but in Laura's experience, construction was like that. Guys wandered around and got comfortable with a project before they actually launched.

She needed to eat something or she'd get a headache, but the thought of food set off waves of stomach upset. She understood the bleak reality of the half-life Maude and Kenneth had led. She so admired the buoyant Freddy, who faltered after every visit but bounced back, affectionate and caring toward the grandmother who now only sometimes knew him.

Would Freddy's mother be surprised that Freddy had not only done the right thing by his grandmother but was trudging on, doing the right thing into the indefinite—and certainly awful—future? Alice Bell had chosen Freddy, not one of her daughters. How painful it must have been to survey four children, deciding which one should be entrusted with the dwindling life of a very old woman.

But maybe the decision had been based entirely on geography, and the three daughters were as wonderful as Freddy but out of the picture only because of distance. Poor Freddy. If he had just known enough to relocate to Australia too, he would have been spared and it would all have been on Kara.

Her heart failed her, thinking of all these trustworthy people when she was not one.

She swallowed half a bowl of cereal and went to chorus rehearsal.

The concert choir practiced in the Congregational Church of Westbrook. Rebuilt after a Christmas Eve fire in 1892, the church had been a charming brown shingle, like the beach cottages of its day. In the 1970s, the brown shingles were pasted over with white vinyl siding. Blessedly, no remodeling committee had attacked the sanctuary, with its high, round ceiling painted a startling indigo blue. Acoustics were outstanding.

The chorus was to perform Haydn's *Mass in the Time of War* with a guest conductor, who turned out to be a wordy doctoral candidate more interested in displaying his scholarly triumphs than rehearsing the subtle dynamics of the *Paukenmesse*. Like all Yalies, Gordon Clary availed himself of every opportunity to wedge the name of his school into any conversation. Laura was approaching comatose when the man added dramatically, "Let us never forget that Charles Ives—about whom I have written two papers for Yale, of course—summered here in Westbrook as a boy. It's entirely possible that this great American composer played the organ in this very sanctuary."

Charles Ives had summered here?

In all her decades in Westbrook, Laura had never heard a mention of Charles Ives. He'd been a Danbury man. Was he also a Westbrook man?

Gordon Clary raised his baton and set a very fast tempo for the Haydn.

What are Charles Ives's dates anyway? she wondered, singing from memory because it was at least her fourth performance of the *Paukenmesse*. I think our doctoral candidate is wrong. I think by the time this building goes up, Charles Ives is at Yale, not hacking around on our organ.

Laura was given to pointless research and this was a fruitful topic: Charles Ives in Westbrook. Impossible to imagine.

But everything about Charlie Ives was impossible to imagine. A composer so chaotic, so wonderfully out of step, not hearing the same tiresome different drummer but church bells, marching bands, yelling children, patriotic songs, anvils, and sweet old hymns, all at the same time, assaulting one another. A composer Laura loved in the abstract, but if she had to sit down and actually listen, she'd rather stick a fork in her eye.

Laura hid her smartphone behind her music folder, went to the online Westbrook library catalog, and here they had a biography of Charles sitting on the shelf. She took the precaution of reserving it, just in case somebody else in the chorus had been paying attention and planned to check it out.

Gordon Clary whipped through the Mass.

Et resurrexit, she sang, and her eyes blurred. She prayed that Maude had been resurrected, that earthly things were gone for her, and that the method of her death no longer had meaning.

And the method of my life, thought Laura. How do I put meaning back into it?

FRIDAY

Twelve

Freddy opened his eyes to find that sleep had worked its glass miracle, filling his mind with color, pattern, and technique. He ran downstairs.

He loved his shop. He loved the posters of spray art taped to the walls. Freddy was not into art crime himself, but he knew a lot of people who were masters of it. He loved the splintery length of four-by-four into which he had drilled a bunch of holes, like a huge pencil holder, in which leftover glass rods in many colors tilted. He loved the crack-off bucket, an orange plastic mixing bowl with some water in it. Catastrophic temperature change caused glass to break off. Unwanted glass usually just fell into the bucket but could turn into projectiles and get you in the eye. Therefore Freddy really loved his big, dark safety glasses.

The kiln was clicking on and off, keeping the temperature at a hundred fifty degrees.

He opened the door and there were his beads waiting for him, warm like fresh baked bread. They cooled quickly in his hands. Last week, he'd overdone some color and the beads had been gaudy instead of glamorous, but this was good stuff.

It was so trippy to be at the level where he totally recognized good from crappy.

Sadly, the nicest bead was cracked. It was important to figure out why it had failed. Could be thermal, going from hot to cold too fast. Freddy added the cracked bead to the Box of Pain, a shallow wooden crate he had discovered in his grandmother's marvelous garage and bolted to the wall next to his bench. Grandma and

Grandpa had never discarded anything. Whenever life was too difficult to consider, Freddy would take another dive into the garage.

Then, surveying his little basement kingdom, Freddy prepared to light up. It was not a ceremony, exactly. More a procedure. He smoked pot out of a scrap of glass tubing because he sold anything good. Sometimes he rolled herb, but he wasn't very adept and half of it ended up on the floor, and Freddy couldn't afford to waste it.

The morning was brisk but sunny. Freddy slouched outside on Grandma's redwood chair with its thick, weather-stained pad, nothing but a recipient for inhaling. He floated, watching an indigo dawn become gaudy fire. Then he had his first cigarette of the day and went upstairs to make coffee.

Coffee was his culinary skill. He loved Grandma's funny old percolator. He loved using her tiny silver tongs to lift sugar cubes and drop them into her old Biltmore Hotel souvenir mug. He loved cream, so thick and perfect, the coffee sliding down like hot snow.

Other than that, Freddy used takeout, unless the minister's wife, Lily Burnworth, brought him a casserole. Her standards were scalloped potatoes with ham and baked spaghetti. How come she brought it so often? Was it funeral overflow? She'd forgotten how to measure and always had extra? Or had she adopted Freddy? Women often did. He was a little worried that Mapes might.

He drank his first cup standing at the counter, planning the day's work, and then carried his second cup downstairs.

He had to make enough beads to have a decent booth at the next bead show and enough pipes to earn a living. He had told the Leper he wasn't doing shows anymore. But in fact, beads hypnotized Freddy. What was more beautiful than a glass sphere?

His sisters liked to say, "Freddy, you can't spend your life making little round things with a hole in them."

Yes, he could. Beads were the most basic adornment of the human body. From the beginning of time, hunter-gatherers had poked holes in shells and bones, strung them together, traded and cherished them.

Freddy tried to think clearly about the presence of Doc and the skinny guy, but it took him weeks or years to see anything clearly. He did know that if he let the Leper run his life, it would last till Freddy was Grandma's age and he and Gary were both in an asylum for old stoners.

At twenty-six, Gary Leperov had already achieved a serious slot in the drug industry, which meant he had epic guts. Doc was no idiot either. He had made it into medical school.

Could it really be that Doc—who had once wanted to heal people—had sneaked into an institution that held the saddest and the weakest and purposely suffocated one of them?

The pipe world referred constantly to peace, love, kindness—all the nouns that went with Christmas cards, although potheads had no sense of grammar and included adjectives, so their list would be peace, love, kindness, pretty... But anyway, let somebody fail to pay for his weed or his pipe, and it was "I'm going to kill him."

Freddy didn't see Doc as a big supporter of peace, love, kindness, or pretty. But he totally didn't see Doc as a smotherer of old ladies asleep in their beds. He decided not to worry about that. The real worry was—could he tolerate another retail bead show?

Nothing compared to the smile of a bead lady who had just purchased a handful of glass jewels and would love him forever. It was the best thing about shows: the dreams in the air. Then of course there was: "Why is this so expensive? What do you mean, you don't take credit cards? You don't trust me?"

Of course he didn't trust a customer. What Freddy trusted was cash. "There's an ATM in the hall," he'd say, smiling right back.

Cash. The reason the Leper had befriended Freddy. How crazy that he'd gotten into hot water in the bead world, which was all middle class and quiet, and not in the pipe world, which ran around with crime all the time.

He'd made a pipe the other day, clean and classic, in Monet

colors. He remembered now that he'd put it up for auction on Instagram. Before he actually checked, he daydreamed about possible bids. Some rich dude who spent thousands on his pipes would see it. The bids would escalate, along with Freddy's fame.

I want a Freddy, somebody would post.
Did you see that Freddy? would be the next post.
What? You don't own a Freddy yet?
And finally, he would be a verb. Do you freddy, bro?

His cell phone rang: Jason, the supplier whose booth was next to his at the Milwaukee convention each year. Jason sold kilns and torches, huge tweezers and paddles, safety glasses and gas equipment. He had two physical shops, a large online presence, and was himself a very large guy. Jason always shared the Tupperware container of cookies his wife packed for his shows.

"Hey, Jase. Whaddup?"

"I got a phone call from the Leper asking about you. He wants to know exactly where you live."

Freddy sat.

"Luckily I don't know where you live," said Jason, "so I couldn't answer. Freddy, are you involved with him? Because Gary Leperov is not some friendly hippie."

Freddy totally trusted Jason, who kept the cashbox for him when Freddy trotted off to take a leak. But even Jason could not be told about the faked sales receipts. "Kind of," said Freddy.

"There's no such thing as 'kind of' with Gary Leperov. Once you're in, you're in. And there's no out."

Freddy resisted this. There was always an out.

"Gary Leperov is not into art, Freddy. He's into money."

"The Lep *is* an artist, Jason. Those toe pipes? The pendants where it's a finger or an ear that's got leprosy and it's necrotizing in glass? He sells a lot of those."

"He hires those out. He's too busy to make glass. Freddy, listen up. Every year in the United States, about a thousand dead bodies are found and never identified."

Freddy was skeptical. "Divide a thousand by fifty states, and you have twenty per state, Jason. You really think each state has twenty unidentified bodies every year?"

Connecticut had a number of tough towns: Bridgeport, Waterbury, Hartford, New Haven, Norwich. Could each one have unidentified corpses? Frozen homeless guys? Faceless murdered guys? Unknown ODs?

Since Jason lived in Brooklyn, he generally referenced New York City. "You know how floaters show up in the rivers around Manhattan? They usually find a dozen bodies in the river each year. And they claim it's suicides jumping off bridges. Well, at least a few of them, they're not suicides. The Leper's guys throw them off."

"The Lep is out of Vegas," protested Freddy. Plus, how many guys could you toss off a bridge when you weren't even thirty yet?

"He has a studio in a Vegas warehouse, where his employees make the toe pipes, but a guy like that, who knows where he's actually based? He's an octopus. Anyway, he's Russian. Second generation in drugs. He wouldn't be connected to Mexican cartels that control Nevada. Russian kingpins are in Brighton Beach and Bergen County."

So Gary wasn't a newbie. He had a father to advise him. And he wasn't a Vegas guy looking for a cheap flight for Doc. He was sending his mutts straight up I-95.

"Gary Leperov wants to know where you live?" said Jason. "This is not a good thing, Freddy. Watch yourself."

He thought of Maude, who could not watch herself. Grandma, who couldn't either. Polly and Philip and Irene and all the others— completely relying on the kindness of strangers. And now there was a stranger, or else Kenneth, who would strangle them.

It was impossible to believe.

Freddy walked into the Way Back: the deep yard he had loved so much as a kid. A belt of grass, an almost impenetrable stretch of forsythia, because each long thin wand arced over and rerooted, the tiny brook, the swamp of skunk cabbage, and finally the strip of sassafras, witch hazel, tulip tree, maple and oak that ran all the way to the railroad tracks. He and his sisters had gotten off the school bus every day at this house, ate afternoon snacks Grandma baked, played in this yard because Grandma and Grandpa believed in fresh air after school, not television, and at five thirty flew across the front yard to leap into their mother's car when she got back from work.

His mother had died in a vehicle. Her tour bus had flipped over, killing two people. Freddy could picture Alice Bell catching the falling bus in her arms and throwing it back up on the road, but he could not picture her trapped, crushed by the impact.

In the photograph his sisters obtained, the bus hadn't fallen into a deep ravine or off a mountainside. It had just fallen. Alice Bell, of all people, died in an accident where practically everybody else just got out, dusted themselves off, and went on.

Oh, Mom, he thought suddenly, and grief shot through him.

He had to pull himself together. He decided to check his Instagram pipe auction. Usually bids were hot for an hour or two and then tapered off and vanished.

> 250. Sweet color.
> 300. Killer work.
> Good one, man. Wish I had money.
> 350. Mine.

Three hundred fifty dollars was way exciting. Freddy had never sold a pipe for that much money. He was laughing with delight when in came another bid.

No, posted the Leper. Mine. 1000. Doc will pick it up at your place, Freddy.

THIRTEEN

Laura walked to the library.

The Ives biography had been written by an expert not from Yale, which was a pleasing bonus. She checked it out, walked home, yelled hello to Howard and Marco, who had arrived in her absence, and sat on her front porch to read.

Charlie, it turned out, had been born in 1874. He had a wonderful childhood with his delightful crazy father and did indeed spend his summers in Westbrook at the home of his uncle, Lyman Brewster.

Great name, thought Laura. Sounds like a Pilgrim or a transcendentalist.

In the 1880s, there had been excellent summer train service between Danbury and the shoreline, and even when he was very young, Charlie caught a train back to Danbury every weekend because he was a church organist there. His brother had had the unenviable job of pumping the organ for him.

In an extant letter from August 1889, Charlie begged his father to sub for him in Danbury, because Charlie wanted to stay in Westbrook—fishing, swimming, rowing, and playing tennis and baseball. (Even in his century, being a musician, let alone an organist, was lame. "What do you play?" a well-meaning adult would ask Charlie, referring to Mr. Ives's marching band. "Shortstop," Charlie would tell them.)

By the time he was a teenager, though, Charlie was organist at St. Thomas's Episcopal in New Haven and attending Hopkins, prepping for Yale. So it seemed unlikely that Charlie had spent much time visiting Westbrook Congregational, or even *any* time, given that he was busy elsewhere on Sundays, and if he had ever been in the church, it would have been the building that burned in 1892.

Many Ives relatives summered next door to each other: Lyman Brewster, the Whites, the Parmelees, and the Seeleys, in whose house Charlie practiced the piano. They called their neighborhood "Cousins' Beach."

Each small beach in Westbrook, separated by little brooks or curves of land, had a name: Chalker Beach and West Beach, New York Beach and Stannard Beach, Middle Beach and Chapman Beach. Laura had never heard of Cousins' Beach, but that might have been family usage, not the official name.

At the town hall, Laura researched the precise location of Lyman Brewster's summer home.

Westbrook had been a popular summer destination since the 1870s. But in that century, houses were not numbered. Laura could not figure out which house had been owned or rented by which Ives cousin. Their houses might have been destroyed in hurricanes, moved away from the beach to save them from future hurricanes, or torn down and replaced.

The Seeley property was easier to work out because it turned over so few times. The Seeleys kept the house where Charles Ives had once practiced the piano from 1882 until 1910. A family named Fairweather bought it in 1910 and kept it as a summer home until 1955. By then, it had a street name: Magna Lane. In 1955, the Valeski family purchased the house. They still owned it.

Freddy was in need of an ally. He drove Grandpa's pickup down to the shoreline, hoping Shawn would be home.

Shawn scored excellent weed, always shared, and never asked

about Grandma, making him the only adult in Freddy's life who did not want to dive into a dementia conversation.

The Aminetti property still had its barn, which had been remade into two apartments. Shawn lived in one and used the other for his glass studio. As far as Freddy knew, Shawn paid no rent, although there were utility dials on the exterior wall of the barn, so he might pay heat and light. His parents and grandparents lived in the farmhouse, which meant that Shawn had great meals whenever he wanted them and probably also when he didn't.

Shawn's grandparents were from Italy and were serious garden-ers. There were grapevines, raised tomato beds, a chicken run, a glass shed, and a row of tiny fruit trees, whose slender branches linked little twiggy fingers. There was a rhubarb bed and thorny assortments of berries. The vegetable garden had raised rows, and fall produce awaited the daily harvest. Freddy wasn't that keen on vegetables and certainly didn't want to raise them, but he liked the garden.

Shawn's truck wasn't parked beside the barn. Freddy had been counting on the camaraderie that only another lampworker could provide. Since he wanted his living arrangements to be temporary, he hadn't made an effort to reach old high-school friends. But want-ing his situation to be temporary was awfully close to wanting his own grandmother to die, so Freddy tried not to go there.

Maude's death hit him again, and again he couldn't believe it. It was too crazy. Too vicious. Too pointless.

He was making a three-point turn to leave when Shawn's mother came out of the house. Freddy put the window down. "Hi, Mrs. Aminetti."

"Freddy, come in. Keep me company. I just made cookies," she added.

Being polite to old women was a large part of his life these days, so he parked and followed her in. In the center of her very large, never remodeled kitchen sat a table with scrubbed oilcloth in a strawberry-and-wicker-basket pattern. Crowded together in the center were an Elvis salt and pepper, a cruet of oil, a cracked sugar bowl, and a chipped china thing packed with paper napkins.

She poured Freddy a glass of milk and set down a plate with a dozen cookies, thick with chocolate chips and oatmeal.

She said, "You heard then." Her voice was raw.

The cookies had had Freddy's attention, but now he looked at Shawn's mother. She'd been crying. "I didn't hear anything. What's wrong? What happened?"

"Shawn's in jail. He got caught buying cocaine in Norwich. They charged him with intent to distribute."

Freddy almost fell off the chair. Shawn? Without an ambition in the entire world except lunch? Deciding to become a drug dealer? You didn't deal coke if you didn't already use it, and Freddy could not believe Shawn was into coke. "Mrs. Aminetti, it has to be a mistake. Shawn would never do that."

"There were cameras. It's on video."

Could Shawn have been set up the way Auburn and Danielle set up Br? What could be achieved by controlling a shoreline constable? It would be like controlling a traffic light.

"Shawn said he was ordered to do it by some horrible person he knows from glass."

How could anybody order Shawn to do anything? Shawn gave the orders; that was what it was to be a cop.

"Oh, Freddy," Mrs. Aminetti burst out. "How could you and Shawn get into this terrible thing? This pipe thing, this nightmare, this evil?"

Freddy did not present a defense. Among themselves, lamp-workers called pipe-making "the degenerate art." Shawn's mother would not want to hear that.

He thought of Shawn behind bars. Behind bars for a long time. Connecticut might make marijuana legal, but it would never make selling cocaine legal. "Shawn give you a name?"

"No. He just said the person was dangerous."

Freddy drank some milk. Could Shawn be mixed up with the same dangerous person Freddy was? But Shawn's glass wasn't even minor league. It was more like T-ball. Glass was just a hobby for him, and Freddy respected that. But whatever it was, it wasn't a channel to Gary Leperov.

"Have a cookie," said Mrs. Aminetti.

"I'm not very hungry, thanks."

Mrs. Aminetti opened a low, deep drawer and took out waxed paper. They still manufactured waxed paper? Mrs. Aminetti had not even converted to plastic bags? I'm living out my life with people who are living *their* lives in the 1950s, Freddy thought.

She tore off a large square, put half a dozen cookies in it, wrapped the cookies in a neat package, and twisted a fat rubber band around it. Probably the rubber band had held the newspaper and been saved for a week or a year.

"Thank you," said Freddy, accepting the cookie packet. "Is there anything I can do to help?" He prayed she would say no. He prayed really hard.

She whirled toward him and glared. "Quit making pipes! Stop using drugs!" Her voice rose. "Grow up, Freddy! Get out of glass!" She slapped her palm on her table.

Glass was his life. He wasn't getting out.

For Shawn, glass was a sideline. Now prison would be Shawn's life.

Shawn was a slow, relaxed kind of guy. Weed magnified these traits, so on his days off, Shawn was a sloth, hanging out on his little deck, binging on TV, taking in the sun. He was addicted to a show where people went naked in snake-infested regions of Central American countries where the natives were smart enough not to live. The Americans would run around bare, knee deep in poisonous frogs and spiders the size of bricks.

Just thinking about jungles made Freddy want to go hug a parking lot.

Shawn had been saving for a boat trip up the Amazon.

Had the Lep promised him airfare? Had Shawn agreed to peddle coke for a cruise?

Freddy couldn't see it. Plus, the Lep's world was marijuana. Cocaine was a whole 'nother universe.

Unless Gary Leperov occupied *two* worlds.

Freddy hadn't let himself use the phrase "money laundering," even though he knew perfectly well that was what he was doing. He liked to think of it as sales receipts—okay, faked, but like, whatever.

But it was money laundering, and the dirt that had to be washed out of Gary Leperov's cash might be from coke. Freddy had agreed in part because it struck him as fun. The first time he got away with it, he thought, *How cool is that?*

If it's coke money, he thought now, there's nothing cool about it.

Mrs. Aminetti said, "There is one thing you could do, Freddy. Take Shawn's dog."

Freddy went into spasm. His fingers crushed the cookie packet.

The dog, Snap, was named for his habit of nipping people. He was cute enough. Medium size, long black-and-white coat, long floppy ears, long sharp teeth. Snap chewed occasionally on Shawn, but Shawn just laughed and rubbed him behind the ears. "He doesn't draw blood," Shawn liked to say. "He just likes to get a grip now and then."

Take Snap? Feed him? Walk him? Protect neighborhood kids from him? Not that Grandma's house was in a neighborhood. What with woods, railroad tracks, and swamps, it was as isolated as you could get on two acres.

Mrs. Aminetti said, "Shawn was so nervous buying drugs he didn't even remember to fasten Snap's leash. The animal-control officer in Norwich called us. They found the dog wandering in some park there."

Snap always rode in the front of Shawn's pickup, the window cracked for the dog to sniff whatever cool things dogs sniffed, something Freddy wished he could do. The passenger window was crusted with dried saliva. Shawn couldn't see any right-side traffic.

"I'll go buy a crate," he said. "I'll be right back."

"You won't be back," said Mrs. Aminetti. "The minute you drive around the corner, you'll know better than to take Snap, and you'll be in the next state under a different name."

Since Freddy frequently planned to be in the next state under a different name, he couldn't laugh.

"I have a crate," she said, leading Freddy down to her truly magnificent cellar, a place even more packed with tantalizing stuff than Grandma's garage, a place where a man could root for days, plus drink homemade wine.

Freddy lugged the crate upstairs.

Next to the barn, Snap waited in his run. He wagged his tail, but this was deceptive. Freddy positioned the open crate against the dog-run gate, slid the gate open, and wiggled his bare fingers through the mesh as bait. Snap leaped forward. Freddy withdrew his fingers just before crunch time and fastened Snap in.

Mrs. Aminetti gave him a case of canned dog food and two huge bags of dry dog food. Freddy hoisted the crate onto the wide front seat and drove home.

Because his sister Emma lived there, Freddy had taken up Alaska reality shows on TV. He followed Alaska state troopers, Alaska railroad engineers, Alaskans living north of the Arctic Circle, Alaska real estate agents, and Alaska cattle ranchers. In most episodes, a man lifted his chin and said into the camera, "I'm here so I can be free." Right after that, the guy would spend a whole day splitting wood in three feet of snow at ten below in a high wind. This was freedom?

With a dog he didn't want whining in his front seat, Freddy pulled into Grandma's driveway. Freddy was living under the radar—no taxes, no bureaucracy, no licenses, car registrations, or diplomas. Instead, he had dementia visits, an ugly raised ranch, somebody else's dog that bit people, and the Leper. This was freedom?

It *is* freedom, he thought. Shawn threw it away.

And maybe I did too, agreeing to do whatever the Lep said.

FOURTEEN

The Valeski house was a huge brown-shingled affair, with a big, old porch facing the beach and a big, old porch facing the lane. Laura bet it had big, old problems and would cost a big, old amount of money to fix. Workmen on high ladders were closing second-floor shutters for the winter, so it was one of the few remaining beach-front houses not remodeled for year-round occupancy.

"Hi, Laura," called a woman.

"Kemmy! Is this your house? Are you a Valeski?" Kemmy sang alto in the concert choir and was one of many friends Laura knew only by voice.

"Nobody's a Valeski," said Kemmy.

"It's on the property records as Valeski."

"Oh, that's true. Nonna Valeski is still alive. She's ninety-six. But she had only daughters, and they all married, so the Valeski name disappeared, like, half a century ago. I married a grandson. What are you doing pawing through property records? Planning to make us an offer? We'll take it. Nonna still comes down for the summer and it's a nightmare, because she can't use stairs, can't manage the stove, can't do anything really, so we take turns staying with her, and she's deaf as a post, so we also take turns shouting."

Laura had enough people like that in her life. "I got interested in Charles Ives," she explained. "The composer."

"Hideous stuff. Gives me headaches. I nearly left the rehearsal when Gordon Clary began blatting about him. Such an annoying man. Gordon, I mean, not Charles Ives. Why does he have to starch his shirt collar so heavily that his neck explodes out of it? And then he tucks the shirt in and tightens his belt and his waist explodes as well. But if you don't look at him, he's fine."

"The whole point of a conductor is that you look at him," said Laura. "Anyway, Charlie Ives summered on this beach and practiced the piano at your house."

"Don't be silly. Nonna would have said so."

Laura had a wild thought. A house that had changed hands only twice in over a century. Had it been redecorated? Or decade after decade, had summer people happily used the same, old shabby stuff? "I don't suppose you have an old piano that Charles Ives might have played."

Kemmy hooted with laughter. "There is a piano but it can't be that old. Nothing lasts that long in unheated, un-air-conditioned waterfront property. Nobody's played it in years. It's a plant stand now."

They went inside to look. The house was cold and ugly and smelled of mothballs, low tide, and onions. It wasn't even a remodeling candidate. It was a teardown. But in Charlie's day, with kids racing in, a salty breeze blowing through open windows, and a dog barking? Perfect.

The piano was an upright grand. Probably weighed a literal ton. Years of icy winters, scorching summer heat, and salt air had destroyed the finish. One side looked as if it had been through a house fire. Even the name of the piano's maker had peeled away.

Kemmy moved a row of dead African violets and wrenched up the warped lid, exposing the keyboard. Some of the ivory had curled but Laura attempted a scale anyway. Only a few keys made sound.

"You want it, you move it," said Kemmy. "And it's not Charles Ives's. It's junk. You were paying way too much attention to Gordon Clary."

Laura tried to be sensible. She actually was quite practical, even thrifty, if you didn't count organ installations and red Cadillacs. But speaking of organ installations, she had two strong men at her house at this very minute. And they had a truck, a ramp, and a dolly.

She called them on her cell.

Howard and Marco had liked Laura Maple before, because they liked anybody who commissioned a pipe organ. But a woman who would buy a dead piano on the off chance it once felt the hands of Charles Ives? When they finally stopped laughing at the sight of the ruined upright, they treated it as piano royalty.

The possible Ives piano would have to live in the same room as the two grands and the future organ, and even after the men condensed the pipe crates, it was a tight fit.

Howard removed the front paneling of the dead piano to see if the works could be restored. Off came the rectangular slab above the keys. The lower door, below the keyboard and above the pedals, seemed to be hinged, which was unusual. Generally this part of the case was held in by pegs. The hinges had rusted shut.

"We'll get to it later," they told her. "Right now, we gotta get back to our organ."

Laura loved the pronoun. It was their organ until it was finished, and then it was hers. But hers or not, she was in their way. Laura retreated to her nicely rearranged parlor, and guilt attacked. Guilt was something Freddy often wanted to discuss. What was it anyway? Why did some people have it and some people didn't?

Laura had hoped that doing good deeds would erase her own guilt about the past, but it hadn't worked out like that. No matter how much decency she displayed now, the ugly past stayed ugly.

She rarely visited MMC two days in a row, but sometimes visiting Aunt Polly assuaged a little of the guilt. She remembered Maude. How could she have set aside the horror of Maude's death? How could she have branched out into some foolish music-history project when there was Maude to think of?

Because I've turned my whole life into silly projects so that I don't have to think of my past. But I should think about Maude. I owe Maude my thoughts.

———————

At Grandma's, Freddy uncrated Snap and fastened his leash. The two of them ran in circles around the house for a while. Maybe all Snap needed was exercise. For sure Shawn never exercised. But it turned out that what Snap mainly wanted to exercise were his jaws.

He led Snap through the Way Back, so full of great smells that Snap was in dog ecstasy. Freddy hauled him over the little swamp and yanked on the ropes of the old tire swing to test them. They hadn't rotted. He took off the leash, gripping Snap's collar with one hand, and tossed the leash around the swing rope, threaded it through its handle, and reattached it to the collar. Snap could now roam about twenty feet.

Snap sat on his haunches and gave Freddy the sad liquid stare that melted most dog owners' hearts, but not one as reluctant as Freddy. The absolute last thing he needed was a bad dog. Back at the house, he filled a water bowl and a kibble bowl and carried them to Snap, who snarfed up the kibble and flung his tongue around in the water.

Freddy walked back to the shop. He didn't have enough focus to eat a cookie, let alone work.

He was awash in anxiety. Shawn dealt drugs? Kenneth suffocated his wife? The Lep threw people off bridges?

He had a jittery sense of needing to put his arm around his grandmother, make sure she was okay.

Freddy never felt *better* after visiting Grandma, exactly, but he always felt good, like his mother might actually be pleased with him. Not proud, she was never proud. But at least not disgusted.

———————

At MMC, Laura found Kenneth once again standing in front of the closed door of his wife's room, staring at the solid wood like a dementia patient who bumps into a wall and can't remember how to go sideways.

"Hello, Kenneth," she said. "I was hoping to read Maude's obituary. Learn more about her life and career. What paper is it in?"

Kenneth twitched the locked doorknob of his wife's room. "I'm not writing an obituary. Maude disapproved of them."

You could disapprove of gambling, bad movies, or a president, but could you really disapprove of obituaries? But then, Laura disapproved of approximately a million things that seemed to be just fine with society.

"If anything happened to her, the staff did it," said Kenneth fiercely, "or one of those jerks pretending to entertain. The residents don't even notice the entertainment. They're just bringing these people in so the staff doesn't get bored. I think it was some activities person. All those cloggers. That creep with the puppets."

The puppet guy *was* creepy. Having dementia was probably a plus during that particular entertainment.

Kenneth rubbed his eyes so hard Laura thought he might avulse his own eyeballs. All of a sudden, he looked older.

He really is Maude's age, she decided. He just has good skin. Everybody has good something: eyesight, hearing, knee joints. His is skin.

Kenneth kept trying the doorknob. "I can't even get her things."

Nobody had valuables here. The poor patients no longer knew what was valuable. And there wasn't space to accessorize. No matter how you had lived before, no matter how grand your possessions and collections, here you were down to a windowsill and a shelf. Maude's room would contain nothing but food-stained blouses and worn-out slippers.

Kenneth gave up on the door and walked away.

Laura found Polly in the art room, crayoning along with half a dozen other residents. Each had been given a page cut from a toddler's coloring book. The volunteer was suggesting good colors for the teddy bear. "Is this brown?" Aunt Polly asked, holding up a green crayon.

Laura couldn't stand it. She walked around the corner, thinking to have a chat with the nurse, but the nurse's office with its top-open Dutch door was empty. Inside, on a deep shelf at eye level, stood a hundred-plus three-ring binders in alphabetical order. Yardley, Maude J., was last on the right.

Movement was slow here in Memory Care.

The nurse would mosey back from whatever she was doing. She was heavy and wore thick-soled neon-bright sneakers, which made squishy noises when she walked.

Laura reached over the shelf of the half door, unlatched it, stepped in, and retrieved Maude's binder. Why was it still here anyway? On the other hand, where would it go?

The first page was the application.

A severely physically ill person could not be accepted as a resident, because this was memory care, not a nursing home. A resident couldn't be violent. Alzheimer's and dementia could cause rage, which led to hitting and biting. MMC wasn't set up for that. Poor Philip had moved to the far edge of acceptability. And third, of course, the family had to have enough money.

This application began with Maude's date of birth, place of birth, husband's full name, residence at the time of application, and the last four digits of her social security number. Because residents could not always identify themselves, the facing page had Maude's current photograph in a plastic sleeve, along with a smaller photo from when she had been a few decades younger. Laura took cell phone photographs of the photos and IDs and replaced the chart.

Laura didn't have a good reason to trespass on Maude Yardley. She didn't have half a reason. She wanted Kenneth *not* to be a murderer. But if he had not killed Maude, it had been a staff member or an outsider, in which case, Polly was at risk.

She had to know.

She let herself out of the record room and latched the half door behind her.

Fifteen

Driving up to Middletown, Freddy came to his senses. Nobody had killed Maude. Certainly not Kenneth. A guy who shows up three or four days a week to sit with a brain-dead wife? He's going to snap? No. He feels homicidal, he skips MMC that week and goes to the casino.

Still. Could Kenneth have killed his wife for money?

But if there's money, he thought, we're all spending every cent of it on MMC. If we don't want to shell out, we don't have our person there. But we all have power of attorney, and if we want money, we just spend it. And he's the husband; he has the money anyway. On the other hand, Maude just keeps on living, MMC is eating up the whole estate, and maybe Kenneth wants something left for himself.

When he got to MMC, he sat in the car and people-searched Kenneth Yardley.

There were two in Connecticut. The one married to Maude Jeanette Kaiser Yardley was in Old Greenwich. Kenneth, the people search informed him, was eighty-eight. Maude was eight-four.

Wow. Mr. Yardley was some well-preserved dude.

Do eighty-eight-year-olds commit murder? Does a person really care that much about anything once he's that old? Isn't it enough just to breathe again the next morning?

Old Greenwich was nowhere near Middletown. Kenneth could not be driving daily from Old Greenwich.

Well, maybe he could. It just seemed like a long way, because Greenwich residents face New York City and hardly know that the rest of Connecticut exists. The drive would be six lanes most of the way: I-95, I-91, and then Route 66, which petered out and became any old road. But even with traffic, it was probably only an hour and a half.

Still, that was three hours of driving plus all that time hanging out at MMC. It made visiting Maude a full-time job.

Real estate in Old Greenwich was seriously expensive. The only people who could afford to buy there were Wall Street types with bonuses. Freddy checked Zillow. The Yardley house looked pretty ordinary on its quarter acre, but its worth was estimated at $1.6 million.

A guy with that kind of house didn't need to murder his wife to get cash. Just sell the house.

Why tuck Maude in an institution too far away for her girl-friends to visit? But Maude had probably outlived most of her friends, while dementia drove away the rest.

Kenneth could have bought the house decades ago when he was a vacuum-cleaner salesman or whatever, and now he was living on social security and couldn't afford memory care in Fairfield County. But then again—just sell the house.

The other Kenneth Yardley lived in New Britain, a city with wild variations in prosperity and neighborhood, about fifteen minutes northwest of Middletown. The street view showed a rather sad two-family near the campus of Central Connecticut, probably a cheap student rental with lots of turnover and parties.

The search listed the same relative—Maude—for both Kenneth Yardleys. So maybe there were not two Kenneths; maybe there was one Kenneth with two houses. Maybe Kenneth had gotten himself housing closer to Maude for these daily visits, which was kind of sweet.

He checked the tax assessor's online records. The New Britain house was owned by a Robert Lansing, so Kenneth was probably a renter. He must have kept the Old Greenwich house but be renting in New Britain so he'd be near Maude.

It was a serious sacrifice. Freddy respected Kenneth for it. He did not want the police deciding that the husband did it.

But if the husband didn't do it, and Doc didn't do it, then somebody on the staff had.

Staff? As in Jade? Heidi? Vera? Constanza? Mary Lou? Grace? No way.

Freddy went in the front door instead of the employee entrance. For the moment, there was no one at the desk.

He leaned over the visitor book. It was a large spiral pad on which you were supposed to write your name, the date and time, the resident you were visiting, and your cell phone number. He took a picture of the day of Maude's death. Kenneth had checked out at 3:00 p.m. Mapes had checked in but forgotten to check out. Freddy of course wasn't there at all. He went backward, capturing several more pages. Kenneth signed in dutifully two or three days a week. Freddy had been thinking he visited a lot more than that. Was Kenneth also a sign-in skipper?

Maude had had only one other visitor he could find. A Virginia Lansing had come once. Was she an owner of the duplex?

You had to be some kind of loyal to visit a woman as deep in dementia as Maude. You can't take a person like Maude to a restaurant or play cards or ask for the latest. You just sit there and then you leave.

Constanza shuffled into the lobby at the pace of an Alzheimer's patient instead of a twenty-year-old clerk.

"Hey, Constanza," said Freddy. "Looking great. Love the earrings." Actually, she looked totally crummy. "Something else happened?" he asked. "What? Tell me."

"The police are checking up on everybody. They found out Mary Lou has a criminal record. She's been fired."

Mary Lou hadn't saved up enough for her dental work. And now she had no income. And she'd have a hard time getting another job. "MMC doesn't run background checks?" he asked.

"Mary Lou came through a temp agency, and the temp agency does the background checks. She was so good, they hired her outright, but it turned out that temp agency just *says* they do a check. And guess what else," said Constanza. "I found a finger on a string. Sitting here on the desk."

Freddy's eyes crossed.

"I'm not joking," said Constanza. "It was a *finger*, all creepy and dusty and dead, like a zombie finger, but it was a bead hanging from a string. They said it's made of glass, although it looked like pottery to me."

Leper pendants were very collectible. The string would be hemp. And Doc would have been wearing one. "A string like a necklace or a Christmas tree decoration?"

"Like a necklace, Freddy. You wouldn't put a dead finger on your tree."

"And the string wasn't broken? It didn't, like, fall off? Somebody set it down on purpose?"

"How would I know? Are you turning into a detective? Everybody else is. It's the new hobby around here."

"When did you find it?"

"Yesterday."

There was no clutter on Constanza's desktop. Along with her computer was the big sign-in book, a little jar filled with pens and pencils, a small digital clock, and a fake plant. A finger on a string could not lurk unnoticed for several days, so it couldn't have been there since late Wednesday night.

Was the finger a sign intended for Freddy? A sign of what? What if Constanza hadn't mentioned it? What was the plan, leaving it on her desk? And whose plan was it?

"The police told us to let them know about anything unusual," said Constanza, "so I gave it to them, and you know what? They recognized it. There's a clothing store down by that Himalayan gift shop, right on Main Street. They sell stuff like that. Like who would buy it?"

The police were probably already in Auburn's shop, questioning her. A woman who had cocaine in her back room would never tell a cop anything.

Except that he now knew Auburn would fabricate anything.

Freddy was suddenly really sorry that his pipes were in a cabinet in her shop.

Sixteen

Mr. Griffin was trying to get out. "Hey, Mr. Griffin," said Freddy. "This is good luck. Let's head on over together."

"I think I'm late," said Mr. Griffin.

"Heck no. Your timing is perfect." Freddy took Mr. Griffin's arm, and together they walked back into the activity room.

He sat on a metal chair with his grandmother in her wheelchair next to him while Mrs. Maple told a long, boring story about the composer Charles Ives being a summer person in Westbrook in the 1880s. Freddy listened because it was better than thinking about everything else converging on him. "You won't believe this," he said, "but I am familiar with Charlie. My mother and my grandmother were strictly classical. NPR was their best friend."

"I wish I had known them!" cried Mrs. Maple, forgetting that she was sitting next to that very grandmother. Of course, there was no way to get to know Cordelia Chase in this incarnation. "I'm reading Charlie's biography," she said.

"Already? You just found out about him."

"If there is a book lying around unread," said Mapes, "I attack. Want to hear a great line? Charlie Ives said that in thinking about composing, he kept in mind a brass band with wings."

A brass band with wings!

He'd seen a trumpet bong on Instagram. He didn't want to copy anything. What else was brass? Maybe he could do a trombone bong. With wings. Awesome.

A trombone was a complex instrument.

Where would the water go? In the bell, of course, which was

cool but problematic, because a trombone's bell was in the center of the slide, so the rig could not stand on its bell like a trumpet. His trombone had to be perfect or people would laugh. Could he put glass feet on the U-turn of the slide so it stood upright, a little trombone person? Tricky.

He'd use clear ruby red for the bell, so you could watch the water bubble, and opaque ruby for the spit valve, braces, and mouthpiece. A water pipe could be any size, and this year, the style was seven or eight inches high.

A real trombone was a metal project, made out of a sheet, and making it from glass was, like, insane. He'd have to build scaffolding to hold his pieces together for when he welded them, glass to glass.

Dude. Seriously difficult. But cool.

He came out of his daydream about the world's most beautiful rig to find that Mrs. Maple was now interrogating Mrs. Reilly. "You sincerely feel the residents are safe?" said Mapes.

"Of course."

"Obviously the *police* do not think the residents are safe," said Mapes, "since they've posted an officer here."

Whoa, thought Freddy. What happened to my cop antenna?

He hadn't even spotted the guy propped up against a wall in the activity room, looking bitter. Probably wondering who he'd offended to get this duty.

Mrs. Reilly went off to do whatever administrators did. Talking low, Freddy filled Mapes in on his Kenneth search: the two houses, the landlord, and the visit of the Lansing woman, who was probably related to the landlord. It was public information, sitting online, waiting to be read, but it felt like a trespass on Kenneth. Mrs. Maple countered with the details of Maude's medical record.

Stuffy old Mapes had gone into a locked (well, latched anyway) office to read private medical records? Now *that* was trespass.

Mrs. Maple handed him her cell phone. "Look at the photo of Maude when she was middle-aged."

Maude Jeanette Kaiser Yardley had been nice looking. Not nice in the sense of pretty but nice in the sense that she looked like the grandmother everyone wanted. A woman who baked a lot and laughed a lot. Like Grandma, except chunky. The resemblance to MMC's Maude was hard to spot, but then, dementia was destructive of personality, and with the personality gone, the face changed.

"What is she standing in front of?" asked Mrs. Maple.

"Definitely stained glass. She's in a church." Freddy had never done stained glass, which he considered basket-weaving, "Kumbaya"-singing 1960s arts-and-crafts crap. Well, not the stained-glass windows in churches, but certainly what hobby stores sold.

"Kenneth told me they didn't believe in anything," said Mapes, "and she didn't want a funeral, but here she is standing in a church."

"Living with dementia could sap anybody's belief," said Freddy. Although in his case, a minister's wife was keeping him in casseroles and the minister was helping with Grandma, so Freddy had, as it were, secondhand faith. And if he had a team in his dementia world, it was not his distant sisters; it was the Burnworths. I should go to church or something, he thought. Show my gratitude.

"We know she lived in Old Greenwich, because that's on the application," said Mrs. Maple, "and therefore I think the church in this photograph is in Old Greenwich. I'm going to call every church secretary in that town to see where Maude was a member."

"Will they tell you?"

"Of course they will. They'll want to put an announcement in the church bulletin so Maude's Old Greenwich friends will know about her death."

Freddy didn't get why Mapes would do that, although certainly *he* never needed a reason to do things. Is it fun? You're on.

"Also under consideration," said Mrs. Maple, "is that your grandmother has called Kenneth a meany beany, and later she said there were other meany beanies. Anything a resident says is suspect, but still."

Freddy's mind skittered to the awful possibility that his grandmother had witnessed the murder. Why leave her alive to tell the tale? If you were going to slaughter one old lady, would you stop at slaughtering another one? He took Grandma's hand to reassure himself that she had not been suffocated. He glanced at the aides, the other residents, the fresh flowers on the tables and the snacks on the tray. He still could not believe that anybody had been murdered.

He pulled out his cell and phoned his Dakota sister. He and Kara never used preliminaries. "Karrie Darrie, can you remember Grandma using the phrase 'meany beany'?"

"She used to call Jenny that. Remember what a bully Jenny was? Always pushing me and Emma around."

"Jenny? Jenny is a total soft touch."

"Well, *now*. She *did* grow up. But *then*. It was always Jenny's toy, Jenny's dessert, Jenny's TV channel, Jenny's shopping trip. Emma and I were just people to yell at."

This sounded fabricated to Freddy. On the other hand, his sisters were a lot older than he was. He hadn't been born when they were battling seven-, eight-, and nine-year-olds or whatever. He said, "Tell me about meany beany."

"Why?" said Kara, leaving out the "h" so the word sounded extra irked.

"Whhhy," he corrected her. "Because Grandma's been saying it."

"Grandma never uses a vulgarity, a swear word, or any syllable that could be construed as ugly or rude. So she never said, 'Jenny, you rotten little shit, cut it out.' She said, 'Jenny! Do not be a meany beany.'"

What could Kenneth have done to merit meany-beany status? He hadn't pulled the chair out from under his wife or smacked her. In fact when Grandma called Kenneth a meany beany, Maude hadn't been murdered yet, had she?

Freddy never had a good time frame. His days slopped into each other, and nights vanished altogether.

"I'm in the car-pool line," said Kara. "Gotta go."

South Dakota vanished and Mrs. Maple leaned forward again. "I need more about Kenneth Yardley. I want to check on money. Money is the reason for most violence and crime."

"Mapes, if Kenneth killed Maude, it's over. We don't have to worry about Aunt Polly or Grandma. We can let go of this."

She gave him the identical disappointed expression of every woman in his family. "And what about Maude?" she asked, gently reproving. "Do we worry about how she died? Do we worry about her pain, suffering, and fear? Or just say, 'Oh well. Whatever.'"

It came to Freddy that *he* was the one who most needed Kenneth to be the murderer. Because otherwise, the murderer might actually be Doc, in which case it would be Freddy's fault.

Heidi burst onto the scene. "Sing-along time, Freddy! You have such a nice voice! And Mrs. Maple! Such a lovely soprano! 'Row, row, row your boat'! 'Here we go, looby loo'! Bring Grandma, Freddy!"

His grandmother croaked, "Looby loo," and Heidi cried, "See? Grandma remembers! Isn't this wonderful?" and Freddy was doomed.

When he was finally back at Grandma's house, Freddy headed straight for the patio and the redwood lounge chair. He needed to get high to make his next phone call. He entertained himself by installing an appropriate ringtone for the Leper. He actually found a ringtone of breaking glass—like a picture window falling ten stories and smashing on concrete.

By the time he'd listened to the satisfying racket of glass crash about a hundred times, he knew that Jason was melodramatic, Gary Leperov's only interest was weed, and Maude hadn't been murdered anyway.

He called Gary's number.

"Yo!" yelled the Leper. "Dude! Timing is everything. I'm here in Austin putting on a demo, got my headset. We can talk while I work."

Freddy could hear the ventilation system of whatever shop the Lep was working in and people in the background talking. There could be fifty or a hundred lampworkers gathered to watch Gary Leperov lampwork; they'd be hanging on his every word. This was not going to be a private conversation.

"Saw that bitch online," said the Leper, meaning Freddy's glass, "and I had to own it. I'm sending Doc for it."

The Lep was not addressing Freddy but his Austin audience, lampworkers already so impressed by the Lep they had bought tickets, and the Lep would make sure they were even more impressed now. Freddy wasn't going to run this conversation, but what else was new? "Thank you for the bid."

"You're all signed in!" shouted the Lep. "Paid for your booth in full. Got your hotel set. And your paperwork, Doc's got that under control."

Freddy tried to sound confident and casual. "Sounds like you're busy, so let's just use PayPal Invoicing and I'll ship the rig. You've been great to me, and I really appreciate it, but I'm not doing another show."

The Lep's voice turned to ice. "Really? After you gave me your word? You're gonna screw me over? I don't think so."

Freddy imagined a crowd of pipe makers listening to this. It would certainly amplify the Russian mafia image.

"I'm just an ordinary guy trying to make a living," said the Lep, and Freddy knew every artist in the studio wished they could be one-tenth of the ordinary that Gary Leperov was. "And you know what?" said the Leper. "You're fulfilling our agreement, or you're getting your head crushed in a car door."

Seventeen

Laura reached the part in the Ives biography where Charlie has composed a "nice" work, which is performed in New Haven, and people say nice things about it, but what his soul yearns to write—the wild cacophony of his musical heart—nobody wants. Probably the worst time in anybody's life: when you realize nobody wants what you have to offer.

She kept coughing from the smell of Kemmy's peeling piano. Was it the stink of ancient varnish dying? Or were there mice inside, their little fleshy bits rotting?

She decided to open the lower panel with the rusted hinges and see if the problem was mice. If so, she was calling somebody who did junk runs to the dump. Down in the cellar, she found a pry bar, and perhaps because she didn't care if she split the wood, it yielded easily. Laura swung the door back.

Fastened to the inside was a slender homemade shelf, with several pieces of sheet music held in place by wooden pins. She lifted the music out carefully and set it on the plastic wrap of the nearest grand piano.

The top piece was an arrangement of Edvard Grieg's "Solveig's Song." The second was Edward MacDowell's "To a Wild Rose." The third, Rimsky-Korsakov's "Flight of the Bumblebee." A predictable vintage pile.

The fourth and final piece was not mass produced.

On a sheet of heavy paper were hand-drawn staffs. A ruler had not been used. Each staff wandered in a pleasant wavy manner over the page. Notes were strewn on the lines and in the spaces.

Accidentals were everywhere. Melodies and chords were scribbled like grocery lists, words scattered like birdseed.

Laura retrieved the library biography and opened to the center package of glossy pages. She studied a photo of a real Charles Ives manuscript.

Her mouth went dry.

———

There probably *was* a real situation somewhere in which somebody got his head crushed in a car door, but Freddy put Gary's threat in the melodrama column and entered his studio. He flicked his lighter and stared into the flame of the torch for a second before putting on his dark safety glasses.

He was ready for the brass band with wings.

It was an almost spiritual aspect of his craft, maybe of any craft— how the inner layers of your mind assessed, designed, prepared, and then nudged you. *We're ready.*

He couldn't rush his trombone project. After all, he wasn't on live TV. Nobody knew what he was doing. He couldn't worry about possible mediocre results, about putting it on Instagram and getting posts that said:

> Good for you, Freddy, you made a boring piece you're pretending is a trombone and it took you three days. Yay.

First, the prep work: each separate part of his trombone.

Freddy worked for hours, floating in the rare assurance that everything he did was good, maybe beyond good.

It was three in the morning when he paused from exhaustion and thirst. Grandma's refrigerator not only didn't have a cold-water tap in the door; it also didn't have an ice maker. You still had to fill little metal trays and get your fingers stuck on the cubes, and Freddy for sure hadn't refilled the trays last time.

The steps up to the rest of the house seemed really tall. Halfway up, Freddy just sat. He was too tired to climb on, and anyway, all the stuff up there would crush him.

It wasn't just Grandma's stuff. When their mother died, his sisters had sold their mother's house quickly in a hot market and divided the profits four ways. Freddy's fourth was sitting wherever Jenny had put it; he needed money, but he didn't need *that* money. The girls had found it too painful to sort their mother's possessions, so a hundred or maybe a thousand sturdy cardboard boxes of Mom's stuff were stored all over Grandma's house. One bedroom was solid to the ceiling with furniture stacked on furniture.

Freddy was oppressed by so many objects whose owners would never use them again. He himself barely owned a thing. He generally slept in the guest room, having cleared out a large collection of dolls dating from who knew when.

The warning light came on.

Freddy had installed motion detectors along the driveway. Nothing lit up outside to tell an intruder that his presence was known, but at the stop of the stairs and in the windowless hall going down to the bedrooms, Freddy had rigged small red bulbs. So far, only deer had set them off. If Freddy turned to deer hunting, he could stand in his doorway or else just mow them down with the car.

He eased into the dark living room. He never closed the drapes because by day, he wanted all the sunlight he could get, and at night, he didn't use that room, so whatever. He peered around the edge of the drapery.

People of goodwill did not drive down a strange driveway at three in the morning. Especially not with their headlights off.

Doc? This property was a fine place to slam Freddy's head in the car door. But the Leper needed Freddy to get on a plane. Fatal injuries would not bring about the desired result.

A crescent moon hung like a shard of white glass in a dark sky. The wind picked up and the clouds shifted. The car was not white. It was dark and ungainly, almost a box. Could it be a Nissan Cube?

Auburn drove a turquoise Cube.

Auburn? How could she know where he lived? Why would she care? Why would she care in the middle of the night? Was she alone or had she brought Doc? Did she want to be in on the head-smashing?

The Cube made a U-turn on the lawn and drove away.

For a moment, Freddy was relieved, and then he thought, *Grandma*.

Auburn had loved getting Br locked up. And hadn't Freddy actually thought that Auburn and Danielle could have dismembered the guy?

Could Auburn have killed Maude?

No. Auburn had nothing to do with anything at MMC. But she had had nothing to do with Br either and had enjoyed ruining his life. Freddy had a vivid, horrifying image of Auburn's long, thin fingers with their heavily decorated nails closing on an old wrinkled throat. He called MMC. It rang six times before a thick, sleepy voice he didn't recognize said, "Middletown Memory Care. Sherry speaking."

"This is Freddy Bell. My grandmother, Cordelia Chase, is a resident." His hands were damp and shaking.

"Yup."

"Is she all right?"

"I checked an hour ago. What exactly you worried about?"

"I don't know. Maude Yardley, I guess." If Grandma was fine an hour ago, Auburn couldn't have done anything to her yet. But what if she checked on Freddy first, before she went up to do something? She could have made sure—

Made sure of what? What was Freddy even thinking here?

"I got my call log here. You never been worried before."

"Maude was never murdered before." He couldn't believe he had to argue in order to get information.

"I'm sorry," Sherry said. "We got reporters calling. We're not supposed to comment. Wait a sec."

There was a long pause.

"Mr. Bell? This is Vera."

The relief that filled Freddy was like helium in a balloon, lifting his whole body. "Oh, hi, Vera. I just all of a sudden panicked. About Grandma and stuff."

"I understand. I will go to her room now, but I am sure that she is fine, because Sherry checked on her an hour ago. Do you wish to hold the line while I look?"

"Yes, please." I'm crazy, he told himself. Auburn has no way of knowing where my grandmother is. Or even that I have a grandmother.

But what about the Leper pendant, which Freddy had totally forgotten to think about? What had it been doing at that front desk?

Freddy had been a hundred percent wrong about his own invisibility. If that had been Auburn out on the grass, he had been wrong that nobody could find him at Grandma's house. He could also be wrong that nobody knew about MMC.

Except, who would care?

"She's fine, Mr. Bell," said Vera. "Sleeping soundly."

Freddy drank tap water, drank some more, and headed back downstairs. He worked until dark was turning to dawn when he stepped outside to taste the air and feel the temperature. From the Way Back came the howls of a dog.

He'd forgotten Snap.

He raced down barely visible paths to find Snap lunging against the noose of his leash. "Sorry," he said to the dog. "I'm really sorry. I forgot I have a dog now. Go ahead, bite me, I deserve it."

Snap obliged, but Freddy was wearing jeans, so not too much happened. He and Snap ran around the property for a while, and then Freddy took Snap into the shop, filled a small heavy mixing bowl with dog food and a medium heavy mixing bowl with water. He scrounged upstairs for old comforters and made a pile in the corner of the studio.

Snap ate, drank, sniffed corners, settled down on the comforters, and went to sleep.

Freddy lit up. For a few minutes, life was simple and he was happy. When you smoked, being a misfit didn't matter. *To thine own self be true*, said literature, teachers, ministers, and parents. But being yourself was no symphony. Your themes and fragments didn't harmonize. Your family didn't want to listen to your music anyway.

SATURDAY

Eighteen

Laura was up way too early on Saturday morning. She had dreamed of Maude. She fixed coffee because she knew she couldn't go back to sleep. Her landline rang, startling her. Who would call at this hour? Had Aunt Polly fallen? Had heart failure? Been murdered?

I have plenty of gas in the car, Laura thought. I can get up there right away. "Hello?" she said anxiously.

"It's Howard, Mrs. Maple. Sorry to bother you so early. We got an emergency. I've been there half the night. This really old Presbyterian church in Westchester County? We rebuilt their whole organ a few years ago, and it's a great instrument, and they were doing roof repairs on the slate roof—slate, you know, not that many people know how to work on it anymore—and they didn't attach the tarps as well as they should, and there was this really serious windstorm, which you didn't get up in your area, you might have seen it on the Weather Channel though, and the rain came in all over the pipes. Can't get to your place this week. I'm really sorry."

Laura stared at her shrink-wrapped grand pianos. Her plastic-covered bookcases. The coffins of pipe, the pieces of console, and the dead, smelly summer piano.

"Or maybe two weeks," he added.

Was she supposed to say *Thank you, you're so kind to call*? If she went all rude on him, she'd wait months for him to show up again. "It sounds difficult," she said. She wanted to cry.

"I'll keep in touch," Howard said brightly, as if he were going to Europe and might send a postcard. "Have a nice day."

———————

Grandma's landline rang. Freddy never paid attention to that phone. He kept it for the same reason he kept the furniture: Grandma wasn't dead. It was still her house and her phone.

But then his cell rang, and the caller ID said Laura Maple. Freddy was freaked. He didn't have her number and she didn't have his. They were MMC buddies but they weren't *buddies*. "Mrs. Maple," he said nervously. "How did you get this number?"

"I called the desk and said I had misplaced your number and they gave me both of yours. No one answered the one with the local area code, so I called this."

So just like that, she knew both Grandma's landline and his cell number. If she knew how to do a reverse phone search, then she knew his (Grandma's) street address. And if she could get it, anybody could.

Yesterday, a rodent was smarter than I am, thought Freddy. Today roadkill is smarter.

"Freddy, have you looked at the news?"

Freddy's interest in the news hovered close to zero. Sometimes less than zero, such as when he really didn't want to hear what the Federal Reserve was up to. "No," said Freddy. He decided to give Mrs. Maple her own ringtone. It should be Bach. Did they have the Toccata in D minor? They had to, it was classic.

"There were television crews at Memory Care," she told him.

He should have expected this. What's more deranged and headliney than murder in a dementia ward?

"Bad publicity is hurtful to institutions," said Mrs. Maple. "We need MMC. We don't want it damaged. I'm going up. Are you?"

Freddy couldn't stand the thought of going to MMC again so soon. His back and arms ached from a whole night of glass. He was hungry, his eyes were burning, and he wanted to sleep all day. "I might," he said cautiously.

"I want to know whether the residents are in danger and precisely what Detective Ames is doing to keep them safe."

Freddy had to laugh. "Get out. You're just dying of curiosity."

"That too," she admitted.

Freddy rounded up dog food, filled a pail with water, woke Snap, got nipped, and dragged Snap back to the tire swing.

Up Grandma's driveway came the oxygen truck.

The truck left the driveway and came down the grassy slope to the patio on the lower level. As the lift gate was coming down, Freddy asked after the driver's kids, and the driver said his daughter had made JV basketball and his son was doing a robot project. The driver was seriously burly and had no trouble wrestling the gleaming stainless-steel tank over to the connection.

Propane you could get anywhere. Oxygen, not so much.

The delivery guy knew Freddy wasn't using this for medical reasons. In fact, he had bought some of Freddy's beads as a gift for his wife's birthday. He wouldn't rat on Freddy, but nobody needed to rat. Doc would check oxygen delivery. There were only two suppliers in this part of the state. The deliveries were made to the house of Vincent Chase, no mention of a guy named Freddy Bell, and that might delay Doc for a day or a minute but not more.

Getting oxygen was like getting a timer. It lasted for about a month, so it was a use-it-or-lose-it asset. He was debating between sleep and more glass when his cell rang again. "Hey, Karrie Darrie."

"Freddy, I believe I've outgrown the nickname 'Karrie Darrie.' I just saw the news. You went national, Freddy. Grandma is in an institution where staff members are murdering people? You didn't call us? We didn't all Skype about where to move her? I certainly hope you now have her safely at home with you."

Home was full of steps and stairs, a gas stove, a yard that led to railroad tracks, and a dog that bit. It was not safe; it never would be. "Kara, Grandma is fine at MMC. The staff is wonderful. I trust them."

"I suppose you know every single one of them well."

"No, I don't. It doesn't matter. They're good people."

Kara lectured her brother on his feckless ways. "If our grandmother is in danger," Kara finished threateningly, "and you aren't working to protect her, Freddy, I will never forgive you."

Kara had not forgiven Freddy for a number of things, and he didn't want to add to her list.

"They're taking steps," he said, although he couldn't think of any.

"Freddy, bring Grandma home," his sister ordered.

"How about I drive her to *your* home instead? Get her room ready. Stock up on disposable adult underpants. You'll need to change her about every two hours. She's leaky. Sitting in her mess will give her infections. You'll feed her, because she forgets. You have to encourage every bite and remind her to swallow. She needs exercise, so you'll force her to use her walker. She'd rather slump in the wheelchair. You have three floors in your house and a lot of stairs, so start remodeling. You need a handicapped bathroom. Half her medications are given before meals and the other half—"

His sister was crying.

"What? You think this is a joke, Kara? You think she's just there because I'm lazy? She needs care twenty-four seven. And MMC is the right place."

"Freddy, drive up there now. Take a photograph of her and send it so I can see you really went."

Yet again, he sat with his grandmother, Aunt Polly, and Mrs. Maple, who had a long, boring saga about a Presbyterian roof leak, a dead piano, and an ancient music manuscript. He was having a hard time listening. Or even breathing. Kara had so little use for him that she wanted proof he visited.

"Freddy," said his grandmother softly. "You don't have school today?"

He took her hand. She smiled her pixie smile, the one that made his heart turn over. "No school today," he told her.

"Were you playing in the Way Back?"

"I was. Just this morning."

She smiled again and his heart hurt. Even George and Lily Burnworth said it was impossible to take care of her at home. But what if Kara was right? What if he had to?

Freddy said to his dead mother, *You should be here. You shouldn't have gone and died on us. I don't know how to do this right, Mom.*

He heard his mother say—as she often had—*You've never done anything right, Freddy.*

He kept an eye on Philip, who was leaning on his cane for balance and therefore couldn't hit anybody with it. If he found something to hang on to, though, he might strike out. Irene, sidling around and muttering her numbers, was within range. There were no aides in sight. If Irene had to be rescued from Philip, Freddy would have to do it. He liked Philip, whose desperate anger seemed perfectly reasonable. He didn't want Philip to go over the edge and be sent away to some other institution.

Philip was a big man. He'd probably been an athlete. What was he thinking inside his all-wrong, half-jailed mind? Could he remember old high school and college triumphs? Or was he blank? Either one would be a taste of hell.

Freddy stood up in case he had to intervene.

"If I approach an expert in Ives music manuscripts," Mrs. Maple said, "and if it's the real thing, I'll have to tell Kemmy it's really hers." She handed Freddy her phone to see a photograph.

He scrolled through a bunch of them and couldn't help laughing. "Mapes, is this thing the Ives piano? Your girlfriend is right—it's a plant stand. And what's on this great, big shelf over it?"

"My smashed brass." She described her collection.

Freddy wanted to run right out and get himself some smashed brass.

"Anyway, that's my dilemma," said Mapes.

Freddy was all too familiar with dilemmas. Commit crimes, don't commit crimes. Stick with the Leper, don't stick. Play it wrong and get head crushed. Play it right and have a brilliant future as a maker of flying glass bands.

Wait.

A whole band? Yes! Next he could make drums. Detachable. Each one a separate pendant.

Freddy was exhilarated, ready to roll. He glanced toward the parking lot and there sat Mrs. Maple's red SRX, sparkling in the sun. What if Doc and Skinny had followed that red SRX to MMC when Mapes picked up Freddy and Grandma last week? What if they had her plate number? They'd have to know somebody in the DMV to get a name and address from the plate. Minor request if you have a cop on the payroll. Or a cop who owes you. Or a cop who buys from you. Like Shawn, say.

But I've already decided they didn't murder Maude, so why would they have the slightest interest in somebody they didn't even see who gave me a ride once?

"I've tried to play it," said Mrs. Maple. "It's definitely based on the old hymn 'In the Sweet By and By.' In the church version, you sort of rock yourself to sleep with the comfort of it. Charlie's piece says—yes, there is a by and by, but you'll be dead, and it won't be what you thought."

Astonishingly, Philip began singing. "In the sweet...by and by...we shall meet on that beautiful shore."

Grandma chimed in. "By and by," she sang.

Outdoors, in the fenced garden, Mr. Griffin rapped courteously on the window, wanting to come back in. How had he gotten out there? The garden door was kept locked, because otherwise residents would be found crouching under shrubbery or hiding behind tree trunks. Freddy walked over and brought Mr. Griffin in. They moved slowly past two visitors talking loudly over the heads of their loved ones.

"Do you think that poor woman really was murdered?"

"Yes! Right there! In *that* room."

Mr. Griffin's hand tightened on Freddy's arm.

Oh great, thought Freddy. The murder is supposed to be a secret from the residents, but those two blurt it out and Mr. Griffin understands.

"I don't think that man is married to her anyway," said Mr. Griffin. Since his conversation was generally confined to the loss of car keys, this was a surprising remark.

"Who isn't married?" Freddy asked.

"That man. But I'm married," said Mr. Griffin. "I'm not sure where she lives. My wife. Do you know?"

"I don't," said Freddy.

"I can't think of her name," he said worriedly.

"It'll come to you, Mr. Griffin. Now sit here next to my grandmother." Freddy was falling apart. He had to bail. "I have to go, Grandma," he said, kissing her cheek. Although he didn't have to go, and it always seemed sly to imply that he did.

Walking past the cop spooked him. They wouldn't station a guy here to comfort Mrs. Reilly. If they were keeping a cop at MMC for a whole shift, then they *were* sure Maude had not died of natural causes, but they *weren't* sure who killed her.

They were fending off another murder.

Thank God for glass, Freddy's own personal beautiful shore. He worked hour after hour. His headband and T-shirt were soaked with sweat. He burned himself a few times. No big deal. He was as excited as if he himself had wings.

The ruby mouthpiece came out so dope. You had to put your lips there: it called to you.

He could hardly wait to work on the wings. Too small and they'd look like fins. Too big and they'd be umbrellas. Placed wrong and the bong would be awkward to hold.

Several hours later, he was ready to pop the hole in the bell for the downstem, a permanently welded straw of glass that turned the trombone into a bong. It was scary ripping a hole in the trombone. If he got it wrong, he was toast.

The weld of the downstem was the functional focal point. The flying trombone might be art, but without a perfect weld, it was trash.

He removed the handle: the temporary glass tubing that made the whole project possible. Now he had to get a piece of thousand-degree glass into the kiln using barbecue tongs wrapped in thermal insulation. Trusting his precious trombone to a two-dollar utensil, he slid it into the kiln, closed the door and turned off the shop lights. The lower level was now lit only by the tiny lights of various devices: the smoke detector, the computer, the digital time display on the cable box.

Through the sliders, he saw only dark. How many hours had he worked? Freddy didn't even know what night it was. Losing track of time scared him, like he might lose track of his entire life.

If he hadn't already.

SUNDAY

Nineteen

Freddy woke up nervous. The remnants of a bad dream shifted before his eyes. Something about Maude, about death, about hands. He checked his phone to see what day of the week it was. Not that it mattered. Freddy's weeks had no meaningful landmarks.

He couldn't open the kiln because his glass had not yet annealed. He had to wait, not one of his major skills. If he had any major skills. The trombone might prove that he had only minor skills.

It was raining out, so he and Snap took a brief run, and then the dog settled down on his comforters while Freddy composed hashtags for his future trombone auction.

#brassbandbongs#glassrigsongs
#glassthatsings#Freddywings

Then he researched Norwich jails online. The site claimed prisoners had telephone privileges, so Mrs. Aminetti would tell Shawn she'd given Snap to Freddy. Shawn would call as soon as he could and Freddy would reassure him that Snap was okay, plus find out if the Leper was the reason for Shawn's arrest.

All three of his sisters texted. They did not follow him on Instagram because they did not know about freddyglass. They were texting about the photo he had dutifully sent from MMC.

> **Emma**—Be sure to visit Grandma again today.
> **Jenny**—When are you bringing her home?
> **Kara**—Grandma needs you to find her another facility.

Freddy sent a group response.

How come she only needs ME? How come she doesn't also need YOU?

How many days in a row had he visited? It felt like a million.

But if he visited again, he could at least settle one of his anxieties. Visiting for an hour didn't really protect Grandma, but he didn't think Grandma *needed* protection. But who knew? Because who, really, would do a thing like that? Strangle the weakest person in a place full of the weak and helpless? He just plain couldn't picture Kenneth doing it. He couldn't picture anybody doing it. And yet it was the only thing he was picturing.

He fed Snap leftovers that would otherwise die in the refrigerator. Snap wolfed down half a meatball sandwich from the deli and mac and cheese warping at the edges. He even ate some old vinegary coleslaw Freddy had bought thinking he should have a vegetable but then forgot to eat.

It was too wet for the Way Back, so he kneed Snap into his crate along with water and kibble. The dog whined sadly.

Shawn and Br were probably in their crates too, whining sadly. Freddy worried more about Br than Shawn. Shawn had chosen his corner. But Br...nightmare.

There was only one other car in the visitor lot.

Out the front door came a man Freddy recognized as Mr. Griffin's son. He was probably fifty or sixty. Maybe even seventy. You thought of sons as being young, but around here, you found out they could be pretty old themselves.

Then came the other son, arm looped in his father's, escorting Mr. Griffin at the shuffling pace common to Alzheimer's patients. Mr. Griffin was using his only topic. "Have you found my car keys? I have to get to work, you know."

"I have the car keys, Dad. I'm going to drive."

They're taking him out for Sunday breakfast, thought Freddy. That's nice.

He couldn't take Grandma anywhere anymore. Her tendency to eat liquids with her fingers was not restaurant appropriate. *Oh, Grandma*, he thought. All those great meals she used to fix, her love of table settings—the place mats, the cloth napkins, the carefully arranged knives and forks and spoons. The insistence on good posture, good manners, good topics.

"Hi, Freddy," said the older son. "I guess we won't see you again. I want to thank you for the times you were so nice to Dad."

"You won't see me again?"

"We're pulling Dad out. We can't risk leaving him in a place where the staff might be involved with a violent death. It's taken two days to finish the paperwork and get everything arranged, but we're finally good to go."

Good to go, thought Freddy, means bad to stay.

"We're not the only ones," said the son. "Will took Irene this morning."

Freddy could not imagine the household that could contain Irene successfully. Poor Will, listening to her count, watching her circle. As for Mr. Griffin, his desire to go to work was intense. The locked doors at MMC kept him off the streets, but at his son's house, Mr. Griffin would find a way out, and off he would go. He would walk into traffic, walk on railroad tracks, walk into rivers for all Freddy knew, trying to get to work.

In the common room, Mrs. Maple's Aunt Polly stood forlornly, clinging to her walker. Polly had tried to dress herself, or maybe undress. She had gotten her bra over one shoulder and forgotten about it. The bra hung uselessly out from under the bottom of her T-shirt, the little beige cup swinging against her side. She was wearing neither pajama bottoms nor pull-ups. Her bare flanks and saggy, naked butt were on display.

Jade hadn't seen Freddy come in. "You're a mess, Miss Polly," she said, laughing out loud, and she photographed the half-naked Polly on her cell phone.

"Jade!" said Freddy. "What are you doing? Don't take a picture of her when she looks like that. Get her dressed!"

Jade turned, saw that it was only Freddy, and shrugged.

"Delete that photo," he said.

"Lighten up. Gonna give me something to share at break."

Freddy was dumbfounded. I trusted her, he thought. I trusted all of them. I said they were fine women. There's nothing fine about Jade right now. And what else does she do to get her jollies? Press a pillow over a complaining mouth? "Jade, I have to tell Mrs. Reilly."

Jade looked at him with loathing and left the common room as if stomping on spiders.

He sat next to Grandma on a couch. "Shall we..." said his grandmother. "Let's..." she frowned. "Prrfkahh—uh." She touched her lips as if maybe the right words were lying in her mouth and she could pick them up. Freddy put his arm around her shoulder, although he was the one in need of comfort. They sat for a while, just holding on, and Mrs. Reilly strode into the common room, glaring.

Freddy tucked his grandmother's hands in her lap and walked over to meet the director. He so didn't want to be the grown-up or rat on anybody ever.

"Mr. Bell," said the administrator severely, "Jade has explained to me that you are making false accusations regarding her treatment of our residents. I stand by my employee. Jade is responsible and hard-working. She has been your grandmother's aide many, many times in the last several months. As for your casting aspersions on my staff, as if I would *ever* let them laugh at one of our residents—as if they would ever *think* of such a thing—I am shocked."

Freddy came unglued. "Jade's taking sick photographs of the people you're responsible for, and you don't give a shit? Your patients are getting murdered on your watch, and you stand here whining about false accusations? Gimme your phone, Jade. We're taking a look."

"He's lying," said Jade. "I don't have no photo like that." Her voice was too belligerent.

Freddy locked eyes with the administrator. Mrs. Reilly blinked, which Freddy had known she would. She said to Jade, "Is an apology in order?"

Freddy said, "She doesn't have to apologize. She has to delete the photograph."

Jade took out her phone. Clicked while Freddy watched. The photo was gone. In its place, he had an enemy.

He sat back down with his grandmother, who had noticed nothing but examined his shirtsleeve as if she had never come across anything like it.

Rule number one in pipes: Trust no one. Maybe it was also true in nursing homes.

Last week, I was as happy as a three-year-old in play school, thought Freddy. Everybody loved me and I loved them. Now I've met the bullies on the playground.

TWENTY

Laura made peanut-butter toast. She was not in the mood for her own church, where everybody would greet her cheerfully and expect her customary cheerful reply, and she didn't want to be cheerful. She wanted to sulk about Howard and the Presbyterians.

Gordon Clary was organist and choir director at a Guilford church. She would attend their service, see what kind of organist Gordon Clary was, and tell the self-proclaimed Charles Ives expert that she might actually have in her possession a very early Charles Ives manuscript.

The drive was pleasant, hardly anybody else on the road, and the autumn leaves were magnificent. The Guilford church was two hundred years old, graceful and beautiful, all white with the original plaster decoration. She began to feel a little of the peace of Sunday.

Gordon Clary played one of her favorite Bach works, Fantasia and Fugue in A minor, but so fast that the notes were a whirlwind. Laura was of the belief that Bach could always be done more slowly.

The sermon was outstanding; the prayers were profound.

But after his postlude, Gordon was in such a rush Laura actually had to block his exit to get him to notice her. "Laura Maple," she said. "I sing soprano in the concert choir."

"Ah," said Gordon Clary. "Of course."

"The Fantasia was splendid."

"Thank you." He tried to steer around her.

"Perhaps you will recall telling us last week that Charles Ives spent his summers as a boy in Westbrook."

"I'm so sorry, Mrs. Maple, but—"

Laura knew she shouldn't proceed. Charlie deserved full attention, and Gordon Clary wasn't giving this any attention. Laura didn't listen to her own wisdom and hurried into her story. "It turns out that his extended family rented houses on Magna Lane."

"No, I'm quite sure he lived at Cousins' Beach." He bustled away.

Laura glared at his back. I could have given you truly fine, one-of-a-kind material for your doctoral paper, she thought. But you're rude and you have bad tempos. You will never catch a glimpse of my manuscript or even be able to gaze upon my smelly piano. So there.

––––––––––––––

Back home, Snap was whining to get outside. Freddy ran around the yard while Snap went after his ankles. It dawned on Freddy that Snap was having a wonderful time. You didn't correct biting by making it more fun.

Freddy got an old towel (all the towels here were old; Grandma was not given to flights of fancy at Bed Bath & Beyond) and rolled it up, and they yanked it back and forth. So much exercise called for a snack. Snap was okay with Mrs. Aminetti's dog food, and Freddy was definitely okay with Mrs. Aminetti's cookies.

At last, holding his breath, Freddy approached the kiln.

He almost said a prayer that the glass trombone would be good, but he wanted God out there feeding the hungry, not distracted by crime glass.

He opened the kiln door.

Oh, yes.

A work of art, elegant but masculine. The clear slides and the ruby bell gleamed like music. The trombone fit perfectly in his hand. Utility was crucial in a water pipe, and his beautiful trombone wasn't bulky or awkward but transferred easily from hand to hand.

The best glass of his life.

He was shaking with excitement. He made a ten-second video, the trombone on its little feet and then in his hand, rotating it to show off all its glory.

He set up an Instagram auction, tapped in his hashtag poetry, and braced himself for applause or contempt.

But if he sat glued to Instagram waiting for results, he'd be mental. He had to wait a while. He clock-watched because if he checked the time on his cell phone, he wouldn't be able to stop himself from checking Instagram too. Grandma's house had a lot of clocks. Some of them he had changed at daylight savings, and some of them he hadn't.

Freddy killed time playing Grandma's piano. It hadn't been tuned in forever, but Freddy liked it out of tune. It gave the notes a shuddery feel, like they were trying to get up and run. He sang along, making up hashtag lyrics for future auctions.

#stacksofglassandverses

#bongsandpipesandcurses

Finally he turned away from the keyboard and tapped Instagram on his phone.

You nailed it, Freddy.
Strike up the band, Freddy! It's gorgeous.

Freddy yelled with delight. Snap tore up the stairs to be part of the excitement. Freddy tossed him a dog treat and read more posts.

Holy herb!
Look at your cool shit!

These were just observations, though. Nice, but not bids. But then in came the first bid. It was for *a thousand dollars*.

Freddy doubled-checked the decimal point.

Yes. One thousand dollars.

Thirty minutes and twelve bidders later, it reached *three* thousand.

Most people never sold anything for hundreds of dollars. Most people never even got up to *one* hundred. Everybody reading these posts was doing miracle math: If Freddy could get three thousand for a few days' work, what could he earn in a year?

He'd just left every bro behind and there would be jealousy and resentment.

On the other hand, it was just a bid. Somebody Freddy didn't know had entered some numbers on a cell phone. They hadn't paid for it, just said they would. If Freddy had learned anything this weekend, it was don't trust people. Even trustworthy people.

> Whattabid! Way to go!
> Love your work, Freddy. So clean.
> Dude!

Even his former girlfriend texted, which was nice, except that Cynthia was trouble. She wanted him to become middle class. Like his sisters, Cyn advocated a job with benefits, a commute, and a wife.

> Freddy! Awesome work! Awesome bids! Cuz u are an awesome guy! Eager to see you at BABE.

How eager? Was she planning to flatten him if he showed up or hoping to save on expenses and share a hotel room? She probably figured he was rich now and could afford a nice hotel.

> Hey Cyn! Good to hear from you.

> Angie has a booth at BABE. I'm going to help.

It was hard to run a booth alone, although Freddy usually did. Going to the bathroom and getting meals was tough because you couldn't leave your booth unsupervised. And it took one person to admire the customer's taste and photograph the necklace she was wearing and a second person to total the sales and wrap the purchase. A third was even better, to keep an eye out for shoplifters. He'd been stunned in the beginning to see nice bead ladies slide away without paying for the beads they were admiring, but now it was just part of the routine.

If he did fly to BABE on the Leper's plane tickets, he'd have a booth with practically nothing to sell. Airline lost my Samsonite, he'd have to say.

They would be incredulous. You *checked* it?

Well, I didn't want to, did I? They made me.

> Lucky Angie, he texted.
> You coming?
> Indecision here.
> Where's here?

Freddy could pick a town. Nashua, New Hampshire. Butte, Montana. Asheville, North Carolina. But then he'd have to keep track of his lie.

> On the road, he wrote. You teaching this semester?
> Third grade. Love it.
> Happy for you. And Happy Birthday next month.
> Freddy! You remembered! See you at BABE!

He went back to Instagram.

The bids did not close at three thousand.

The next bid was *five* thousand.

Five thousand dollars. For one piece of glass.

Freddy read and reread this staggering number.

His glass was so brilliant, so beautiful, so awesome—

Wait.

The bid was from **Blowupallmedschools**.

Had to be Doc. Except (a) Doc didn't care about a glass trombone, and (b) Doc didn't have five thousand dollars to drop on a piece of glass.

The bid was fake. It was just another notice from Gary Leperov.

Freddy sat down heavily.

The Leper wouldn't pay Freddy a thing. He was destroying Freddy's auction instead.

The very next post was the sentence he had yearned to read his whole glass life.

I want a Freddy.

It was meaningless.

Like me, thought Freddy. Like my life.

MONDAY

TWENTY-ONE

"Maude Yardley," repeated the secretary at the third church Laura phoned Monday morning. "She was a pillar of the church. Before my time, but people still get teary telling me how she went downhill with Alzheimer's."

"Downhill" was the favored adjective for Alzheimer's patients. An easy euphemism, dismissive of the details that made the disease so grim.

"And then I think her husband started to get it too."

Kenneth had early-stage Alzheimer's? It made perfect sense. It explained the teetering in doorways. He really *didn't* know whether he was coming or going.

This awful news put Maude's death in another light. It was entirely possible that if Kenneth suffocated his own wife, he only half knew he was doing it. Right now, he would only half know that he *had* done it. Or half not know. It was why Alzheimer's patients could be so frantic and irritable. They only half knew anything, and they only knew *that* half the time.

"Oh my goodness!" shrieked the secretary. "I'm Googling Maude! She was murdered!"

Laura and the secretary had a ghastly conversation about how much Maude might have suffered. Laura thought that suffering, like living, was different for a person in profound dementia. It could be far worse, with fear and horror hideously magnified. Or the opposite: all sensors too slow and damaged to process anything.

"I'll put an announcement in our daily email," said the secretary, "but I'll just say *died suddenly*. Those go out to hundreds of people. I'll add Kenneth Yardley to our email prayer list. Do you have his email address so people can send their sympathy?"

Laura opened the screenshot of Maude's admission page and recited it.

If Kenneth is innocent, she thought, it will be so uplifting to hear from old friends, and if he's guilty, he'll feel worse, which is only fair.

She hadn't even fixed a second cup of coffee when her cell phone rang. "Mrs. Maple? My name is Betty Sherwood. Forty years ago, Maude Yardley and I lived in Old Greenwich on the same street. She was my dear friend. My granddaughter Tiffany gets the prayer list on her cell phone, and she just read it to me."

That was quick. The secretary must have sent out the news while she and Laura were still on the phone.

"Tiff called the church for the details of Maude's funeral, and she was told that my poor Maude was murdered. They gave Tiffany your phone number. Please tell me more. I'm beside myself."

Laura gave her everything she knew, which was very little.

"I'm heartsick," said Betty. "She was a good, dear woman. That's such a brutal ending for a fine life. Tiffany took the morning off from work to come over and comfort me. She pulled out my old photograph albums. I lost a foot and most of my sight from diabetes, so I can't see the photos anymore, but Tiff is reading all the labels from when we lived on Highview Avenue. Maude and Kenneth were just two doors down, and we used to have barbecues. We still used charcoal. It was so hard to light. People would bring their own hamburgers or hot dogs and everybody would bring a salad or a dessert—we had just discovered cake mixes—and all summer, the neighbors would congregate. My husband would say the blessing, and we'd sit in the backyard. We had folding aluminum chairs, the kind with webbing. Now I'm in assisted living and I don't even have an oven."

Laura still paused in the cake-mix aisle. The boxes were so pretty. But she hadn't baked in a decade. Possibly two.

"The church secretary told us that Kenneth is still alive," said

Betty. "Kenneth had Alzheimer's first, of course, and I expected him to be long gone. Kenneth must be ninety or more."

Could Kenneth really and truly be in his nineties? Managing his Alzheimer's so well that he was still driving, paying bills, renting out houses? Using an astounding skin cream and a wig? Or had Betty, along with being blind and one-footed, lost track over the years?

"There was a cousin," said Betty. "He put Kenneth in a home somewhere. Tiffany, read the barbeque photo captions to me. I can't remember the cousins and I'll need to call them."

The album pages are probably black, thought Laura, and Betty wrote in white ink, and pasted on four little photo corners to hold each picture.

"Hank and Evelyn," read Tiffany. "Kenneth and Maude. Jim and Janet. Stephen and Lucille. That's the first page. Now over here, Hank and Evelyn are not around, but we've added Morris and Eunice. Nana, how come you always list the man's name first?"

"Tiffany, don't start with me. Next you'll be telling me not to call the women in my club 'the girls.' Pull yourself together and keep reading."

"Here's some excitement," she heard Tiffany say. "A new couple on the block. They're way young, compared to you middle-aged guys. Bobby and Virginia."

"How fortuitous!" cried Betty. "Bobby and Virginia are the cousins. Well, Bobby was the cousin. Virginia was his wife. I even remember their last name now! Lansing."

The name Freddy had found in his searches.

"Betty," said Laura, "since your lovely granddaughter is staying for the morning, how about I bring lunch and stay for the afternoon? Because I am also upset about Maude's death."

Tiffany said she would arrange for two meals to be sent up from the dining room.

"Meals here are bland," said Betty sadly. "No salt, no grease. Probably you should bring your own lunch from McDonald's."

The sound of broken glass crashed through Grandma's kitchen.

The point of installing the special ringtone was to remind Freddy *not* to answer. But a guy who bid five thousand dollars for your rig, you had to answer, even if his master plan was to ruin you. "Hey, Lep. Is that your bid on the trombone? Thanks. I'm honored."

"The trombone is sick, Freddy. How did you even think of a winged trombone?"

"A friend of mine is researching an American composer named Charles Ives, and Charles Ives said that when he was writing music, he kept in mind a brass band with wings. So I decided I'd make the band. But in glass."

"Dude. Isn't Charles Ives the guy who writes music nobody can listen to but it's trendy?"

"Pretty much."

"And are you making beads between brass band pieces?"

"We already talked about this, Gary. I'm not doing more bead shows."

"Freddy, what's the matter with you?" said Gary tiredly. "I'm not asking you to steal anything. You're just scribbling your name on some sheets of paper and handing *my cash* over to a clerk for the sales tax."

"I guess I don't want to go in that direction."

"*I'm* the one going that direction. Listen. I got expenses. I got a four-carat wife, she drives a Lexus, I wear Fair Trade pants, we got a kid in a pricey nursery school, I am stretched to the max, I'm sponsoring your career by bidding up that rig, *and you are doing BABE for me.*"

"Gary, you're a big deal. You're not stretched."

"What are you talking about? I'm just an ordinary guy trying to make a living."

"Come on. You know what people say about you."

"They're quoting me, Freddy. I make it all up. That Russian gangster stuff—that's just advertising. People love that shit."

Freddy didn't believe it. If Jason knew, everybody knew. Probably the police on both coasts knew. And you didn't hire real, true muscle like Doc unless you needed real, true muscle.

But what does it matter? he asked himself. What does it actually matter if I stand firm with Gary Leperov? Nobody on earth cares but me.

It was the terrifying theme song of his existence. Nobody actually cared.

Freddy felt a desperation so deep he could not imagine climbing out.

"Freddy, I've invested in you for a year," said the Leper. "I have expectations. And you're not withdrawing. No one withdraws from me. Ask your little friend Cynthia."

Cynthia had texted because Gary Leperov told her to?

Freddy felt even worse.

Cynthia was mixed up with the Leper. A sweet, wholesome third-grade teacher who even made girlish little pastel beads. How could Cynthia even know that Gary Leperov existed?

But Freddy would not have believed Shawn would make coke buys either.

TWENTY-TWO

Laura smuggled the McDonald's bag past the front desk and gave it to Betty. They both giggled. "It was a guess," said Laura. "My feeling is, at our age, it's our choice what we eat."

"If only," said Betty. She happily unwrapped her burger while Laura ate the dining room meal, sprinkling it with a tiny packet of McDonald's salt. "Mmm! French fries!" said Betty. She dug in while Laura talked about MMC and her drive up there and her new best friend Freddy and her sad, ruined aunt Polly.

"You visit Polly three times a week?" said Betty. "You are a saint."

People often told Laura this. Surely it was harder to qualify for sainthood than just driving up Route 9 now and then. "When I visit, Polly might mumble meaningless syllables or wants to go shoe shopping."

"The horror of dementia," agreed Betty. "The sensation that your loved one is still there, but she can't get out and you can't get in. You know, Laura, I think Bobby and Virginia may have moved to Farmington. Next time Tiffany comes, I will ask her how I might reach them."

"We can find that out right now." Laura opened her phone, located Robert Lansing in Farmington on Schoolhouse Road, pressed the number, and handed the cell phone to Betty.

Betty held the phone nervously. "I lost most of my sight prior to the advent of cell phones, Laura. Tiffany lives on her phone, whatever that means, but I don't own one. Oh dear. A voice is repeating the phone number."

"That's good. Wait for a little beep. Then leave your message."

Betty gulped. "Hello, Virginia!" she shouted. "And Bobby! Good afternoon! It's Betty Sherwood from Old Greenwich days. I just heard the tragic news of dear Maude's death. Do, please do, phone me." She recited her landline number and handed the cell back with visible relief.

They visited another half hour and then Laura stood up to go.

"Why don't you take the album home to leaf through?" said Betty.

Laura wasn't interested in Betty's photo collection, but she well understood that the loan ensured a second visit. She thought of the huge world of desperate old ladies, gamely going on, supported by exhausted children and grandchildren, nieces and nephews. "How lovely," she said.

I-95 was busier than Laura had expected, which was always the case. This part had been constructed when they believed in entrances with crossover exits, so Laura kept to the middle lane, hoping not to sideswipe or be sideswiped. She was approaching New Haven. She could continue east on 95 and go home or turn north on 91 to Farmington, home of Virginia and Robert Lansing.

Virginia Lansing still cares about Maude, thought Laura, because she visited MMC just last month. She must be torn to pieces about Maude's death. I bet she's as eager to talk as Betty. And I am in need of information.

She went north on 91, exhilarated to be hot on the trail.

But...trail of what, exactly? She wanted it to be Kenneth who killed Maude, not some insane staff member. But did she really want to creep around in people's lives, lying and prying? A sort of murder voyeur? Yes, she did, so she mustn't.

Laura took the Route 66 exit and drove to Middletown instead. Mrs. Reilly was at the front desk.

"Why, hello," said Laura. "You don't usually have desk duty."

"We're short-staffed."

"You are?"

"Not every employee is comfortable working where there has been a murder."

It had not occurred to Laura that the staff would be afraid. But of course they were. Whoever the murderer was, the staff probably knew or had met the person. Or worked with them.

"Please excuse me," said Mrs. Reilly, "but I am dealing"— she seemed to debate how to finish this sentence and then openly shrugged—"with a family removing their loved one because of what happened to Maude Yardley."

It's starting, thought Laura. Staff and residents are leaving the ship. If too many leave, we sink.

She crossed the pretty lobby to the locked door and entered the code.

The door didn't open.

She entered the code again and still the door didn't open.

I can't remember four numbers I've tapped a thousand times. I'm getting Alzheimer's too.

She would end up here, spoon-fed, wearing pull-ups and smiling at nothing. Beloved faces would fade away and music would just be noise. And her children. Oh, the children. Would they bother?

Mrs. Reilly hastened over. "I'm so sorry, Mrs. Maple. The police told us to change the code."

In times of joy, boredom, fear, or, for that matter, any emotion, Freddy's solution was glass.

He decided to start the band with one drum in his favorite dark green, streaky with garnet. Maybe a face in the drumhead, something distorted, with long ears and drooping nose like an Easter Island statue. Grotesque sold well in pipe circles.

If he made the drum too drummy, it would look like a Christmas tree ornament. *Twelve drummers drumming, eleven pipers piping.*

This was distracting. A Christmas card with eleven glass-pipe guys piping? He might have to design a poster. What should the partridge in a pear tree be?

Speaking of trees, he should make Tree Lady a rig. You didn't see that many maple tree rigs. If any.

Freddy recognized that he was seriously high. Now of course his cell phone had to go and ring, and the caller ID said Auburn. He had forgotten to think about her middle-of-the-night trespass. Her Cube. Her dealing. Her necrotic finger that turned up on the MMC desk. He totally didn't want to talk to Auburn, but not talking to her could be just as crummy. "Hey, Aub," he said, super casual.

"You hear about Shawn?"

Auburn knew Shawn? She knew Shawn and Freddy were friends?

Freddy had never wondered where Shawn bought his herb. Now he thought: *from Auburn.*

"I guess he had an issue with coke," said Freddy carefully.

"What happened was, the Leper needed a cop. The Leper is so smart, Freddy. How he made Shawn deal? His guys caught Shawn's dog, some old mutt Shawn loves. I don't see the point in dogs myself. Then he told Shawn to do what he was told or they'd slice off the dog's paws, so Shawn said yes, but he's so stupid he worked a parking lot with video cameras and he got caught."

Cut off Snap's paws?

Would anybody actually grab a dog and whap down on its little legs with a machete?

Doc, who had planned to be a healer? Mutilate a dog? Or was that a job for the skinny sidekick? But would they really do that?

Shawn must have believed they would.

You heard about dogs that died to save their masters, but you didn't hear that often about a master dying to save his dog. Because that could happen to Shawn. A cop might not survive prison.

How could Shawn have run into the Leper to start with? He didn't do glass shows. He didn't even attend shows.

Freddy had been having nightmares about hands around throats. Now he was going to have nightmares about machetes and paws.

TWENTY-THREE

In the common room, Laura found most residents napping while a few played bingo with a volunteer. Bingo was quite a challenge when you were no longer numerate. Freddy's grandmother dozed in an armchair. Evie, whom Laura rarely saw, sat blankly on a sofa. Evie was one of the silent ones who mainly slept.

Kenneth was once again standing at Maude's door.

Maybe Kenneth *did* have Alzheimer's and couldn't remember that his wife had died. Many patients didn't remember that they had children and would argue with an adult child who kept insisting they were related.

Poor Philip was panting and frantic over something or nothing. He tried to turn his table over, but the table was heavily braced. He began pounding it with his big fists.

"Grace!" Kenneth yelled. "Jade! Give that monster a shot and calm him down!"

Which did not sound like decades of Alzheimer's but just a short-tempered man losing control.

Grace poked her head out of a resident's room. "Can't without doctors' orders. But plus, you give a trank, he can't balance anymore, and he falls. Might break bones." Grace coaxed Philip to his room while he called her names and tried to trip her.

Philip had a lift chair, which launched him upright, but if the aides set the control on the floor, Philip could neither see nor reach it. He'd be stuck in his chair. It was one of many awful but necessary ways in which residents were controlled. Grace shut Philip's door and returned to her tasks.

"The guy's a menace," said Kenneth.

Philip's not a menace, thought Laura. He's a sorrow.

In her room, Aunt Polly was sipping her fortified chocolate drink. "Hi, Aunt Polly. Shall we read the next chapter?"

"Laura," said Polly affectionately. "I like your hair. You had it cut."

Laura had not, but she said "Thank you," because anytime Polly knew her made up for all the times Polly didn't.

Through Polly's open bedroom door, Laura could see Grace at the big center island, fixing somebody a banana and cracker snack. She couldn't see the rest of the common room, but each ceiling corner had a large circular mirror, the sort people with dangerous driveways use to check oncoming traffic. In one, Jade was walking a resident Laura didn't recognize to his room. In the other mirror, Kenneth remained in Maude's door, looking left and right as if dealing with heavy traffic. Very Alzheimery. The poor man, sliding in and out of normalcy like that.

Kenneth darted away and was no longer in the mirror. A minute later, he scuttled back. Neither Jade nor Grace was now in view.

It was like watching a soap opera with only a fraction of the screen available. Laura forgot to read to Polly, and Polly continued to sip chocolate.

Now Philip appeared, stumbling over to the sofas. How had he gotten his door open? He was a fall waiting to happen.

Kenneth went to Philip's aid before Laura could, which was unexpected and nice. The men had a sort of tussle as Kenneth tried and failed to keep Philip upright.

Philip fell heavily on top of Evie.

Evie was a toothpick under the freight truck that was Philip. Laura shouted for help and rushed forward. Jade and Grace came running.

Philip's muscles were flaccid and his coordination long gone. He was helpless. It took all four of them to hoist such a tall man to his feet.

Philip's weight could have cracked Evie's ribs or damaged

internal organs. Silent Evie couldn't tell them if it hurt. They called the ambulance. She would have to have X-rays.

"I bet that's what's happened to my Maude," said Kenneth. "This monster came in and lay down on her."

Laura was horrified. Could Maude have been suffocated by Philip's dingy, old terry-cloth bathrobe? What if Philip had reached out and the only thing he could grab hold of was a throat?

And then she had a worse thought. Why had Kenneth suddenly darted away from Maude's room? Had Kenneth opened Philip's door? Given Philip the chair control? Or pushed the buttons himself? When Philip came back in the common room, had Kenneth tried to help? *Or had he intentionally pushed Philip down onto Evie?*

Stop it! she told herself.

Bad enough she had nearly driven to Farmington to interrogate a stranger named Virginia in some sneaky, we're-all-in-this-together kind of way. Now she was pretending Kenneth shoved helpless people to the floor and Philip strangled old ladies without knowing.

Laura said goodbye to her now dozing aunt and walked out of the common room. Kenneth caught up to her at the locked door. He blocked it, glaring at her. He was not a large man, but he was certainly a furious one. "You interfering bitch," he whispered. "You called that church Maude used to belong to. You told people to send sympathy emails and crap. The goddamn minister called me to pray."

Laura was more shocked by his language than by the possibility that he had shoved Philip. However, Alzheimer's made some victims deeply angry. If Kenneth had been floating in some grim low-level Alzheimer's for years, this might be how it manifested.

Laura was afraid of him.

On the other side of the reinforced glass panes, a middle-aged couple tapped the code and opened the door. Reluctant children trailed behind them, scuffing the floor and looking irritably at their silenced devices. Laura slid through, leaving Kenneth's sick rage and her own sick curiosity behind.

Twenty-Four

There was never a pause in glass. Stop for two seconds and gravity took over; the glass drooped like honey on the end of a spoon. Molten glass was orange, so when he was actually working on a piece, he couldn't see its real color. He loved that: the mystery of chemistry. Well, it wasn't mysterious really—he could explain it— and yet the truth of any glass was hidden during its creation.

There was a sharp knock on the sliding glass door behind him. Freddy was startled but too experienced to flinch when holding glass whose temperature was over two thousand degrees. He glanced over his shoulder.

The detective from MMC was standing with his nose actually in the crack of the sliding glass doors.

To Freddy, a cop was a known predator, complete with gun, truncheon, and satellite radio. A cop in his studio was unthinkable. I have a seriously stupid studio design, he thought. My bench should face the door. But no, I arranged this place so somebody can sneak up on me.

He did not turn off the torch. He did not remove his huge, dark safety glasses.

He turned to face the cop, glass rod still in his right hand, still spinning it, keeping the glob aloft, like a softball on a stick.

Freddy circled his bench.

The cop unwisely slid the door open all the way.

Freddy held the glass upright, not pointing it like a weapon, but it was a weapon, because nobody stands still with molten glass advancing toward his face.

Freddy stepped forward. "Oh, hey, how ya doin'?" he asked, all friendly, as the cop backed away.

The little poured-concrete patio had a partial ring of fieldstone, stacked about a foot high. Grandpa had built it from stones he turned up in the soil when they were putting in the perennial gardens. Freddy remembered towing a little sledge on which Grandpa set the fieldstones. Grandma always lined the ring with baskets of scarlet geraniums and orange marigolds. She never had any use for pastels.

If the cop backed up another inch, he'd trip on the fieldstone. Freddy weighed the pleasure of seeing him fall and the punishment for damaging a cop.

He stopped.

The cop couldn't take his eyes off the spinning glass knob, which was rapidly cooling but would be capable of delivering a hideous burn for quite a while. "How come you don't burn your hand?"

"Glass is an insulator, not a conductor."

"You like glassblowing?"

No, thought Freddy. I've dedicated my life to something I despise. "I'm not a glassblower. This is called lampwork."

"Is it what Dale Chihuly does?"

"No."

"What's the gas?"

"Propane."

"There's a second tube."

"Oxygen."

"How does it work?"

"Propane accepts a lot of oxygen. Controlling the mix is a torch art." Control the mix, Freddy told himself. Stay calm.

"Flammable gas," said the cop. "Sounds tricky. If somebody wanted to wreck your studio, what would they do?"

Huh? What was up with that? "Take my lucky tweezers, probably," said Freddy lightly. They were sparring, but Freddy didn't know why. He couldn't pace himself because he couldn't guess how long he had to last.

"You know," said the guy chattily, "somehow I didn't expect a raised ranch tucked back here. I figured a cute old colonial."

Freddy's loathing for the cop was eclipsed by despair for his grandmother, soldiering on, so brave and so lost. No doubt she, too, had expected a more gracious life and a more beautiful house. But she made the best of what she had.

She's still making the best of it, he thought.

"The house belongs to you now?"

"My grandmother isn't dead yet."

"Sorry. So. Auburn, with the store on Main Street. One-name Auburn. She visited Middletown Memory Care."

Seriously? Then Freddy needed to check on Grandma right this second. He had left his cell phone on the bench and didn't want to let the cop in and didn't want to set down the glass and didn't want the cop to know that he was suddenly, completely terrified for Grandma.

Auburn might actually suffocate an old lady.

Because the Leper told her to.

Because she was showing off for Danielle.

Because she wanted to know Freddy's last name.

Because it was fun, like trapping Br.

Maybe Auburn was trapping Freddy. For sure, she'd had something to do with trapping Shawn. Or everything. She could even have thrown in the Leper's name for fun while in fact she set Shawn up herself.

"Auburn didn't get past the front desk," said the cop. "She didn't give her name and she didn't sign in."

She'd go in next time. His sisters were right. He had to get Grandma out of there. But how? And take her where?

To Emma in Australia? Grandma couldn't last one hour on a plane, never mind twenty-four or whatever it was to Sydney.

Jenny in Alaska? It was possible to drive there but not possible for Grandma.

South Dakota. Drivable. He and Grandma would have to share a hotel room. What would he do when she had to go potty? Bring her into the men's room and change her pull-ups? How many bathroom stops between here and South Dakota?

Freddy transferred the molten glass to his other hand. He was tiring.

"One of the housekeeping staff happened to walk by when Auburn was at the desk and recognize her, because she's a customer at Auburn's shop."

Auburn did not currently stock a single accessory that a maid could afford. So either the maid had shopped in the store's previous incarnation or she was there buying pot. Or coke.

"We had a little chat with Auburn."

Middletown cops probably knew Auburn better than Freddy did. They probably wanted to question Auburn pretty much any time, and once they recognized that pendant, they would have trotted right over.

He wondered if Ames was also the cop who had dealt with poor Br. No, because the guy who pulled Br over would not have been a detective.

Wait.

Why had Auburn told Danielle not to use names in Br's story? Auburn wouldn't protect Br. Her whole goal was to ruin Br.

Maybe she didn't want *me* to know the name, thought Freddy. Which means *I know Br*.

Freddy had grown up on the shoreline. His high-school graduating class had had only seventy-eight kids. He knew most people who'd been one, two, and three grades ahead and behind. He knew his sisters' friends and classmates, even though they were a lot older, like Shawn. He knew tons of people from the church he grew up in. Br, he thought. Brian? Brent? Brady? "Did Auburn tell you who bought that finger on a string?" Freddy asked.

"How do you know about the finger?"

"Come on. The whole staff is talking about it."

"It's pretty clever, that finger," said the cop. "It's actually a cocaine jar."

Freddy had seen quite a few Leper pendants, and that was what they were: cool jewels. This had been a jar? So Gary had yet another line, and Doc wholesaled it to retailers like Auburn. Not good news. It meant that Freddy really was laundering coke money.

And then he realized something else: Auburn didn't know the Leper. She knew only his reputation, or she'd have been calling him Gary. It would have been crucial for her to call him Gary and prove they were on close terms. So it wasn't the Leper Auburn knew.

It was Doc.

Twenty-Five

By the time the cop finally left, it was getting dark.

Snap seriously did not want to be tied up in the Way Back. He not only tried to bite but also growled. His barks and howls followed Freddy all the way to the house. Good thing there were no close neighbors.

Freddy wished he could like Snap. He and his dog could go through life together: trade shows, angry landlords, repo men, girlfriends, glass burns, and blisters. But if he ever got his own dog, Freddy would want a dog whose eyes yearned for affection, not a dog whose teeth yearned to break skin.

It was late when he drove into the visitor lot at MMC. An extremely heavy man was getting out of a Prius. Philip's son, Martin. He and his entire family always came for Sunday dinner, and now and then Martin showed up during the week. Mrs. Maple liked them a lot because of the regularity of their visits. Sometimes Freddy thought Mrs. Maple was grading all these relatives: people who got an A, people who were C minus, people who failed and would have to repeat their dementia year.

"Freddy!" cried Martin. "Have you heard? Kenneth Yardley called the police and accused my father of murdering Maude! They're taking him seriously! They're here right now! Kenneth says that my father falls on people and probably fell on Maude and crushed her to death. They believe him! I don't know what we're going to do! It's insane."

A cop came out of MMC. He must have been waiting for Martin. What could be worse?

"Wait," said Freddy, who needed this syllable a lot while he worked on elusive thoughts and tried to reach intelligent conclusions. Or even any conclusion. "Nobody here can get up," he told the cop. "Once they're down, they're down. Philip is a big guy, but he can't get up from a chair by himself. He sure couldn't get up off a bed or a floor. If Philip fell on top of Maude, he'd be there till the staff found him. He didn't do it, and it didn't happen."

"Why didn't the aides just tell us that?" asked the cop.

"Come on. They're scared of you. They can't think straight."

The three of them processed into the building. Martin gripped Freddy's arm for support.

We're all on the verge of collapse, thought Freddy. Our person is fragile, our lives are shaky, and the police are crawling all over us.

The cop stopped in the foyer to make calls while Freddy and Martin went on in.

He didn't know a single aide on the evening shift, but a pleasant, very chubby woman named Monica was expecting him. She rolled out a folding cot from a closet filled with them. "For emergencies," she explained. "Like if the town loses power, staff have to sleep over or maybe we get extra patients from other places or whatever. And when a family member wants to spend the night, like sometimes visitors stay for a week if they live far away."

You really had to love your person to live on a dementia ward for a week.

Grandma did not notice that she was getting a roommate.

The sheets were for single beds, too big for a cot, so the fitted bottom came right back off. He couldn't imagine sleeping well, but on the other hand, he didn't want to sleep well. He wanted to sleep lightly, so he could intercept Auburn if she showed up.

But why would she show up? What was any of this nightmare *for*? He couldn't get a grip on Maude's death. He couldn't figure out Auburn or Br or Shawn or Jade.

Monica said gently, "You don't have to do this, Mr. Bell. I know you're afraid. Everybody is afraid. But your grandmother is fine. I'm not going to sleep through my shift. Plus we have an officer here for the night," she added, pointing at a guy in rumpled old clothes. Freddy had figured him for a patient. He spotted the distinctive shape of a cigarette pack in the cop's shirt pocket. No cigarettes, lighters, matches, birthday-cake candles, or any kind of fire at all were allowed in a place like this.

"At night," Monica reminded him, "the regular front doors are locked. Nobody can get into the lobby. A visitor talks into the inter- com. One of us answers. If we're satisfied the person is legit, we go to the door and let them in. Then I take them through the coded door to the resident wings. If I felt nervous, I wouldn't open that door. I'd call the officer here to come out."

"And I'll come quick," said the cop. "I'm in and out a lot anyway because I have to go outside for a smoke."

Freddy lay down on a mattress so thin he could feel the cross- wire supports under his back. Around midnight, he got up, bored and restless. The common room was fully lit. An aide he didn't know was sorting laundry. A patient he didn't know was asking when they would serve lunch. In his room, Philip was swearing.

Freddy lay back down. He couldn't close his eyes, never mind sleep.

At one in the morning, he heard sharp footsteps, crisper than slippers or sneakers. He got up, cracked the door, and peered out. It was the cop, returning from a cigarette break. The delicious scent wafted past Freddy, and immediately he was desperate for a smoke himself. He almost went out to bum a cigarette off the cop. Instead, he took a selfie and sent it to his sisters, so they'd know he was being responsible.

He didn't feel responsible. He felt like a man in prison. Like Br. Like Shawn.

His grandmother slept silently. He couldn't hear her breathing and got up twice to lean close and make sure she was still alive.

He said to his mother, *I'm trying, okay? I'm trying to do something right. But you know what, Mom?* Right *is kind of elusive in my world.*

He actually heard her from heaven. Or memory. *Then change worlds, Freddy.*

TUESDAY

Twenty-Six

Morning finally came to MMC. The day shift took over. Grandma slept on and on, motionless, as if she had crossed the threshold into death. Freddy wanted to see her up and going before he left. If he could stand it. It would be a test.

At eight thirty a deeply anxious family of five began moving their grandfather into Maude's old room. Good news that people still wanted to move in. The new people must think MMC was nice and safe. Or they were desperate. Freddy felt acquainted with desperate.

"James!" the grandfather kept calling.

"I'm here, Dad," the adult son said.

"The children! Did you leave the children in the car?"

"We're here, PopPop," said the teenage boys.

"Let's go home now," said the grandfather nervously.

The grandsons muscled a recliner through the bedroom door. "That isn't mine!" cried the grandfather. "Where's mine?"

The boys tried to comfort him. "Yours was too big for this room, PopPop. So we stole Dad's. Cool, huh? You have a stolen recliner. Let's try it out. Let's sit in it." They patted the seat. The grandfather backed away.

Freddy so understood. The grandfather was thinking—I sit in that thing, and they'll leave, and I won't be able to get up and run after them.

Freddy found an unoccupied corner of the common room and called his minister.

"Hello, Freddy," said George Burnworth in a voice that tried and failed to be enthusiastic. Probably he'd been up all night with some dying member of the church or maybe writing a sermon, which would certainly sap Freddy's strength. "How are you? I meant to call. I've been swept up in other situations. What a nightmare at MMC. How are you faring?"

"I'm fine, thanks, and so is Grandma."

"Lily and I haven't been able to visit Cordelia for a few weeks," said the minister, "but we'll drive up shortly."

"My sisters want to move Grandma."

"That might be a good idea. Nobody seems to know why that poor patient was killed or by whom. There could be some maniac on the staff, although everybody I've encountered is kind and good. What are your thoughts?"

"Mixed," said Freddy. "But that's not why I called, Dr. Burnworth."

"When are you going to call me George?"

"Probably never. Listen, do you happen to know any criminal lawyers in Middletown? I mean, you probably don't ever run into that kind of thing, but I thought I'd ask."

The minister said wearily, "Is this your crime, Freddy?"

"I'm researching for a friend."

"Right," said the pastor skeptically. "I'll text a Middletown attorney I like and ask him to fit you into his schedule ASAP. I'll text you his phone number and you set it up. Meanwhile, how can I help, Freddy?"

"This helps. I really appreciate it."

"Call and let me know how it goes," said the minister, but Freddy could tell the last thing George Burnworth wanted was to know how it went. He wanted a nice world, a smooth world, a Mrs. Maple world.

Me too, thought Freddy, checking on Grandma again.

She was waking up and trying to get her bearings. She thrashed around, clearly needing the bathroom. There were no aides in sight.

Freddy helped her out of bed, walked her into her bathroom, guided her into position, and closed her right hand on the pull bar attached to the wall.

She didn't know what to do next. Freddy did know; he just didn't want to. He stilled himself, helped her with her pajama bottoms, pulled her pull-up down, and she sat, having finally remembered how to go potty.

Freddy shut the door, not so Grandma could have privacy, because she didn't know what that was anymore, but so he had privacy. He washed up at a sink in the common room kitchen and went back to wait.

Grandma was taking a long time. Finally, Freddy knocked. "You okay, Grandma?" he yelled.

No answer.

He opened the bathroom door.

Grandma had had a poop event on the floor and tried to clean it up with her bare hands. When that hadn't worked, she'd slipped her feet out of her slippers and was using them as scoops.

"Jade!" Freddy yelled and added in a normal voice, "Sorry, shouldn't yell. Please help Grandma." He pointed to the bathroom.

Glaring at him, Jade marched in. But the glare didn't apply to her patient. In a sweet, cheerful voice, she said, "Uh-oh, Miss Cordelia. Oopsy. Now you just sit back down on the toilet and let me glove up, and we're going to get sparkly clean."

Freddy felt as if he were sinking into some sort of delirium. Complete with tremens.

Jade finally brought Grandma out, freshly dressed and wearing moccasins. "I couldn't save the slippers," said Jade. "You gotta buy new ones."

"You're a peach," he told her, wondering where you bought bedroom slippers.

"True story."

Okay, so she photographs patients at their worst, thought Freddy. But she cleans up stuff like this and she's nice about it.

To hustle in Freddy's world, you needed to be a good judge of character, because you were always on thin ice in heavy drug traffic. But Freddy wasn't a good judge of character, and he didn't believe anybody else was either, because people shifted and wavered and changed. There were good bad people and bad good people, and Freddy least of all knew who was who.

TWENTY-SEVEN

When Laura went into the kitchen to fix breakfast, the stink of the dead piano choked her. It was an almost visible miasma. She opened every window, the front, back, and side doors, and lugged out the fans. Then she started phone calls to find somebody to take the piano to the dump. She got two "Leave a message" responses and one live answer. "We can't make it today," the junk guy said rather proudly. "We're way too booked."

"I'll pay you double."

"We still can't make it today. Maybe tomorrow."

They agreed that he would come as soon as he could.

With nothing else to do, Laura opened Betty Sherwood's album. How pretty Maude had been in those lovely midcalf swishing skirts they wore in the fifties, ironed so primly, with the big square pocket. Her hair hung to her shoulders, a tortoiseshell barrette holding it back.

But the Highview Avenue photographs contained a major surprise: It wasn't *Kenneth* who visited Maude at MMC. It was the *cousin*, Bobby.

Mr. Griffin had told Freddy he didn't think that man was married to that woman, and Mr. Griffin was right. The man who called himself Maude's husband was in fact her cousin.

Laura was dumbfounded. A cousin had a perfectly good right to visit. Why would sixty-ish Bobby represent himself as ninety-ish Kenneth?

Maybe Cousin Bobby had taken over Kenneth's bank accounts?

But Laura had taken over Aunt Polly's money, and Freddy and

his sisters had taken over their grandmother's. Everybody had to. And if Bobby was spending some of the real Kenneth's money on himself instead of on Maude, he'd inherit it anyway, and meanwhile, he certainly wasn't stinting Maude.

Why go to all the trouble of calling himself by his cousin's name?

Was that why he wore a white wig? To look more like a very old woman's very old husband?

The masquerade was creepy, but she was not ready to consign Bobby Lansing/Kenneth Yardley to some circle of hell. Anybody who visited Memory Care several times a week deserved praise, not censure. No one knew that better than Laura Maple.

What had happened to the real Kenneth?

Was he still alive, tucked in some upstairs bedroom in one of those houses? He'd be in his nineties. If his Alzheimer's had indeed begun years ago when they were in Old Greenwich, he'd be beyond muddled now. He'd be a stone.

If Bobby was comfortable having Maude in an institution, though, wouldn't he also put the real Kenneth in one? Perhaps he couldn't afford two, which would be ruinous for almost anybody.

But then why not just sell the Old Greenwich house?

More likely, the real Kenneth was dead.

Laura Googled the *Hartford Courant*, *Greenwich Time*, *Stamford Advocate*, and *Middletown Press* and checked obituaries for Kenneth Yardley. There were none. Of course, Kenneth— well, Bobby—had said he didn't believe in obituaries, and obituaries weren't mandatory. No law proclaimed that people had to publish them.

Could Bobby have hidden the real Kenneth's death? How could he accomplish that? Bury the body in his backyard? She couldn't picture Kenneth/Bobby with a shovel or a backhoe.

Maybe the poor old man was buried under another name. What other name? Well, Bobby wasn't using his own name right now, which freed up the name Robert Lansing.

Laura Googled again. Robert Lansing Senior had died five years ago. That was no detailed obituary, just a two-line announcement.

Wind was now actively blowing through her house, which was good. Dead piano stench was dwindling. Laura was shivering, but if she closed the house, the smell would build up again. She put on a heavy coat. Added a scarf.

It occurred to her that if Kenneth wasn't Kenneth, maybe Maude wasn't Maude. Maybe she was Bobby's mother or Virginia's mother. Maybe the Lansings were getting free Memory Care by substituting their loved one for Maude and using her long-term insurance and social security and pensions.

Laura studied photographs of Maude in the album and the one on her phone from the nursing record. Maude was Maude. But Kenneth was Bobby.

Was he the meany beany to whom Freddy's grandmother had referred? What could he have been doing that Cordelia Chase would decide he was a meany beany? Or even notice? Noticing was not a dementia characteristic.

And why did Kenneth/Bobby visit MMC so often? Why come several times a week to visit a woman to whom you were not married, and she didn't recognize you anyway?

Fingers tapped her shoulder.

Kenneth Yardley stood next to her.

How could she not have heard him walk in? Was she going deaf? What a horrible fate.

And now she was alone in her house with a man not using his real name who might be the killer of his own cousin and who hated her guts for phoning a church. She picked up the coffeepot. Thank goodness she still used a percolator. Boiling water was a weapon. "Mr. Yardley. What a surprise."

"No more surprising than you digging up Betty Sherwood and making her call us."

I'm an old fool, thought Laura. I gave Betty my phone to call Bobby and Virginia, so my caller ID—of course—ID'd me.

"Why are you butting into my life?" he yelled. "What kind of sick person are you? I have suffered a terrible loss! The death by violence of my dear wife. And you're poking at it, as if you're toasting marshmallows or something. *It's not a game.*"

But it *is* a game, thought Laura. She's not your wife. You are using a false name at MMC. You even have a false head of hair.

He took a step forward. She took two back. She was now cornered. She really would have to exit by crawling under one of the grand pianos. She could probably scootch down and creep out, find something to hang on to, and haul herself to her feet on the other side, but Kenneth would long since have walked around to kick her.

She could not meet his glare and dropped her eyes. Lying on the counter was Betty Sherwood's faux leather album, her name embossed in gold on the cover. She looked quickly away. "How did you get this address?"

"I stopped at MMC first thing this morning," said Kenneth, "and told the desk you wanted to help me write the obituary but, oh dear me, I lost your address and phone number. So they gave it to me. I drive down here, your front door's literally open, and I walk in." He pointed to her music room. "You are some sick hoarder. Normal people don't live like this. You've got broken stuff on your shelves? And what are you collecting in those boxes? They're big enough to hold cannon." He frowned at the shrink wrap on the nearest piano. Then he looked her up and down, in her heavy coat and long scarf, clutching her coffeepot. His voice turned gentle, a man dealing with a psycho. "Mrs. Maple, we're all shaken by how my poor Maude died. I don't believe the police are right. I don't believe she died by violence. It was natural causes or an accident. I know families are removing their loved ones from MMC as fast as they can. I know you poked into my life in some misguided attempt to find out what happened, maybe hoping to pin the blame on me, *but I wasn't there*. You know that. The police told you."

He sounded so nice. He probably was nice. Only nice people visited MMC anyway. And if you had to have a fake husband, you might as well have a nice fake husband.

With Kenneth over by the pianos, she slipped into the hall. "It's pleasant on the front porch," she said, heading out.

Kenneth's courtesy evaporated. "What is this?" he shouted. He snatched up Betty Sherwood's album. "Where did you get this?" His face began to twitch. His cheek and one side of his lip leaped.

Please don't have a stroke. "Kenneth, that album is precious to Betty. I need to return it."

Kenneth stomped out of the house and over the grass, threw the album onto his passenger seat, and drove off so violently he left a patch.

She didn't want to face Betty over a lost album. She didn't want to think about Bobby Lansing and Kenneth Yardley and the suffocation of poor Maude. She wanted the dead piano gone and the practice pipe organ built, and above all, she wanted to hear from her children.

Why was she always the one to call them?

Why didn't they ever say to themselves, *Gosh, I haven't talked to Mom in ages, I can't wait to hear her voice.*

She was close to tears. If she started crying, she wouldn't be able to stop.

Wayne Ames pulled into the driveway.

It wasn't fair! She couldn't deal with him too.

The detective trotted right up to the front door where she stood.

Should she tell him that Kenneth Yardley was actually Robert Lansing? No. Whether or not he was Bobby, Kenneth had not been at MMC the night Maude was murdered. No matter how weird, illegal, or wrong it was to call himself somebody else, he wasn't the murderer.

She walked back to the kitchen. The detective took this as an invitation and came in, closing the front door after himself. The rest of the downstairs was still open, cold, and literally windy. "You like it chilly, huh?" he said.

She lacked the energy to discuss dead piano smells. She didn't invite him to sit because there wasn't anywhere. She poured him a cup of coffee. He wanted sugar. She gave him sugar.

"We've been looking into Mr. Bell's situation," said the detective, leaning on the counter. "What do you know about him?"

"He's a sweet, good soul. His mother instructed him that if anything should happen to her, Freddy was in charge of his grandmother. His mother did in fact die. Freddy has shouldered that responsibility with grace."

Laura prayed for grace.

Her own mother had been fifty-eight when she got Alzheimer's. Susan Chamberlain turned into a wreck so fast, she was like a sped-up film of decay. Her beautiful face went slack, her voice became a monotone, she slouched when she walked and missed her mouth when she lifted the spoon.

Laura could have dealt with that.

But her mother became sly and vicious. Her speech was mostly swear words. She accused Laura of stealing from her, and she threw things at people.

The doctors said this behavior was not uncommon; paranoia was a feature of Alzheimer's.

Laura hated being around her mother. Hated looking at her destroyed features and hearing her four-letter words. And the terrible day came when Laura simply hated her mother.

She put her mother in an institution because aides wouldn't stay. Susan bit them.

Laura explained to everybody that she had to be excused from the burden of visiting and thus be able remember her mother as the warm, good woman she had once been, not the creature she'd become.

That was what Laura called her mother. A burden. A creature. Susan Chamberlain lived two more years.

Laura didn't visit.

Not once.

Alzheimer's ate Susan up and spit her out. Laura not only paid other people to deal with it; she didn't check to see if they bothered.

Mother wouldn't want me to suffer, Laura told everybody in a lofty voice. *She would want me to celebrate life.*

So Laura had celebrated life. Her own. She had dismissed the angry, desperate, terrified woman who was formerly her mother and let her sink.

There were residents at MMC who had no visitors, and oh, how Laura understood. *You'll pay a price*, she wanted to tell their families. *You'll always know that you are weak and cruel.*

"Taking care of an old woman with dementia can't be the life plan of a twenty-six-year-old man," said Wayne Ames.

She had forgotten the detective was even here. "No," she said sadly. "That's what makes Freddy so admirable."

"Do you know what Mr. Bell does for a living?" asked Wayne Ames.

"He makes glass beads." She dug into her purse for the little plastic baggie with his gift. "Aren't they beautiful? Look how the colors bleed into each other. I haven't had them made into a necklace yet. I have a neighbor who beads and she'd do it for me, but I enjoy having them loose and taking them out to admire."

Wayne Ames had a strange expression on his face. After a while, he said, "Freddy never signs in or out. And we know now that the staff is frequently too busy to notice visitors. They're off in some bedroom or bathroom, the activity room, the nurses' record room. Freddy could have been there the night of Maude's murder, and no one would know."

"What are you implying?"

"Last night," he said, "Freddy slept in his grandmother's room."

"Really? I love to think of him doing that." She had never spent a minute in her mother's room, let alone slept there. She had never even worried about her mother. She just wrote her off, like a bad debt.

"He's a druggie, Mrs. Maple. They're all dangerous. Why do you suppose he spent the night there? What do you think he had in mind?"

Laura swung her handbag around and whacked Wayne Ames in the face.

She did not carry an entry-level bag. Her purse was serious. Her whole life was in there. She had her iPad for music and books and a real book as well, her reading glasses, cell phone, tissues, hand wipes, lipsticks, compact, notebook for lists, Charlie Ives material, a catalog to peruse, and a little envelope fat with grocery coupons.

He was not expecting the attack. She got him straight on.

Generally speaking, it was probably unwise to hit policemen, bruise their lips, and give them bloody noses. Probably if Freddy had done it, he'd be jailed.

But she was thin and gray and decades older than Wayne Ames. She realized with pleasure that this gave her a certain power. What was he going to do about this? Admit it?

She pulled a tissue pack out of her purse and handed it over.

He sighed, squished the sides of his nose together, and blotted the blood. "Mr. Yardley told me that you're taking an unhealthy interest in his wife's demise. He must *really* think that, since he just drove down here to yell at you."

"I'm taking a sensible interest. My vulnerable aunt lives steps away from where that murder happened."

"You told a number of people that dying is not necessarily a bad thing."

Laura used his first name to diminish him. "Wayne, dying comes to everybody. It is natural. Maude's death wasn't natural. That's why it is dreadful. But prior to senility, I am sure every resident of

Middletown Memory Care would have chosen death over the life they lead now."

"A lot of those people seem content."

"How do you define contentment? Are you thinking of Mr. Griffin perhaps? Who has spent *years* trying to find his car keys, his car, and his parking lot? Desperately trying to get to work on time? Knocking on doors and pleading for guidance? Is *he* content?"

"So you think it's a good idea to help someone die."

"Somebody suffocated Maude, young man. You are looking for somebody vicious and cruel. That person could be a crazy passerby or a brutal staff member or a greedy relative. But do not so carelessly use the word 'help,' because nobody *helped* Maude Yardley."

She escorted him to the door. She would never forgive him for implying that Freddy could be the murderer.

TWENTY-EIGHT

Freddy had just merged onto Route 9 on his way home when his cell rang. Laura Maple.

Freddy wanted a life without old ladies. He wanted a life where Br and Shawn lived free. He wanted to be rid of the Leper and Doc. He wanted never to cross paths with Auburn again.

I'm just a guy, he thought. All I want is food and a friend and flamework. Like Snap. He's just a dog. All he wants is food and somebody to chew on. "Hey, Mapes."

"Freddy, the police think I did it."

"No, they don't."

"Kenneth Yardley told them that I am taking an unhealthy interest in the funeral. And then they found Aunt Polly's watch in Maude's room."

This was meaningless. Half the residents didn't know what room they lived in anyway and were always going in the wrong one, while the wanderer crowd would go through any door, sit on any chair, pick up anybody's possession, or abandon their own. The aides generally recognized knickknacks and could return them to their proper owners, but there was a constant drift of stuff.

"Ames is just poking," he told her. "Police do that. They're like wild dogs. They smell fear. They smell secrets. But not to worry. The police have to have evidence, and there isn't any, for you or anybody else."

Although Br was going to be convicted by planted evidence and false statements. In one effortless minute, Auburn and Danielle had destroyed Br.

"They're probably going to suspect everybody," he comforted Mrs. Maple. "They'll probably suspect me next."

Freddy so did not want to be suspected next.

He was not paying income tax.

He was driving two vehicles not his own on which he had no insurance.

He had failed to notify Social Security that Alice Bell was no longer alive, and he was living off his mother's monthly income.

He was making drug paraphernalia.

He was laundering money.

And the best glass of his life had died through a fake bid.

Mrs. Maple told him about Betty Sherwood and the photograph album, proof that Kenneth was in fact Robert Lansing.

Freddy didn't give cops much credit, but anything Mrs. Maple could find out, the cops could find out. They had to know by now about Kenneth/Bobby.

The impersonation made it even harder to believe that Kenneth had murdered Maude. If Kenneth really was Cousin Bobby, he'd be out buying beachfront with Kenneth's cash, not spooning pudding into Maude's mouth.

Except you could spoon something other than pudding. Suppose you crushed up strong heart medication and mixed that in. Suppose you came often so you could overdose her. Nobody would do an autopsy if an old lady's heart stopped. It was supposed to stop.

But if she was such a tough old bird that her heart kept beating no matter what you slugged down her throat?

If all you did was spoon pudding, you could pretend you weren't killing her. But hold her down hard enough to bruise her, jamming that cloth into her mouth and over her nose, you'd know you were a murderer. You'd feel Maude's agony in your own personal fingers.

You probably wouldn't be caught taking the pudding route. But the suffocation route—you had to be some desperate to consider that.

What was the desperate part?

"Kenneth walked right into my house this morning," said Mrs. Maple.

"Well, definitely start locking your doors," said Freddy, hoping he had remembered to lock Grandma's, especially now that Doc, the Leper, and Auburn were all in the picture. Come to think of it, so was that detective, asking about how to wreck a glass shop.

It was pretty much a cinch to blow up a glass shop. Just get yourself a good combination of oxygen and propane and figure out how to ignite it without killing yourself.

Freddy thought of fire consuming generations of family stuff. Photographs since photography began. Teacups and crochet and paint-by-number oil paintings Alice had done when she was ten and they still hung on the wall. In a hideous way, it wouldn't be so bad. Freddy and his sisters didn't know what to do with all that stuff anyway.

Freddy was too worn out to drive, which had never happened to him before. He exited 9 and headed for a coffee shop. At the bottom of the ramp, with no car behind him, he came to a full stop and checked his texts.

Kara had written.

I'm flying down.

Kara? In his actual house, by his actual side?

There was enough going on without his bossy sister invading. What would happen when Kara gave the bottom level of Grandma's house a thorough inspection?

No worries. She'll see a lot of equipment she doesn't understand, I'll give her a pretty bead and shoo her upstairs. If she does catch on to the pipes, I'll shrug. *What did you think I was doing? And it's none of your business, unless you want to buy one. Or two. And if you think I'm too morally corrupt to take care of Grandma, you do it.*

Freddy realized with a catch in his throat that he did not want his sister to take over Grandma. Kara loved the grandma who had existed in their childhood. But that grandma did not live here anymore. This grandma would not know Kara and, very possibly, had no memory of Kara at all. Kara would be dutiful, but would she love Grandma anyway?

Because that was the trick. Loving your person anyway.

Plus he couldn't let Kara be alone in a house when Doc or Auburn might come calling.

"Yet another thing happened early this morning, Freddy," said Mrs. Maple. "That detective, Wayne Ames, came to my house and all but accused *you* of suffocating Maude. I hit him in the face with my handbag and gave him a bloody nose."

Freddy was rather braced by the idea that somebody out there could make even stupider decisions than he did. Mapes, of all people. "It was nice of you to defend me. But what made Ames think about me to start with?"

"I don't know. He had a peculiar expression on his face when I showed him your beautiful beads. And he called you—Freddy, these are not my words—he called you a druggie."

Freddy parked at the diner. He began thinking of bacon.

"The policeman said that what you actually do, Freddy, is make drug paraphernalia."

Don't lecture me, Freddy prayed. We're not gonna be friends if you do.

"Oh, Freddy!" she cried, his mother reincarnated. "Surely you could go back to school and find a nicer occupation, like being an accountant or something."

"Glass isn't an occupation really," he said lightly. "Making pipes is more like a sport. Prison to avoid, taxes to dodge, gang members to be invisible to, and all the time, creating things of great beauty for which college men will pay insane amounts of money. Their parents' money, that is. Come on, Mapes. You hang out with me in nursing homes. You know I'm not a dirty, long-haired dope fiend. See you later."

He hung up, and then, remembering other possible dope fiends, called to make an appointment with the Middletown lawyer.

They put him on hold. He thought about skipping the whole thing, and then, just when he expected to be squeezed in next month, they said to come right now.

Whoa. Dr. Burnworth's name was some powerful.

Once more, Freddy drove north up 9. How could a person make glass with all this commuting? It was probably a good thing he was living rent-free.

He parked where he was least likely to run into Auburn or Doc: the county courthouse.

Jenny called before he could get out of the truck. She refused to discuss Australia, although it was having wildfires right now, and Freddy thought fire was a fine topic. "I'm calling because you won't listen to Kara. I want you to move Grandma out of there. You don't do anything all day anyway. Find another home for her. That minister will help you."

Jenny knew perfectly well who "that minister" was. She had grown up in his church. Plus Dr. Burnworth's joy was teaching delinquent kids to play tennis, because he believed in the discipline of sports, and Jenny had been a partner with various semi-willing participants and even written her college application essay about it. Furthermore, "that minister" had performed Jenny's wedding.

But wherever Jenny had dumped religion, Freddy didn't go there. He half thought his sisters were jealous of Lily and George Burnworth because they really did visit the needy, the jailed, and the sick, whereas Freddy's sisters just gave orders from a distance.

"Kara has researched online, Freddy, and set up interviews at two other memory-care institutions where people are not murdering each other."

Freddy had received this email and paid no attention to it. "Jenny, those places are in northwest Connecticut. There are no direct routes from here. There are hardly any indirect routes. It'll be local two-lane roads with a million traffic lights. How am I going to visit? It's gotta be hours each way."

"Freddy, you make *beads*. You can take time off. Don't be selfish."

"You're the one being selfish. We can't ask Grandma to adjust to another place."

"She has dementia," yelled Jenny. "What kind of adjustment is there?"

Freddy thought of his grandmother's first week at MMC: her confusion and despair, how she clung to him, begging to go home. She couldn't eat, sleep, or figure out who all these blurry strangers were. He thought of the terrible second afternoon when she crawled onto his lap and lifted a tearstained, runny-nosed face. Mrs. Burnworth had peeled her off, told Freddy to leave, and put her own arms around Cordelia Chase.

When Freddy had stumbled out of MMC that day, sick that he had inflicted this agony on his poor grandmother, he ran into Will, husband of Irene. Will took Freddy out for a drink although Freddy wasn't into alcohol, being satisfied with nicotine and weed. "Your grandmother will calm down by the end of the week," Will told him. "She'll get into a routine and won't remember how awful it was. It's the only blessing there is with memory loss. They really do forget."

Freddy loved Jenny. He loved all his sisters. But his allies in this nightmare were strangers like Will, ministers like Dr. Burnworth—there were plenty of other ministers and priests who stopped by MMC—and new friends like Tree Lady. "Talk to you later, Jenny," he said. "I have an appointment."

"Freddy! My time zone—"

Freddy abandoned her to the Australian wildfires and walked two blocks to a nice, old brick building, the kind that says *Sturdy, reliable, and historic. Lawyers here overcharge.*

The guy turned out to be a hefty middle-aged man with great hanging jowls. Freddy hoped his own face wouldn't end up like that. How did you shave? You'd have to yank on the puddles of your cheeks, smoothening them so you could move a razor around.

He had a hard time spitting out the story, and when he was finally done, the attorney studied Freddy thoughtfully. "Not much surprises me anymore. But this does."

"I can pay you. It shouldn't be that many hours." He certainly hoped it wouldn't be that many hours.

"Pay me from making pipes?"

Freddy thought of the trombone with wings that Gary Leperov would probably not pay for. "Well, yeah, I don't earn enough from beads." Or pay out of Mom's social security, he thought, ordering himself to call Social Security and deal with that and knowing he wouldn't. "I can't be part of this. You do it. The fingerprints on that baggie are not going to be Br's. The fingerprints are Auburn's and Danielle's."

"Auburn told you she was in Br's car with a 'big baggie of coke,' right?" asked the attorney. "So she's a dealer?"

Freddy nodded, but now he was confused all over again. Would a dealer give away her supply just to sucker punch a stranger? Dealers didn't want losses; they wanted gains. What would Auburn gain by destroying Br?

On the other hand, it was a psycho stalker thing to do. "I don't have the whole picture," he said. My motto, he thought glumly.

The attorney rocked back in his swivel chair, which had several handles for the proper adjustment to height and weight. Freddy, who stood up to work, had no knowledge of chairs, but it looked pretty comfy. "Done," said the attorney, offering his hand.

"You didn't tell me the fee."

The guy shrugged, whatever that meant. "You say hello to George Burnworth for me."

Freddy didn't actually skip back to the truck, but he felt kind of lighthearted. Br was getting saved, or maybe, or partly, and—

"Freddy."

Doc was leaning against the truck, a fleshy barricade in a T-shirt with the sleeves slit to fit his biceps. Freddy did not think of himself as small, but next to Doc, he was a twig. If Doc swatted Freddy with the flat of his hand, he'd break Freddy's jaw. And if he wanted to crush Freddy's head in a car door, he could grip Freddy's skull in one hand—the hand whose massive fingers wore sharply protruding rings.

Still and all, Freddy couldn't see Doc mutilating Shawn's dog.

"You're getting on the Leper's nerves," said Doc. "This is the second time I've had to drive to your stupid little state with all its stupid trees." He handed his phone to Freddy, and the phone began ringing wherever Gary Leperov was.

It went to voicemail, which was worse. Whatever he said would last forever. "Gary, now that I know it's cocaine, I *really* can't do it. I'm out." He handed the phone back.

"Where did you get the idea that he's in coke?" said Doc. "We're weed, all weed."

"What about the cocaine jar pendants you're selling at Auburn's?"

"Huh?"

"The Leper fingers."

"They're pendants, Freddy. Regular old pendants."

Freddy looked away, trying to gather his thoughts. Doc's white Toyota Corolla was parked right next to his truck, and he hadn't even noticed. The passenger window was down, and Skinny was sitting there.

The guy was scary thin, like he ate a week ago and might eat again next week, because all his calories were drug calories. Even his hair was thin and his pitiful beard. Around his neck, Skinny wore a Leper nose. He was grinning. His teeth were rotted out, and his lips were crusty and swollen. He actually resembled his pendant.

You didn't get like that from weed. This looked like meth.

And this was Doc's sidekick? Freddy could totally see this guy with a machete and paws.

"The Lep is building your career, Freddy," said Doc, using his best bedside manner. "Every bid he makes on your glass impresses everybody else. You're going to be somebody someday. Or you're going to be dead meat. You choose." Doc took off his cap to scratch his head. He was going bald.

He's too old for this game, thought Freddy. He wanted to be a surgeon, but he's just running errands, and the years are turning into decades.

Doc held out a large yellow envelope. "Sales receipts. Your BABE information, your hotel and plane. I've got you flying out of Providence."

Freddy didn't take it.

Doc let go. The envelope fell flat on the sidewalk. "Your name's on everything, Freddy. And just so you know, down Main Street here, cops are walking into Auburn's. You want some advice? Stay away from Auburn. She's a predator."

"*You* deal with her."

"Freddy, *I'm* a predator. We're a match. You're prey."

Twenty-Nine

Laura looked at her previously beautiful, currently hideous music room.

She considered covering the piano shrink-wraps with her white damask tablecloths and setting bouquets on them, but that would look even more peculiar.

She had inherited linens, silver, crystal, and ridiculous amounts of china. Her children had no interest. When Laura died, everything she cherished would go to the thrift shop. Her daughter and daughter-in-law were not going to set the table with silver and crystal. In fact, they didn't set a table at all but ate like scavengers. Watching her grandchildren dine was like watching a nature show, where the vultures flew in, ripped off a piece of flesh, and flew away.

"I changed my mind," said Kemmy. "I want to see it."

"Kemmy! You're shortening my life, creeping up like this."

"You didn't lock your front door," said Kemmy severely. "When you come inside your house, you lock it behind you, Laura. How hard is that? At least answer when somebody knocks and yells. I thought you had fallen. That's why I walked in. I bet you need hearing aids."

"My hearing is perfect!"

"No, it isn't. Is that it? On the piano?"

Laura nodded. She already cherished her possible Charles Ives more than any music in her library. Kemmy stroked the soft old page and inspected each side.

According to the biographer, there was quite a bit of lost Charles Ives music. In 1891 and '92, when he was in his late teens, he composed dozens of pieces for organ, chorus, band, and voice, including elegies for departed pets, and much of this had vanished without being published.

"I Googled Charles Ives," said Kemmy. "Pictures of his manuscripts look kind of like this, but not really. This looks fake."

Laura bristled.

"All these wavy lines and cross-outs and jottings," said Kemmy skeptically.

"The paper itself is very old," Laura pointed out. "Nobody makes paper like this now."

"Somebody could have forged it."

"Oh, please. Back then, nobody thought highly enough of Charlie to bother." Laura forced herself to present the likelier possibility. "It could have been written by his father, though. 'Sweet By and By' was George Ives's trademark hymn. And since this is the Seeley family piano, Seeley people also played it. One of them could have been a musician."

"We have to get this authenticated," said Kemmy briskly. "Luckily we know a doctoral candidate who has an Ives background."

"You mean Gordon Clary? He's a jerk," said Laura.

"That's a little strong. But he's our jerk and he's been bragging about his Ives knowledge, so I'll ask him to look at it."

Kemmy left with the manuscript. The empty house loomed around Laura: all her silly projects, ridiculous collections, and foolish plans. If only she liked shopping. Then she'd always have a destination because there was always another store.

But it wasn't possessions for which she yearned.

———————

Doc and Skinny drove away without slamming Freddy's head in the door. Freddy was tense around Doc but not scared. He *was* scared of Skinny. And *definitely* scared of Auburn.

Freddy looked down at the envelope.

Probably should pick that up, he thought. Probably incriminating.

Instead he backed out of his parking space and drove over it. He left Middletown by a weird little road next to the railroad tracks, got on 9, immediately exited, made a turn, and circled a block.

No white Toyota Corolla followed him.

He was taking a slow, circuitous country-lane route back to Grandma's house when Dr. Burnworth called. Did the minister want to check on why Freddy needed a criminal attorney? He so didn't want a discussion.

But it was way worse. "Kara phoned," said Dr. Burnworth.

"Yeah, she wants to visit," said Freddy glumly. "Tell her the house is sliding into a sinkhole and it isn't safe."

"My worry, Freddy, is that Middletown Memory Care is sliding into a sinkhole. How about you have dinner here tonight and we'll talk about our options?"

If the pastor was straight from a conversation with Kara, the option they had in mind was for Freddy to shop around for new nursing homes. Plus work out interim raised-ranch care.

"Pie for dessert," said Dr. Burnworth.

Freddy said nothing.

Dr. Burnworth upped the ante. "Home-baked, fresh-from-the-oven pie using local apples. Brown-sugar crumb topping. Real whipped cream. No spray cans, no plastic tubs."

Oh, well then. "What time?" asked Freddy.

"Five. We're eating early because I have a church committee meeting this evening."

Freddy didn't often have dinner at five, but it could also be said that Freddy didn't often have dinner. He ate when he was starved or it was convenient.

"Wow!" said Freddy, full of pie and food happiness. "Mrs. Burnworth, you are a great baker."

"George told you the pie was home baked," said Lily Burnworth, "but I don't think he said I baked it. I haven't baked in a hundred years. I buy these from a neighbor, so we always have homemade goodies around, and people think I'm an outstanding pastor's wife, which I am. I'm just not the baker."

Freddy liked that. He didn't like the Skype call Mrs. Burnworth now set up with Kara. "Really?" he said. "The pie was a trick?"

Lily Burnworth smiled. "Sit next to me, Freddy."

South Dakota came into focus.

How beautiful Kara was. She resembled their dead mother so much it hurt.

Kara gave him a stretched-tight smile. "Freddy, I check my Facebook all day long. Our high school class has a website. So I know about Shawn. On top of everything else, your best friend on the shoreline deals coke?"

The Burnworths gasped.

Freddy didn't think they would have known Shawn. Their only kid was a lot younger and had gone to a different high school, plus the Aminettis were Catholic so they wouldn't cross paths in church. But the Burnworths sure didn't like finding out that Freddy hung around with dealers. If he wanted more pie, he'd have to cut his own slice.

"I'll send you my flight number and arrival time as soon as I have arranged it, Freddy," said Kara sternly, "and you will pick me up at Bradley Airport. Write this down, Freddy. I need you to buy me vanilla soy milk. I need—"

Freddy walked away.

Mrs. Burnworth leaned into Skype view. "Kara, darling, we so want you to stay with us instead. Freddy is a young bachelor, and perhaps housekeeping is not his strength, but our guest room is charming and we love your company. Now give me the shopping list."

Why am I fighting Kara's visit? Freddy wondered. It's good that she's coming. I can resign from all this. It's Kara's turn anyway, and she wants her turn, and she'll be good at it. Better than I am.

Freddy left the Burnworths, went to Grandma's and fed Snap, got back on 9, and drove to Middletown for the third time that day. Night, actually. By the time he took the MMC exit, it was nearly eleven. He wasn't going back because of Auburn. Not because of Doc either. Maybe because of Skinny. Maybe because of his sisters. Definitely because of Grandma.

He was bone tired. He could probably sleep tight even on cot wires.

A block away, he saw a sea of bright-red and white circling lights.

By the time he turned into MMC, he was in full panic mode. He expected an ambulance, a fire truck, and a rescue vehicle: those were protocol. But the visitor lot was also full of cop cars. So it wasn't a fall. It must be a homicide.

His sisters had been way right. But they always were. How come he kept pretending he knew anything?

Please, God, he prayed, *please let it not be Grandma*. He managed to park, turn off the car, and drop the keys in his pocket. When he ran toward the front entrance, his legs felt like they were different lengths.

A cop stopped him, hands up, like for cars in traffic. He was in uniform, heavily equipped. Burly. Big gut.

Don't shove him, Freddy told himself. Don't get in a fight. "My grandmother," he said. "I gotta check on her."

"Yeah? How'd you find out anything was going on?" asked the cop, as if Freddy might be the murderer, coming back to gloat and observe.

Freddy was instantly furious. "Wild guess," he said, gesturing at the badly parked, idling emergency vehicles. "I have to check on my grandmother," he repeated, trying to get past.

"Calm down," said the cop.

People who told him to calm down went straight to Freddy's hate list.

"The victim is male," said the cop.

Victim. People weren't "victims" of falls. So his guess had been right. Somebody else had been suffocated. And at this hour, who could have done it but a staff member?

Freddy's thoughts throbbed in circular blinking color, like the lights on the roof of each squad car. He couldn't grab a thought and make it go anywhere. The cop was holding his arm, which normally Freddy would not ignore, but he had better things to do than worry about a cop's grip. On his cell, he clicked the MMH contact.

"Middletown Memory Care. Constanza speaking. How may I direct your call?"

"Constanza, it's Freddy. I'm outside. They won't let me in. Is my grandmother all right? Mrs. Chase? Cordelia Chase?" He thought, Wait. Constanza works days. What does it mean that she's here tonight? The old short-staffing excuse? Or getting herself in position to commit a homicide?

But he couldn't imagine Constanza ever hurting anybody.

"I'm sure she's fine, Freddy," said Constanza. "I'll have an aide from her wing call you, though. But it's Philip, Freddy. They're all here for Philip."

"Philip?"

"They found him outside in the garden. In the dark. Alone. By himself. He didn't have his cane or his walker. He was just there on the grass. And he was dead. And how did he even get out there? Who opened the door for him? Who walked him there? Freddy, they're talking to everybody because they think... Oh, yes, Mrs.

Reilly, I'm simply reassuring Mrs. Chase's grandson that she's fine. Excuse me, Freddy, I have to put you on hold."

Philip.

Poor angry, desperate Philip.

Freddy's eyes smarted. He wiped at them. Philip, always trying to protect his desk. Philip, singing "In the sweet by and by."

And then the detective guy was next to him. Wayne Ames. Who had asked how to destroy a glass studio. "Mr. Bell," said the detective in a slow, skeptical drawl. "What are you doing here?"

Like it was a crime to show up. "Checking on my grandmother."

"The staff just finished a check on every single resident. So she's fine."

"I'm not taking your word for it. I have to see her. Anyway, I'm spending the night."

"Not tonight. We have plenty of people here to make sure the residents are safe. How did you find out anything was happening here, Freddy?"

"I guess the cop cars, the fire truck, and the ambulance tipped me off."

A swarm of cops were floating around the building. A few of them headed in Freddy's direction.

"Okay, I'm back," said Constanza in his ear. "Sherry, she's the night nurse tonight, she thinks Philip just fell or maybe had a heart attack because he had several over the years before he came here. But still, somehow he got out, or somebody took him out, and the police are calling it a suspicious death. They don't actually know what killed him. I mean, there's no blood or anything. It's just that he couldn't have gotten outside by himself."

He could have actually. Rather easily.

When an employee or a family person went out to the garden, they'd put in the code, and the heavy exit door could then be pushed open. It would slowly close by itself, leaving time for a wheelchair or walker to get through, and its own weight would cause it to relock.

But you could catch it before it closed and slow its momentum, and then it would rest against the lock instead of catching it. There was also a wooden wedge you could kick under the door to keep it open. You might do that if you were going out for just a moment, to water a hanging pot of flowers, say, or if you needed the door to stay open while you brought a whole group of residents outdoors for an activity.

He remembered suddenly that Mr. Griffin had gotten himself locked outside in that garden a few days ago. He, Freddy, had let Mr. Griffin back in. It hadn't occurred to Freddy to report the incident. It hadn't even occurred to him to wonder about it.

He didn't think there was a patient on the wing who could learn, let alone apply, the code. Certainly not Mr. Griffin or Philip.

He had a chilling image of a serial accident causer, some lunatic staff member smirking as a resident fell.

But it could be an accident. The door could have been left ajar this evening because somebody had previously gone outside or was still outside.

Constanza said Philip didn't have his cane or walker, but Philip could have used the walls as support to reach the door. He was definitely strong enough to open it, which Grandma, say, could never do. He could have tottered along one of the paths. Tripped out there. Fallen facedown and broken his neck. Fallen backward and hit his head. Or had another heart attack and collapsed.

Except—Freddy glanced at his phone—it must have happened after dinner. Say after eight or nine or ten.

Nobody took excursions then. But who would entice Philip outside? Who could possibly want to hurt him?

His phone rang again. Jade—not calling on the MMC phone but her own cell. Jade working evenings? Double shifts? He should be impressed and grateful, but he remembered with nausea how Jade got her jollies.

"Constanza told me to call you," she said irritably. She had definitely not forgiven him for the whole Polly video thing. "Your grandmother's fine, Freddy. Slept through most of it. Woke up a few minutes ago for the bathroom. I tucked her back in."

"I was going to spend the night again."

"They won't let you. But she'll be safer than toast with all these people here."

"Toast?" repeated Freddy.

"Yeah, you know. Bread. With butter. Can you think of anything safer?"

Freddy had never thought of toast in terms of safety, but okay. Whatever. "Thanks, Jade." His phone had barely any power left. It upped his anxiety to think that he could be phoneless in a minute.

For Philip to die was not a shock. Everyone here was going to die relatively soon. Their poor sad bodies were decomposing in place. It was only a shock if somebody had *caused* it to happen, *meant* it to happen. If Philip hadn't fallen or had a heart attack, had he been killed like Maude? This didn't sound like suffocation, and anyway, Philip was strong enough to shove somebody away or strangle them back.

For Maude's death, the only suspect outside of staff was Kenneth, and Kenneth loathed Philip. He'd called the cops on Philip, called him names like "monster." But how could it profit Kenneth to hurt Philip? Mapes had that over-the-top theory that Kenneth had shoved Philip onto Irene in order to blame Philip for Maude's death. But if that were true, Kenneth wouldn't kill off the guy he wanted to have carry the blame.

Why go to all the trouble of getting Philip into the garden? If you tried to hustle Philip anywhere he didn't want to go, he'd be swearing the whole way. Somebody would hear it. So Philip had gone willingly or gone out on his own.

Freddy couldn't imagine Auburn, Doc, or Skinny getting into the building at this hour and coaxing a great big guy to tiptoe out a garden door at night. Anyway, there were no unknown visitors at night, because a visitor had to be specially admitted after staff answered the front intercom. Come to think of it, Kenneth wouldn't be here at night either; he didn't have a person here anymore.

Which meant it was one of the staff.

Jade, who was suddenly working double shifts?

Vera? Sherry? Grace? Mrs. Reilly? Constanza? Heidi? Monica? Aides and workers he hadn't met?

Freddy's heart was racing. It was like an overdose without the drugs: paranoia, delusions, panic, extreme confusion. Freddy felt them all coming on.

What was happening in this place?

It would hit the news.

Second homicide at Memory Care.

He didn't want to leave. He wanted to see Grandma.

"Mr. Bell," said the detective in a kindergarten-teacher voice. *Now, little boy, do as you are told.* "Get in your car and go home."

There was practically a platoon of cops standing here now. Freddy could feel the necessary self-discipline off to his side somewhere, but it was his third trip up here, they weren't letting him in to see Grandma, and his sisters were going to go berserk when this hit the fan. He wasn't leaving.

He recognized the night cop from last night's sleepover, still in the rumpled clothing that made him look like another Alzheimer's patient. You were here? You were supposed to be protecting everybody, thought Freddy. What were you doing while this happening?

The cop looked as jangled as Freddy felt. He was smoking, but it hadn't helped his nerves. "You were negligent," he said to the cop, wondering if he'd ever used that word before. "You weren't paying any attention or this wouldn't have happened."

Cops never dropped their eyes. Their stare was another weapon. The guy locked eyes on Freddy, and his whole body got belligerent, chest swelling, chin projecting. Hey, two could play that game.

Wayne Ames butted in and said, "Listen, sport," like he was dealing with vermin, "*go home*. We're covering all the bases here."

"No, you're not! Your cop was supposed to cover the bases."

They were all spoiling for a fight, especially Freddy, but he ran out of energy. Cops protected each other. They'd never admit screwing up. Freddy hated to admit defeat, but there was no way for him to reach Grandma, and if he actually socked one of these guys, visits to Grandma would be seriously crimped.

He trudged back to the car, thinking of Marty, Philip's son. He needed to call Marty and talk about Philip. Maybe tomorrow. Maybe ask about the funeral. Mapes would go with him.

He was almost at the car and he sure hoped he had some cigarettes in there because he needed nicotine or he wouldn't have enough zip even to start the engine. And then Freddy knew.

"It's *you*!" he yelled, turning around and racing back. He would have attacked the night cop if he could have, but the other cops instantly formed a row, elbows out, hands closing in on their weapons, or so it seemed in the shadowy confusion of night.

"You went out for a smoke, didn't you?" Freddy yelled at the overnight guy, who was hidden by his buddies or had fled. "*You* propped the door open! Philip didn't *get* out. You *let* him while nobody was looking including *you* because you wanted your cigarette. *You killed him!*"

The cops were a wall. Their chests, their equipment, their badges, their snarls.

"Leave," said Wayne Ames. "Just leave."

The garden gate opened. The one with the latch too high for most people to reach.

A stretcher was wheeled out of the garden and toward the ambulance. The whirling lights of cop cars and fire truck illuminated the sheets over Philip's body, changed their color, left them dark, and then covered them with shivery stars.

Oh, Philip, thought Freddy. Whatever happened to you, you

didn't deserve it. Nobody here deserves it. And even though I'm sure it was an accident and it was the cop's fault, I've been wrong about everything. Just the way my sisters and my mother always say I am.

It could be staff, and it could be murder and I have to bring Grandma home tomorrow.

WEDNESDAY

THIRTY

Freddy had turned on all the lights in Grandma's house and walked around for hours, trying to figure out how he was going to bring her home. He even had a pencil and paper, and he was not a list person. He was an oh-well-it'll-probably-work-out person.

She would want to sleep in her old bedroom, but the bed was high and she could no longer get up on it. If he took away the box spring, the mattress would fall through the slats. He could get rid of the frame and bedstead and put the box spring and mattress on the floor. But then it would be too low, and she could never get up. He probably had to rent a hospital bed.

How would he block the stairs so she wouldn't fall down them?

What would he do about Snap?

What about Grandma's medications?

And food. He'd have to ask what her diet was. How to fix it. Where to buy it.

And the bathroom.

What was he going to do about Grandma and the bathroom?

He was so tense he couldn't sit in a chair, never mind lie down in bed.

Had a stupid, negligent cop left a door open so that Philip ended up in an unsafe place in the dark? Had Jade or Sherry or Grace or Monica walked Philip outside and shoved him? He realized that it was irrelevant to bringing Grandma home. No matter what had happened to Philip, murder had happened to Maude.

Freddy mourned for Philip, who had never caught a break from anger and despair. Maybe it was a natural death, he told himself.

Maybe Philip knew death was coming and he wanted fresh air and freedom for his last minute on earth.

At five in the morning, his cell phone rang. It had to be one of his sisters, Googling MMC at this hour and finding out.

But it was Jade.

Freddy's heart almost stopped. Grandma had been hurt after all. And he had left! He had driven away when she needed him.

"Freddy, I'm telling you, but you can't let anybody know I'm telling you. At the hospital? They did an X-ray of Philip's body. He don't have no broken bones. His throat, the little bone that breaks if they strangle you? It's not broken. He don't have bruises either. They think he just kind of folded up and died. His son was here, that really nice son? The heavy one? He thinks it was another heart attack."

Freddy's rigid muscles and tendons gave way. He sat heavily on the nearest chair, an ugly maple captain's chair with a thick tufted pad. It was a pretty great chair actually.

"But the big news, Freddy?" Her voice was hot and gloating. "Guess what the real news is, Freddy?"

Freddy couldn't guess.

"That night cop who looked homeless?" she said gladly. "He admitted he went out for a cigarette and maybe left the door open." So Jade was definitely part of the vast suspicious population that never wanted a cop around and cheered when a cop was in trouble.

So the cops had followed through. Checked the garden, found the cigarette butts. Or maybe the guy himself stepped up and told them.

Philip had not been murdered. It was probably still a homicide, manslaughter maybe, because that cop was responsible. But it didn't have anything to do with Maude. And maybe, just maybe, he didn't have to bring Grandma home immediately. He had time to hire an aide and get hold of a bed and deal with food and meds and a hundred other things he wouldn't think of until it was too late. "Thanks for letting me know, Jade. Are you calling everybody?"

"Just you." Her voice was sneaky. "Doing you a favor, Freddy. So...Freddy? I'm into what you're into. Maybe send me a certain type of flower?"

She didn't want roses, but he wasn't going to be anybody's supplier. Ever. Still, he did owe her because now he knew there wasn't a serial killer on the staff. If the killer was on the staff, they were a one-time killer. "I hear you," he said and hung up.

He couldn't get over that the cop had admitted doing wrong. His admission must be public, or Jade wouldn't have known.

Wait.

A *cop* told me that the pendant on Constanza's desk was a cocaine jar. Since when do cops tell the truth? Cops want information. They'll say anything. Lying is their trade.

Freddy was seized by a wild hope. There was no dirty drug money at those bead shows because the drug in question was not coke. It was marijuana, which was legal, or sort of, or going to be, so whatever.

Sagging in the embrace of the captain's chair, he looked across the room and saw the stairs, which he didn't have to gate or fence after all, or at least not today, and remembered that he made glass down there, that he had glass in the kiln!

He hopped out of the chair and ran down the steps.

He had completed the snare drum for his future drum set rig, and now he took it from the kiln. Its body was gold with a scarlet hoop, the drumhead amber streaked in green, with a fat knob to string a gold chain. The face on the drum was sick.

Totally stoked, he put it on line for auction.

#drumsmadeofglass#borosilicateclass

#dogsthatsnap#snapsthatdog

The Snap hashtags had nothing to do with the pendant and didn't rhyme, but he loved them and he'd already sent them, so whatever.

Wait.

The drum was supposed to be a removable part of a drummer

rig he hadn't yet made, and he shouldn't be selling it separately. Once again, Freddy recognized that he had the brains of gravel.

He wrapped up in the comforter he'd thrown on the floor for Snap, went outside to sit on Grandma's redwood lounge chair, and fell asleep.

His ringing cell phone woke him up.

He was bleary and cold, Snap was barking, he was starving.

It was the Bach Toccata so it was Mrs. Maple. She must have heard about Philip. She'd have another conspiracy theory to run by him. Freddy tried to pull himself together. Then he thought, Face it. Pulled together is not my thing.

Mrs. Maple didn't even bother to say hello. "I need to tell you something, Freddy. I need you to know something in my past. Very few people in my life are aware of this." Her voice was trembling, an intro voice; something's coming. But this was apparently not about Philip. It dawned on him that if Philip had died from a regular old heart attack (which, were they going to take Marty's word for it or do an autopsy?)—anyway, they didn't have to notify everybody's family. They wouldn't have notified Mapes.

Except MMC probably did have to admit negligence, even when it wasn't theirs.

There would be inspectors or social workers or whatever. The entrance and exit doors would be set up differently. New protocols. A totally annoying word that really meant, We're adding more rules and you have to follow them.

Freddy had enough to think about without Mrs. Maple's past. "Whatever it is, I don't want to know," said Freddy. "Please don't confess anything. I love ignorance."

Like all the women in Freddy's life, she didn't even pretend to listen. "I'm at the cemetery, Freddy. At the grave of my husband."

Hadn't he been firm? Don't tell me anything. He thought about Jade. He wasn't going to give her weed so maybe he'd give her glass when he went up today. What did he have around?

"My husband was a cocaine addict, Freddy. I loved him so but it turned out that he loved coke. I am very fond of you and so impressed by the beautiful beads you gave me, but the pipes... Oh, Freddy, I wish you weren't making pipes. I cannot accept that the way to a righteous life is smoking pot."

In his circle, "righteous" meant cool. Sweet. Epic. Mrs. Maple meant obeying the Lord's commandments. I've got one of 'em down anyway, he thought. I'm honoring my mother, and I'm honoring *her* mother.

"*And* you get lung cancer," said Mrs. Maple.

"Not from herb," Freddy corrected her. "But people who smoke pot usually smoke cigarettes, so you're right. Lung cancer's out there." He didn't tell her whether he was making beads or pipes, the particulate from glass could lodge in the lungs and that would never heal, that glare and particulate often caused severe eye problems, that color dust could be poisonous.

Freddy did not believe marijuana was a gateway drug: that people who loved weed would one day decide they'd love cocaine even more. Freddy could skip weed for a week, but he couldn't skip cigarettes for an afternoon, and if he had an addiction that would kill him one day, it was tobacco.

"My husband was out for his daily run, and he collapsed on the sidewalk. We found out about the cocaine from the autopsy. The doctors said that arrhythmia and tachycardia are common with cocaine. He was an athlete in good condition. I'm sure he never expected death. The children were in college when it happened. They couldn't believe I hadn't picked up on the symptoms. Like the runny nose..He said it was an allergy. That sounded logical to me. And the mood swings. Who doesn't have those?"

Freddy didn't. He was a happy kind of guy. Until now anyway. October had shattered like glass, and the whole month belonged in the Box of Pain.

"After the funeral," said Mrs. Maple, "the children searched the house. They said their father had to have a stash somewhere. But they never found it. The family counselor said that he probably used whatever he bought as soon as he bought it and there never had been a stash."

People didn't stockpile. That was how guys on the street made their money and how cops caught the buyers. All that activity. He thought about Auburn, casting around for high-end clientele: people like Mrs. Maple's husband, who had money.

"My children hold me responsible," said Mrs. Maple dully.

Freddy had known this woman for months, and many of their conversations had been profound. On the graph of life, he would have given her a boring suburban straight line, but she was talking serious peaks and valleys here.

"You know, Freddy, if I visit MMC routinely, I'm okay. It's just something I do. But if I let a week go by, I stand at that door full of fear. As if, when I go through that door, I'll be the patient. They'll take my things and lock me up and I will never get out. No one will hug me or sit with me except people who are paid to do it. That's the punishment waiting for me."

"Come on," said Freddy. "There's no punishment waiting for you, Mrs. Maple. You're a saint."

She hung up on him.

THIRTY-ONE

Laura couldn't believe she had made that phone call to Freddy, let alone chastised him. Why take out her despair on a boy who had his own problems?

She had barely gotten home from the cemetery when another difficulty surfaced. Betty Sherwood's niece Tiffany texted, asking her to visit again soon and please bring back the album.

Kenneth/Bobby was presumably at that Farmington house where Betty had placed the call. Laura couldn't phone Kenneth and request that he bring the album back. She sent Freddy a text, asking *him* to go get the album, since he was always in Middletown anyway, and Farmington was sort of close. It was a major demand, especially right after haranguing him and hanging up on him, but Freddy was used to women asking a lot, and she thought he'd do it for her.

The front doorbell rang. She dragged herself through the dark house.

"It's me, Kemmy!" yelled Kemmy.

Laura opened the door.

"Put the lights on," said Kemmy irritably. "Open the curtains. You're turning into a mole. It happens to people who live alone." Kemmy walked around hitting light switches. "Where've you been? I stopped by earlier."

Earlier? It was barely midmorning. Of course, anybody who knew Laura knew she was up before dawn, so Kemmy had probably figured early was good.

"I was at Memory Care," said Laura, which was a lie, but she couldn't talk about the cemetery. She couldn't tell anybody that sometimes her grief for her husband was so deep she had to drive there and stand over his grave and cry aloud, *How could you? We loved you!*

She yearned to weep. Sometimes tears helped, like a faucet letting out pain, but more often tears gave her a throbbing headache. She grit her teeth and postponed sobbing until after Kemmy's departure.

"You've already been up to Memory Care and back? Do you have breakfast with your aunt? That's so sweet, Laura," said Kemmy, giving Laura a not-touching hug. "I love how devoted you are. You set such a good example for us all. You're a saint. So yesterday, I gave the manuscript to Gordon Clary." Kemmy plopped down on the parlor sofa, as if she planned to stay for hours. "He was so excited."

"You *gave* it to him?"

"Well, loaned. It's still mine. He was positively greedy over it, stroking the paper. But I ran into a problem."

What did Kemmy know of problems? The battle against crying was lost. Laura tried to pretend she was coughing, but sobs vaulted out of her chest and tears rained on her cheeks.

Kemmy pulled her down onto the little sofa, and Laura surrendered, weeping.

"I know," Kemmy said in a warm, comfort-the-two-year-old voice. "I know how hard it must be. Even for saints, it must be hard."

Laura jerked away. "I'm not a saint!"

"What did you do, cut your visit short by ten minutes? Come on, Laura. You're the best person I know."

"I'm the *worst* person you know. I didn't visit my own mother, Kemmy, when she got Alzheimer's. She was one of the bitter, angry, swearing, paranoiac types, and I hated being around her, and when she didn't even recognize me, why suffer through visits? She bit the aides, she threw things, she swore at me, and I abandoned her. She lasted two more years. She was a wonderful mother, and when she needed me, I paid other people to deal with it. At her funeral, Kemmy, I was relieved."

Kemmy's arms tightened around Laura. "I can't even imagine it," she said. "My mother died of breast cancer when I was thirty-one, and I would have given anything for more time with her. But years like you're describing—maybe not."

"My children went on loving their grandmother. They visited. They seemed to be okay with whoever she was at the moment, even when she wasn't anybody, even when she was worse than anybody. They used to ask me along."

She remembered Lindsay's long, slow look. Jonathan's silence.

Laura had read another hundred pages of Charlie's biography. Charlie's mother was rarely mentioned. The biographer eventually explained that nobody in the Ives family mentioned her. Hundreds of extant letters…and nobody referred to the mother.

Laura, too, was invisible to her children. In a lifetime of shocks, that was the most shocking. These two wonderful beloved people, for whom she had sacrificed so much and whom she adored, had largely forgotten her. She had to beg for holidays. They always had other plans. Reluctantly, they would agree to fit her in. She never came first.

"Did the children forgive you for not going?" asked Kemmy.

Laura's headache increased. "I don't think the children considered it in those terms," she said finally. "But I taught them a lesson. And they learned it well. Visiting your mother is optional."

Freddy and Snap wrestled with a towel. Then he collected food and water and fastened Snap to the tire swing in the Way Back.

He thought about Philip. Last night, he had decided Doc or Skinny or Auburn could have nothing to do with it, because they couldn't have offed Philip. But nobody had offed Philip, if Jade's information was correct, so Doc and Skinny and Auburn were still in the running.

Back at the house, he discovered a loaf of bread in the freezer, which was a pleasant surprise. He fixed toast and buttered it heavily. Jade was absolutely right. Toast was safe. Way too safe. He needed to go out for a real breakfast. He thought about bacon and all the ways that bacon could appear on a menu, and then Emma called.

If Mrs. Maple didn't know about Philip, neither did Emma, which was a very good thing.

How had he acquired so many women in his life? All of them disapproving and not one of them a girlfriend?

The best way to find a girlfriend around here was to get in touch with his high school crowd. But somehow he didn't want to. Kara said it was because he was ashamed that he did nothing but make silly little beads while his classmates were having worthwhile careers and starting families. Kara wanted to set pieces of Freddy on her little shelf of inspection and rearrange him to suit.

Freddy prayed that Kara wouldn't visit after all. It was kind of a selfish prayer, but Freddy thought all prayer was selfish. *Come on, God. Do it my way.*

"Frederick," said Emma from Alaska, "how are you? How are beads?"

Freddy thought of his Alaska TV shows. How many of those guys lived above the Arctic Circle because they were running away from the law? Probably not the ones who chose to be featured on the National Geographic channel. Freddy didn't want to live in a below-zero world. Plus he couldn't live there anyway. No oxygen delivery.

"Kara's bent out of shape that you have not yet taken Grandma home with you. I know that would be impossible. I know you're doing the best you can."

Traditionally, Emma figured her little brother was doing the worst he could. Freddy wondered what was up with the new phase.

"Listen, Emma. What would you think of looking for a place for Grandma in Alaska?"

"Freddy, even if I thought for one minute that our ninety-three-year-old grandmother could tolerate the upheaval, the plane flights, the new spaces, and the new faces, I couldn't consider it because we could be transferred next week to New Mexico or whatever. But you don't need me. Kara is flying down to give you a break. Although a break from what, I'd like to know," she said, her real attitude showing. "You make *beads*. Your whole life is a vacation. I have two children. They're in school. They have sports. They need supper. They have a truly monumental amount of laundry. You don't have anybody but yourself."

"I have Grandma," he countered.

"No, you don't. MMC has Grandma. You whip up there for a minute or two and then whip back to your glass studio. Kara's not too thrilled that she has to stay with the Burnworths."

"George and Lily Burnworth are the best."

"He performed my wedding, you remember."

"Sure," said Freddy, who didn't remember a thing about Emma's wedding. She'd had one. All three sisters had had one. But brides looked alike, that white thing going on, and the flowers and stuff. He did remember the annoyance of renting a tux. But he didn't remember it separately, per wedding.

"I'm not that into Mrs. Burnworth," said Emma. "She's a bit judgy, you know."

Freddy thought Mrs. Burnworth was totally nonjudgy. "She bakes a great pie," he offered. "Well, except she doesn't. They buy homemade pies from a neighbor."

"No! Then she's a hypocrite on top of everything else!" Emma launched happily into a discussion of hypocrisy in establishment religion, which Freddy thought was a little harsh considering it was just a slice of pie.

"What's this rumor about Josh Burnworth?" asked Emma.

Josh Burnworth was way younger than Emma. Younger than Freddy for that matter. How old was Emma anyway? Freddy was twenty-six, so Emma must be thirty-five. And Josh was maybe twenty-two. Could somebody in Alaska hear rumors about somebody she didn't even know in Connecticut who was, like, twelve or thirteen years younger? "I haven't heard any," he said.

"It was on Facebook," said Emma. "Josh was picked up for possession. Not grass either. Coke. Preacher's kids, you know. All that religion. It's not good for them."

"*Josh?*" This was impossible. Josh was a totally decent guy. Volunteered weekends for something really do-goodery. A Big Brother or something. Maybe ran a soup kitchen.

...or maybe tried to rescue Danielle and Auburn.

Br.

Burnworth?

No wonder the pastor hadn't found time to visit MMC.

THIRTY-TWO

When Kemmy had left and Laura was alone again, she felt the dark engulfing her. Before it took over, she made herself phone her daughter.

"Oh, hi, Mom," said Lindsay in the surprised voice she always used, like, *I thought you were dead.*

Laura cut to the chase. "Lindsay, I miss you. And the worries I have about MMC and Aunt Polly and life in general and so many other things are closing in on me. Honey, can you visit? Maybe spend the night?"

There was the usual long pause, the mental sorting through of appointments and obligations, the choosing of a good excuse, the postponement of any physical association between mother and daughter.

The pause continued until it was too much to bear. Laura touched the cell phone lightly, ending the call with the faintest pressure from one finger. She turned her phone off and silenced the ringer for good measure. She wanted to walk away from everything—house, town, music, children.

But could she walk away from her aunt?

Polly had never married, though she held out hope for many years. Never had children of her own, though she ached for a family. Polly accepted being a gym teacher as her calling. Sports and teams, balls and rackets and other people's kids were her life. Polly never set aside her cheerful exuberance until she met the only opponent she could never defeat: Alzheimer's.

But Polly kept smiling, and Laura never looked at that smile without pride that she was related to this brave woman and grief that Polly never had what she so deeply wanted: somebody to love her back.

A pickup truck pulled into Laura's driveway.

Could it be the organ crew? But it wasn't their truck, and she didn't recognize the skanky men who got out. Laura had a moment of intense fear. Had Maude felt this way, looking up at her murderer? Lock the door, Laura told herself. Call the police.

But the men were already at her back door, and Laura in her sluggishness had not gotten there first.

———————————

On Instagram, Freddy followed guys who collaborated on rigs, one making the prep, one making the pipe. What a great life, going cross-country from studio to studio.

As soon as Kara gets here, that's what I'll do. No one will ever find me, because even I will never know where I'm going.

But crossing all those state lines, probably ought to have car insurance.

Freddy telephoned his grandmother's insurance agent. It turned out that getting car insurance was not that simple. He had let it lapse. They couldn't start it up in two minutes, especially since the vehicles weren't his. The fact that he had power of attorney for his grandmother did not seem to impress the agent. It would be a slow process.

"I'll pay cash," Freddy offered. "I'll drive straight to your office."

They did not take cash. All payments went to their central office by check or direct withdrawal.

Freddy gave him the VIN numbers for the truck and the Avalon. The agent would call him back.

Being called back was just another form of nagging. Freddy's commitment to going middle class with insurance and everything faded away.

He picked out a pipe for Jade. Last year, before Cynthia broke up with him and destroyed his studio, he'd made her a sort of a glass Cinderella slipper, actually a glittering, crazy high-heeled shoe, but you could smoke out of it. It was totally awesome. It would be good to get rid of it, even though he still had daydreams where he and Cynthia got back together and the glass slipper would be a great peace offering.

The phones rang continually. He ignored Kara, Jenny, and Dr. Burnworth, but then came the only call he could not ignore. "Mr. Bell, this is Vera, the nurse. Your grandmother is not doing well. Can you get up here?"

Freddy took Route 9 at rocket speed. All he could think of was Philip.

What if it *hadn't* been an accident? What if there *was* somebody up there shoving people to their death? Just because the cop left the door open didn't mean some insane staff person didn't walk Philip outside and give him a push onto a rock! He should never have driven away last night.

His grandmother was in her room, an ugly generic tissue box in her lap. At one time, she had cared deeply about tissue-box design and color. She even crocheted tissue-box covers. The Bible on her coffee table still held its hand-crocheted bookmark. The empty fruit bowl still sat on its doily.

Grandma saw Freddy, drew a shuddery deep breath, and held out her skinny arms. "Oh, Arthur!" she cried. Her face was streaked with tears.

The wheelchair boxed her in. There was no sofa or armchair in her little bedroom so Freddy picked her up, settled himself on the bed with her sideways on his lap, and rocked her. "Tell me," he said, realizing that no, he could not become a migrant collab flameworker. He could not abandon Grandma to Kara unless Kara wanted to have her. He was pretty sure the calls he had ignored from Kara were postponing her visit; a child had a fever or a horse had an abscess. Anyway, what would he do with Snap if he headed for the horizon? Give him to a charity?

"What's wrong, Grandma?"

She raised a stricken face. "Arthur, I think she died."

Wayne Ames walked in, with Vera right behind him. Freddy couldn't believe the guy was intruding again. "Later," he mouthed, letting his fury show only in his face, because he couldn't let Grandma hear it in his voice. "I think so too, Grandma," he said. "It's very sad."

"What was she doing?" said his grandmother urgently. "Where was she going?"

"Peru."

Grandma was incredulous. "Peru?"

"I know. You wouldn't catch me going. She wanted to see Machu Picchu."

"Ask her who died," said Ames.

Freddy glared at the detective, drew his finger across his throat, and pointed to the door. *Get out*, he mouthed.

Jade peered in the doorway, scoping out the action. No doubt she had her cell phone ready to take a video.

Instead of leaving, the cop went down on one knee, looked into Grandma's eyes, and said, "How did she die, Mrs. Bell? Did you see it happen?"

Freddy thought, I'm going to ambush him in some alley. Or just kill him here, with witnesses, and get credit for ridding the world of a cop who makes my grandmother cry.

Grandma began a rare series of complete sentences. "Freddy, how did she die? Isn't she younger than I am? Freddy, where's Arthur? He was here. I'm sure he was here."

Freddy was not equipped to handle this. He wasn't sure

anybody was equipped. There were residents who wept, trembled, and begged. Their minds froze and unfroze, and they could find no peace. He so didn't want his grandmother feeling that way. His only tool was distraction.

"You know what, Grandma?" he said, smiling into her face. "It's October! The trees are yellow and red. That maple tree over by the old elementary school, the tree you painted every year, when you did watercolors? It's gorgeous again this year. Let's go for a drive. We'll collect good leaves. You used to press leaves in the dictionary. I bet there's still a leaf or two in our dictionary. And maybe we'll find horse chestnuts. You like to have a bowl of chestnuts on the table in the fall."

Vera handed Freddy a damp washcloth. He wiped his grandmother's face.

It bothered Freddy that all these women seemed to be working double shifts. Okay, they were short-staffed and it was an act of decency to work long hours. Unless you were offing your patients and needed those extra hours to cover your tracks or set up your next one.

But he really liked Vera. He respected her. She couldn't possibly be out there harming helpless people. Unless she was. As for Jade, she could be in the doorway from curiosity, from wanting to see if Freddy had brought her the right flowers or to find out what the cops knew about the deaths of Philip and Maude.

"Do I need a sweater?" asked Grandma uncertainly.

She was already wearing a sweater.

"I'll get your coat, Mrs. Chase," said Vera.

Over Grandma's head, Freddy said very quietly to the cop, "She's talking about my mother. Her daughter, Alice. Beat it."

"I don't think she was talking about Alice," said Wayne Ames in a loud, belligerent voice. "I've been questioning her about her meany-beany statement."

Freddy lost it. "You questioned my grandmother?" he shouted.

"You piece of shit! You stay away from my grandmother!" He felt himself becoming molten, like glass. He was going to burn himself and everyone around him.

Vera said, "Now, Freddy," in the universal voice of women who want docile men.

Jade held up her cell phone, taking the video.

"If I weren't holding my grandmother in my arms, I'd break your jaw," he yelled at the cop. "What I'd really like is for *you* to get dementia. I'd love to see you frightened and lost and your whole life upside down and inside out and then you're locked up in an institution and you can't even salt your food and some cop barges in asking you about murder, which until then you hadn't even realized *happened* and now some cop has ruined any possibility of feeling safe or good."

Freddy was shaking.

Jade was filming.

"OxyContin" said his grandmother.

THIRTY-THREE

"Hi, Mrs. Maple!" called the skanky guys. "We're here for your piano."

Oh, for heaven's sake. Laura held the door for them instead of having a nervous collapse.

The junk run guys didn't comment on the smell of the summer piano or the state of her music room. They accepted the cash and the dump fee, popped the piano on a dolly as easily as if it were Tupperware, bumped it down the back step, shoved it up a ramp onto their truck, and drove away.

At least something had gotten done today, even if the junk-run guys were the ones who had done it. The stinking piano was gone. Check. She was still upright. Check. She wasn't currently weeping. Check.

She couldn't bring herself to go back inside where the smell lingered and gloom reigned. She forced herself to stop thinking of Lindsay. Having disposed of Charlie's practice piano (which it probably hadn't been anyway), she thought about Charlie's practice organ. His father had rigged out their old square piano in Danbury with dummy organ pedals so poor Charlie could practice at home in silence. Wasn't there a Charles Ives Museum in Danbury? She should visit.

She walked on and on. She didn't feel better. Her throat was closed. She was probably getting diphtheria.

A white sedan honked and pulled over to the curb next to her. Its windows were shaded, and Laura couldn't see who was driving. Her heart lurched.

The driver lowered the shaded windows. "Hop in, Laura," said Kemmy decisively. "I'll give you a ride home."

"Oh, thank you, but I'm headed the opposite direction."

"I know, but we have things to talk about."

"Kemmy, didn't we have an emotionally draining session just a minute ago? Let's not have another episode."

"It was an hour ago, and in the midst of all that sharing, I forgot about the problem with Gordon Clary. I just now made my third stop at your house in one morning."

"Second," said Laura.

"No, remember, I stopped by *before* we sobbed on the couch, so the sobbing was the *second* visit. This is my *third*. We're going back to your house to discuss the piano. That'll be my *fourth* visit before lunch. My life isn't usually this ridiculous."

"Don't worry about the piano. I had it taken to the dump."

"*You what?*"

"Kemmy, it was smelly. The junk guys just left with it."

"We have to get it back!"

"It's a dead piano," said Laura, "and it's my dead piano. You gave it to me. But you were right all along. The only thing it was good for is a beach bonfire. But fires are outlawed now, so I sent it to the dump."

"Laura! Gordon Clary called me back yesterday evening, informing me that he knew best and *he* would decide what to do with the manuscript. You were absolutely right. The combined arrogance of youth and Yale is not to be believed. I drove right down to New Haven and took it back. Early this morning, when you should have been home, you *weren't* home, and the front door was literally open! I dropped the manuscript off. Then the second time I came, I got you so upset, I forgot to tell you. I mean, who cares about a piece of paper when a friend is weeping?" Kemmy leaned way across her front seat and opened the passenger door. "Your house was wide open each time, Laura," she scolded. "When are you going to start locking it anyway?"

She's right, thought Laura. I just wander off. Why can't I remember the simple, basic task of using keys? Probably because I'm opposed to all this locking of doors.

In her childhood, they hadn't even taken the car keys out of the ignition.

"Well, it's your house," said Kemmy. "You want people to break in, it's your problem. Although they don't have to break, they can just saunter. Listen. We have to get the piano back. Call the junk-run people."

"I don't have their number on my cell. I used my landline."

"Get rid of the landline. It's a waste of money. We'll drive back to your house, you'll look up their number and pay them to bring the piano back."

"Remind me," said Laura. "Why do we want a dead, smelly piano back?"

"Because when I walked into your empty unlocked house and I didn't find you, I stored the manuscript where it belongs. In the piano. I love that crazy little shelf inside the knee door."

Laura was amazed and touched by this romantic maneuver. Kemmy! Who was as practical as a dishrag—tucking Charlie's manuscript back on Charlie's secret shelf.

At Laura's house, they huddled over the kitchen landline and finally reached the junk-run guys, who had already dumped the piano and were not interested in bringing it back. They didn't think they could get the manuscript out anyway, because the piano had fallen face-down. They'd need a backhoe to flip the thing.

"Or an ax," said Kemmy. "Just chop up the piano."

Laura offered another hundred dollars to the junk-run guys. No, they said, we're busy, we have a client we're already late for.

Kemmy, using her cell phone at the same time as Laura used her landline, could not reach a supervisor or, for that matter, a minor grunt at the dump.

Laura went up to two hundred. Three. They settled on five.

"We're paying five hundred dollars for these guys to flip a piano and take out a piece of paper," she said to Kemmy.

They giggled hysterically. "Your share is only two hundred fifty," Kemmy pointed out.

"Do we believe they'll really do it? Carefully? Right this very minute, before it rains, or the piano gets covered with the contents of port-a-potties?"

"Yes, because they want their five hundred. Here's my share."

"You carry that much cash with you?"

"Sure. I'm going shopping."

"You don't use your debit or your credit card? That's silly, Kemmy. It's like me not getting rid of my landline. Hey. Where are you going?"

"I told you. Shopping. You can handle a manuscript return by yourself, Laura. I have a coupon I need to use today, and I have to be back home in time to get my husband to his doctor's appointment because he won't drive himself, he'll pretend he didn't remember the appointment, and then we'll have to wait another month for an opening."

Laura remembered this kind of marital detail.

If only she could have it back.

THIRTY-FOUR

The cop ignored Freddy's rant. "Mrs. Chase? Tell me about OxyContin."

Freddy thought Grandma regarded Ames with exactly the right expression. *You're who? You want what?* "Grandma," he said, "you don't take opiates, do you?"

Silly question. No resident had the slightest idea what meds they took. Faceless people held out little white pleated paper cups full of pills plus a glass of water and told them to swallow. "Who here does take it?" he asked Vera.

"Not your grandmother. And only one resident. That is a narcotic pain reliever, and generally in this facility, there is no need for such a strong pharmaceutical. We provide memory care but not intensive medical care."

"Did Maude Yardley take it?"

"Physical pain was not one of Maude Yardley's difficulties."

Lily Burnworth had told Freddy to count his blessings, which mainly he couldn't think of any, but now he did have one to count: Grandma was not in pain. How much worse would this be if she hurt to the point of needing narcotics? How would she even tell the doctor it hurt? Would the doctor believe her?

"However," said Vera, "the autopsy of Maude Yardley turned up OxyContin. One must wonder how it got into her system and why Mrs. Chase would be thinking of it now."

Had Kenneth fed Maude an opiate crushed up in her soft food? When this failed to kill her, had he squeezed the life out of her instead? That would take a level of rage Freddy hadn't seen in Kenneth. On the other hand, Freddy had just experienced that level. Out of nowhere had come anger so intense he was lucky he'd had his arms full of grandmother and couldn't squeeze the life out of Wayne Ames. Maybe that had happened to Kenneth.

The big wall clock over the exit doors said twelve. Which must mean noon, although it felt like midnight. Freddy was exhausted. But at least Grandma had forgotten tears, fears, and OxyContin. She was dozing in his arms.

"Maybe the med techs made a mistake?" said Jade. "I know we got a new policy for meds. I know that's why you're on today, Vera. To get that going."

Nightmare. MMC would need new policies on everything. Or get closed down. *Should* they get closed down?

Vera gave the detective a serious stare-down. "It would be helpful if you were to give me more information, Detective Ames, because I am responsible for the safety of my residents and my staff. To say the least, your people let us down last night. My faith in you is low. Now. Do you believe that Mr. Yardley is involved in his wife's death?"

"Maude Yardley did not die from a drug overdose," said the cop, skipping the Philip issue. "She got suffocated. Kenneth Yardley was definitely *not* here the night she was suffocated."

So the cops knew for sure that Kenneth hadn't killed Maude, thought Freddy. They wouldn't base that on faulty sign-in sheets, so they had knowledge Freddy didn't, like maybe Kenneth's bowling team vouched for him or something. Freddy was relieved but now seriously worried about the staff. Because if Kenneth was out of the running, who was left?

"Freddy, we need to talk," said the cop. "Want to follow me down to the station?"

Want? Half a million U.S. citizens were arrested last year for marijuana possession even though it's mainly legal—and you think I might *want* to follow you down to your little police station?

They wouldn't find anything if they searched him. In his pockets were his key fob, wallet, a little change, cell phone, pocketknife. Grandpa had given him the pocketknife when he was maybe seven years old, refusing to accept that boys today were no longer allowed to have knives. Freddy's mother agreed he could keep it, but he was never to take it out of the house, or she would be arrested for bad parenting. (Grandpa had said, "Huh? What's that supposed to mean, Alice?") Freddy loved his knife and always took it out of the house, except when flying on planes, which in his opinion was when he needed it most. If there were hijackers, what was Freddy supposed to do? Frown at them?

"Detective Ames," said Vera, drawing herself to her full tower position, "it was necessary for me to telephone Mrs. Chase's only family member to drive all the way up here to resolve a situation *caused by your questioning*. You should have asked me for permission prior to approaching my resident. I wholly agree with Mr. Bell that you were unnecessarily forceful in your approach, thus bringing his grandmother to tears. Mr. Bell's duty is here, at his grandmother's side. He will not be going to your police station."

Whoa, thought Freddy. I seriously have to get to know Vera better.

The detective held up his hands in surrender. "I apologize. I was completely in the wrong."

A humble cop? No such thing. This was technique, although where it led, Freddy didn't know.

"How about I just drop in tomorrow at your studio?" he said to Freddy.

Nicely done. If Freddy refused to talk now, he'd have cops on his property again, and overnight was plenty of time to get a search warrant, on what grounds he couldn't imagine, but guaranteeing a one hundred percent lousy experience.

Freddy's cell phone rang. Broken glass smashed on pavement.

Jade jumped, Vera flinched, the cop blinked, and even Grandma woke up.

The glass crashed a second time and then a third, and Freddy touched the green button. The Leper's voice began immediately. "I'm sick of this, Freddy. I got hundreds of people watching Instagram where I'm supporting your career, and they know you aren't supporting me back. You haven't accepted the bids, and you're making me look like a fool."

"I'm sick of this too," said Freddy. "I'm here at my grandmother's with a cop who wants to question me about OxyContin."

"No, I don't," said Wayne Ames irritably.

"A cop?" repeated the Leper in an entirely different voice.

"Because of the murder," said Freddy.

"What murder? Freddy, what's up with you? Nobody's murdered anybody. Nobody's going to. I'm not the Mafia or whatever. I'm your goddamn *friend*. You owe me. Do the right thing. Now. Or else. Got it?" The Leper disconnected.

I'm your goddamn friend. Car salesman talk. Although the Leper just sounded honestly peeved. But what was honest about a Russian gangster who dealt drugs, laundered money, and mutilated dogs? Well, threatened to mutilate. Once again, Freddy had forgotten to ask him about Snap's paws and Shawn's jail. "Thank you for calling me about Grandma," he said to Vera. "I'd be grateful if you wrote up an incident report regarding Detective Ames's actions."

"It will be done," said Vera regally.

But the cop had the last word. "See you in the morning, Freddy."

Ames left. Vera and Jade went back to work. Grandma slept. In his anxiety and fury, Freddy had not asked for details about Philip's death, and what kind of incident report Vera was filing on *that*, and what Marty was going to do, and a hundred other things that Freddy couldn't keep straight. He soothed himself by checking messages, which were anything but soothing.

Mrs. Maple had the nerve to ask him to go to Kenneth/Bobby's house and collect Betty Sherwood's photo album for her. He had to run her errands as well as hear her confessions? No thanks.

Kara. He didn't open that one. She'd be staying with the Burnworths. Let her call them.

Mrs. Aminetti. He'd already taken the dog. He didn't even want to think about her next request.

The only thing Freddy was sure of was that the cops knew Kenneth hadn't killed Maude. That was probably enough sureness for one day.

Grandma smiled at him, her real smile, as if she'd been hiding in there all along, so Freddy kissed her forehead and left the ward. He was still starving. He'd go to a diner and have breakfast for lunch.

Jade lifted a palm, telling him to wait until she could leave her patient.

He was pretty sure he'd put Cynthia's pipe in the glove compartment. Was he going to give it to Jade or not? He thought about the OxyContin, which in fact, one patient took. Jade was not a med tech and did not have access to the med cart. Except maybe they all colluded, the way they all looked at snapshots that should never have been taken.

Snap.

Snap.

Auburn knows where I live. Therefore the Leper knows where I live. Therefore Doc knows. And they all know I have Snap, because I put Snap in my hashtag poetry.

Did Freddy believe that anybody would slice the paws off a dog? Shawn had believed it.

Freddy forgot Jade, tore out of the building, and got on 9 South. It was a divided parkway, with woodsy acres running down the middle, sometimes so sparse you could see traffic going the opposite direction but more often deep, wide, and rocky. Freddy had always meant to explore the wilder parts, which looked like great places to hide out. Again today, he didn't have time. The divider stretch just before his exit was not woods, just fifty feet of grass, and he glanced across to see a turquoise Cube going the opposite direction.

Off 9, Freddy raced down a bunch of roads, whipped up Grandma's driveway, drove over the grass, around the house, and right up to the row of forsythia. He leaped out and ran, jumping over the tiny brook, crossing the swamp of skunk cabbage, and crashing through the woods.

"Snap!" he shouted.

Snap was gone.

No leash hung from the tire swing branch. Snap could maybe bite through the leather, but he could not have removed the leash.

If they were going to mutilate him, they'd have done it here, leaving an agonized, bleeding dog for Freddy to find, because that was the point.

So somebody had taken Snap. Couldn't be Shawn; he was in jail. Couldn't be Mrs. Aminetti; she was sane and had just unloaded this biting mutt.

An animal-control officer? Neighbors complained about barking? What neighbors? There weren't any back here.

Auburn, who considered dogs worthless? Had that been Auburn's turquoise Cube? She drove up 9 every day. But why take Snap?

Had the Leper closed in on Auburn as well? Ordered her to get Shawn's dog? Maybe Doc was busy? Maybe Auburn was retailing Doc's rip-off cocaine-jar finger pendants and those two were in business together? But Doc didn't seem to think the pendants were anything but pendants.

Was Shawn thinking of ratting on Auburn? Was Auburn thinking that a video of Snap in agony would stop him?

But he's in jail, thought Freddy. His cell phone's been confiscated. She can't send him a video, and he can't see it anyway.

Freddy checked every door of Grandma's house. The place was

locked up nice and tight. No windows were broken, so the dognapper was not also a burglar. Snap had no dollar value, while the house was packed with value, floor to ceiling, already in cartons ready to carry. A good opportunity to trash or steal, and the Snap-taker had passed.

Freddy got back on 9. If that had been Auburn, he was ten or fifteen minutes behind her. He caught up with two other cars also going way over the speed limit, and they huddled together, hoping for safety in numbers.

What would he do if he found Auburn cutting Snap to pieces?

In Middletown, he turned left at the red light, went over the railroad tracks, turned right on Main, passed Auburn's shop, street-parked in front of the Hispanic grocery, squeezed between buildings, and trotted down the alley behind the long block of stores. Auburn's Cube was parked at her back door.

A wet black nose poked out of a window left open two inches.

Stooping to keep the body of the Cube between himself and the little window in Auburn's back door, Freddy tried the car door handle. Locked.

He wrapped his fingers over the open window and pulled down with his whole body weight. The window sank just enough for him to wriggle his arm down, accept a nip from Snap, and unlock the door. Gripping Snap's collar, he ran crouching back to the Avalon.

Freddy didn't have a crate, and Snap was a very poorly trained animal. Freddy cracked the windows to entertain the dog with scents he hoped were interesting enough to keep Snap from chewing on his exposed forearm.

He drove a few blocks to the same parking lot he had used to visit the lawyer, which reminded him that at some point, he needed to call up and find out if Br was Josh Burnworth. He Googled Norwich jails and called the visitor line. They did not have a prisoner named Shawn Aminetti. Great. Shawn had already been transferred or whatever. Freddy couldn't ask what Shawn wanted him to do with the dog.

He Googled Middletown boarding kennels and clicked on one with five stars. It cost as much as a motel, with separate fees for playtime and trail walks.

Seriously? Playtime fees?

The kennel was several miles northwest of Middletown. It looked like a nice place, and the owner looked like a nice woman. Too bad she wasn't getting a nice dog. "Snap is a little nippy. Sorry about that."

"We can handle it." She produced a muzzle.

It had not crossed Freddy's mind to consider an appliance. Snap, you're in jaw prison. But you have all four paws and that's cool.

"May I ask you to prepay for the week?" the woman said.

Luckily, he was a cash kind of guy. He peeled bills off a fat roll.

She looked startled. Probably going to call the police and say, "Only drug dealers carry wads of cash. Check him out."

But no, she beamed. "Love income I don't have to report."

"Do I get a break for cash?"

"Nice try."

They both laughed. It was easier for her.

Freddy got back into the Avalon and tried to figure out his priorities.

Two weeks ago, I didn't have a single priority, he thought. I did a little lampwork and ate takeout.

Freddy started the engine, and the GPS map materialized on the dashboard screen. He studied routes home and nearby fast-food places. He was starving. Having come north from Middletown, he now wasn't far from Farmington. Maybe six, eight miles.

Whether the man was Kenneth or Bobby, the guy was exonerated. Did he even know that? Cops loved mental torture, and Ames would enjoy leaving Kenneth terrified, especially if they were still looking at him for pill crushing. "Oh," they might say a few days later, "did we forget to tell you? You're in the clear, Maude-murder-wise."

Freddy decided to drive on to Farmington. Let Kenneth know that the cops were cool with his alibi. Maybe not let on that he knew Kenneth wasn't Kenneth, but for sure collect that photo album Mrs. Maple was so tense about. That would give him a peace offering for Mapes, which was key, because visits to MMC would go on, and he needed an ally, even one who dumped on him. He bet Mapes was already feeling sorry about that. She was the reserved New England type who would be a lifelong holdout against Twitter, Facebook, and all the personal-detail rest of them. She'd never refer to her husband again, and they'd be back on their same old footing.

Freddy turned onto Schoolhouse Road.

THIRTY-FIVE

With Kemmy huddled at her side, calling the junk-run guys had been a giggly adventure. But alone in her kitchen waiting for their return, Laura felt beyond stupid.

The junk-run guys were probably laughing so hard they couldn't steer. Five hundred dollars from some pathetic woman who left a piece of paper in her dead piano? They were probably calling a reality show to describe a seriously deranged hoarder for the next episode. On top of everything else, they would tell the producer, she has two other pianos, which she shrink-wraps so they can't be played.

A white car of indeterminate make drifted slowly up her driveway. It was the kind of sedan Laura had driven her entire adult life, and she couldn't help the little bump of superiority she felt because her red Cadillac was so much more exciting. She did vaguely wonder why the men weren't driving their pickup, but then, they weren't loading a piano this time, so a truck wasn't necessary. She stood in the open door and waved.

She had paid cash before and now had Kemmy's cash and her own check. The men got out of the car and came toward her.

They were not carrying anything, let alone a large page of music manuscript.

She didn't remember one of the junk-run guys being so thin he could hardly keep his pants up. She didn't remember the ponytail.

She definitely didn't remember the other man being the size of a closet.

The anorexic guy grinned. His mouth was full of gold, as if he had substituted a bracelet for his teeth. His eyes were too wide or maybe too bright. His skin was leprous.

The closet guy's bare arms were covered with purple and green tattoos.

They weren't the junk-run guys.

Laura tried to get back in the house, slam the door, lock herself in, and call 911, but she had left it too late. The massive one literally set her aside, his huge hands closing on her upper arms, moving her as easily as Laura would move a glass of water. His hands were tattooed all the way down the fingers, which were laden with rings so large they were weapons.

Laura had never stood next to a human being as large as this. He was a wall of flesh.

Once inside, the ponytail guy stopped short, staring through the wide hall arch blocked by shrink-wrapped pianos and long wooden crates.

The closet guy bent his face toward hers. Even his lips and nose were huge. He spoke in a voice as heavy as his body. "Looking for Freddy," he told her.

These terrifying creatures she would expect to be out robbing a convenience store were Freddy's friends? Or enemies? What were they doing at *her* house? Freddy had never been here.

"Freddy you gave a ride to," said the thin one, walking through the kitchen to examine the music room. "He had a ole woman in a wheelchair."

Freddy. Wheelchairs. Rides. She remembered now. What pleasure she had felt when Freddy flagged her down, loving the idea that she was helping this sweet boy and his dear grandmother.

But Freddy was not a sweet boy. He was in drugs.

Making pipes is a sport, Freddy had told her. Prison to avoid. Taxes to dodge. Gang members to be invisible to.

Evidently, Freddy had ceased to be invisible because Laura Maple had two gang members in her house looking for him.

They found me because I gave Freddy a ride, she thought, which means they found me through my license plate. So they are able to bribe or terrify somebody at the DMV or the police department. Or deal drugs to them. Because that's why the skinny guy's eyes are blaring like trumpets. He's on something.

It had taken these creatures a week to get here. Why the delay? Maybe they'd found out her address earlier but zoned out or forgot to follow up.

Perhaps they were the reason Freddy had needed a ride to start with. He had lied that his grandmother was ill. He had been running from Closet and Ponytail and up she drove, so he threw his grandmother in the front seat and Laura under the bus.

Freddy was probably home free. But Laura Maple was home trapped.

The skinny ponytail guy was giggling, a high wheezy chortle coming out of his gold bracelet mouth.

Many years ago, there had been a notorious Connecticut home invasion where the violence had been extreme: ropes and rape and the young victims burned alive. And now, thanks to Freddy Bell, it was happening to her, Laura Maple, of Bach fugues and overdue library books.

She would tell these two how to find him. So there!

Except Freddy was her friend. She who had betrayed her own mother... Was she also going to betray her friend?

It was the worst thing you could say of a person: *He'd sell his own mother if it got him somewhere.* For anyone but Laura, that was hyperbole. Laura had, in fact, sold her mother to the lowest-bidding institution and walked off.

Whereas Freddy had closed up his life in Chicago, left every friend behind, moved into his grandmother's isolated house to care for her at home. Took her to church, figured out how to get her into Memory Care when he couldn't manage the slimy details of home care, and now took her out for fresh air and sunshine, holding her in his arms when things were at their worst.

No, she could not give Freddy to these creatures. "The woman in the wheelchair was my aunt," she improvised, surprised to find that she was speaking with a British accent. Perhaps her inner self thought that Masterpiece Theatre diction would create an invisibility cloak. "I don't know which aide was pushing her," she explained, her English lilt ridiculously overdone. "Some man who works at the nursing home."

Closet Man was almost quaintly taken aback by her answer or perhaps her pathetic fake accent. "What's your aunt's name?"

She named a different aunt from the one living at MMC. "Esther Johnstone," she said. Aunt Esther had died years ago out in California.

"What nursing home?"

"Three Pines." The name of a long-ago summer place she and her husband had rented when the children were little. Three Pines, four people, two dogs, one lake. Oh, those sunny, perfect days. Her husband and the children swimming and fishing and canoeing and always, always hungry. She saw herself in the funny old kitchen, each appliance standing alone on its side of the room, and no counter at all, just the table in the center.

The Closet looked at his smartphone. It was the size of a domino in his massive hand. He would soon find that she had made up the Three Pines nursing home in Middletown. Freddy didn't work there because it didn't exist. She did not want to think about what these two could do to her. She backed into the kitchen, thinking, I have knives, I have a landline.

But Closet followed her. She had cornered herself, no way out except crawling under a piano.

Ponytail Guy was working his way through the shrink-wrapped grand pianos, plastic-covered bookcases, and pieces of future organ. His hair was too thin to be called a ponytail; it was more of a greasy rat's tail. He kicked the biggest crate, which was over ten feet long. The claw hammer still lay on its lid. "What's in these?" he said belligerently, as if they'd been arguing.

"Pipes," she said, thinking, I'll never play my practice organ. Its pipes will stay in their coffins, and I will end up in mine. Freddy, how could you? You've sicced an actual gang on me.

"No way! You're in pipes? These are serious containers! You ship 'em? How many does each crate hold anyway? You could put thousands of pipes in there! Where do you buy 'em? Where do you sell 'em? Freddy's your partner?"

Laura had not stopped to consider that she and Freddy sought the same thing, except that his pipes inhaled drugs and hers exhaled music. She wanted to share the joke with him, but she might not share a laugh with anybody again.

"I need to find Freddy Bell," said the huge man. "He's making me crazy, he's making my boss crazy, I gotta straighten the little shit out. All you gotta do is tell me where he is."

"I don't talk to the aides," Laura said, trying to insert a little British disdain into her voice. She could hardly form syllables. It was like at the dentist's, when the Novocain set in, and half of your jaw was useless. "I don't know if the aide's name was Freddy."

Ponytail Guy picked up the hammer and tapped the claw head against his palm, grinning his gold bracelet grin.

Some anorexic moron druggie is going to hit me in the face with a hammer, Laura thought, and I won't be able to stop him.

Where had these two come from? What did Freddy have in common with them? Sweet Freddy, who teased all the aides and kissed his grandmother hello? Freddy didn't plan on being good, she thought. He isn't in a good profession. But life required him to be good and so he is. Life required *me* to be good and I just shrugged.

Closet Guy looked toward the front of the house and cocked his head in the posture of listening.

Laura didn't hear a thing. I really am going deaf, she thought, as horrified by that as by the home invaders.

Ponytail Guy set the hammer down. Out of his pocket, where Laura would stuff a pack of tissues, he pulled a gun. He smiled at the gun as if it were an old friend and they were glad to see each other. He took a quick sneaky look at Closet, who was facing the other way. Giggling silently, he pointed the gun at Laura.

Then she heard what Closet heard: a car engine. The junk-run guys had arrived.

Because of the kitchen wall, she couldn't see her back door, but it was literally open; she could feel the cold draft. The junk-run guys were young. Probably had wives and babies. She opened her mouth to scream a warning, but Closet slammed his hand over her mouth and swung her around. The hand was the size of her entire face. If he dug those huge fingernails into her flesh and yanked, she would relive yet another Connecticut nightmare, where somebody's pet chimpanzee ripped a woman's face off, blinding her and discarding her lips.

There was a loud drumbeat-style knock and a cheery bright call. "Hello there! I'm looking for Mrs. Maple!"

THIRTY-SIX

Talk about autumn leaves. Kenneth's street was like glass gone wild—orange, red, and gold shards thrown in the air, piled in the street. Up the block, landscaping crews were blowing leaves to the curb and sucking them up in trucks. One woman with a rake was attacking her own yard. She looked militant, a lone warrior against a million leafy invaders, her little metal tines spending hours on a chore those crews could do in ten minutes.

She waved. Freddy saluted her.

The white clapboard house was low-slung and rather pretty. Kenneth/Bobby's car was in the drive, along with a car Freddy didn't recognize. The name Virginia filtered into his mind—the only visitor Maude had had besides Kenneth. Betty had told Mrs. Maple that Virginia was married to Cousin Bobby. So maybe Virginia drove that second car, because maybe here, these two were a regular old couple named Lansing. Not that it was a regular old thing to have a fake wife and a fake name and fake hair.

Freddy parked behind the two cars and walked up to the front of the house. A brass pineapple knocker on the wooden door was behind a flimsy aluminum storm door that didn't close right, making it useless summer or winter.

Every clapboard needed paint and every windowpane needed caulk. Every shrub needed to be removed. If Kenneth/Bobby had been spending Maude's money, he sure wasn't throwing it away on maintenance.

Freddy leaned on the doorbell and waited.

After a minute, the door opened a few inches, revealing the little piddly kind of chain Freddy could kick through if he felt like it. "Yes?" The hoarse voice wasn't Kenneth's.

"Hi, I'm Freddy Bell. My grandmother is at Middletown Memory Care. I'm here to see Kenneth."

The door closed.

The woman across the street leaned on her rake, watching.

The chain was removed, the door opened, and there stood a frazzled-looking old woman. Heavy, with weird yellow hair—not blond, not honey, sort of lemon—and smeared lipstick. "Heyyyyy," said Freddy, as if greeting a bead lady.

"Come in," she said, biting her lip in a flirty fashion and even batting her eyes. She was down to about four lashes, each caked with mascara. She was wearing garden gloves but had them on the wrong hands, so the empty thumbs stuck out at the sides, and she was clutching some statue thing to her chest, like a wooden doll.

Could this possibly be Virginia? Whoa.

This was what Kenneth came home to? The poor guy had one dementia relative tucked in an institution and lived with a second one at home?

Freddy decided to make this a very short visit. He opened the storm door himself and stepped into a little hall painted a green so dark it verged on black. There was no furniture and very little light. "I just came for a photo album Kenneth borrowed," he said. "I'm picking it up for Mrs. Maple."

"Kenneth's in the other room," said the woman.

"Are you Virginia?" he asked. "Mrs. Lansing?"

She gave him a sly smile, very Alzheimery. Freddy couldn't imagine how awful this must be for Kenneth/Bobby. Had the poor guy taken up the real Kenneth's name and money and houses, planning on some distant, dreamy good life, only to find himself walled in by dementia? Had Kenneth showed up at MMC in order to *escape* dementia at home? Why didn't he just get in the car and ride off into the sunset?

But Freddy knew all too well that riding off into the sunset was harder than it sounded.

They passed through two very low, very narrow doorways, which proved that the house really was as old as it looked. The living room was painted dark mustard and had mustard-colored couches and brown plaid recliners. It made Grandma's stuff look pretty sophisticated. Every window was covered by drapes, and only one small lamp cast a little circle of light.

"Here," said the possible Virginia. "Hold this for me." She handed Freddy the statue thing. It was heavier than it looked and grubby, no surprise given the state of the house. "This way," she said.

Freddy shifted the statue. It might be two people embracing or it might be a deformed lamp base. Women always wanted you to do stuff for them. Next she'd probably ask him to fix her garbage disposal. Listen, as his grandmother would have said, this place was a vineyard in which you could labor forever.

Kenneth was lying on the floor, watching TV from the rug, like a little kid.

Freddy set the statue on the coffee table. "Kenneth?"

The woman went back the way they had come. Trotted, actually. Sprinted, maybe.

Freddy dropped to his knees.

Kenneth's head was turned sideways, and the back of his skull was covered with something like black cherry Jell-O. It took Freddy a moment to grasp that it must be clotted blood. Kenneth's hair had detached and stood up in little bloody forests. It was either a wig or he had been scalped. His eyes were open. The eyes didn't try to blink away the flecks of blood.

Freddy had never actually seen a dead body. It was way more shocking than he would have expected. He panted for a moment and then looked back at the coffee table. The heavy statue thing was grubby because it had its own share of black cherry Jell-O.

She handed me the murder weapon, thought Freddy. She wore gloves but I held it in my bare hands.

That was what she wanted me to do for her.

Take the rap.

THIRTY-SEVEN

The newcomer walked right into the kitchen, beaming.

He was Laura's height and rather pudgy. His tight button-down collar with heavy starch made his neck squash out. He wore a bright-blue bow tie, a spiffy jacket, and a scarf tossed artfully around his shoulders.

Closet let go of Laura's face and backed her into the wall of kitchen cabinets. In the music room, Ponytail scratched his head with the barrel of his gun. There might be a safety catch on the weapon, but Laura doubted that there was a safety catch in Ponytail's thinking.

"Gordon Clary," said the doctoral candidate, beaming at Closet. "I talked to Kemmy, Mrs. Maple," he said, leaning around the Closet's huge waist to make eye contact, as if he routinely found sopranos crushed by giants. "I know it's on its way back, and I'm so relieved and excited. I didn't handle things well. I went overboard, it's a tendency I have, and of course I also apologize for being short with you last Sunday. Its price is beyond dollars, and when I called back, Kemmy reconsidered and gave me permission to make appointments with the proper experts."

Oh, Gordon, thought Laura, your tempos are too fast. You shouldn't have waltzed in like this. You should have waited. You're so young. If I die, at least I've had my life. If you die, you haven't started yet. How do I get you out of here? Do I give up Freddy to save you?

But if she did tell Closet Guy how to reach Freddy, he wouldn't say "Oh, thanks for the information" and head on out. These men were here for entertainment, and the entertainment value had just doubled.

Gordon extended his hand to shake with Closet Guy.

Classical musicians, thought Laura. They're near-sighted whether they wear glasses or not. He doesn't see how scary these men are. Or perhaps he thinks they're my sons, because they are the right age and they're in my house. Perhaps he's thinking: tattoos—ponytails—creepy teeth—that's her problem. I'm just here for the manuscript.

Closet Guy ignored him, walked into the little hall, and bolted the back door.

Gordon, unfazed by the refusal to shake hands, moved deeper in the kitchen. "Gordon Clary," he greeted the Ponytail.

Ponytail Guy held the real gun in one hand and, with the thumb and first finger of his other hand, pretend-shot Gordon.

Gordon came to a halt.

Closet was back in the kitchen. "What exactly is beyond price?" His street accent was gone. He sounded like a Yale man himself.

The grunge stuff was an act, thought Laura. But then, everything about drugs is an act. Lying is part of the culture. *It still makes me so mad at you*, she thought at her dead husband. *All that lying and acting. With me! Who loved you so.*

They were evenly distributed on the limited floor space. Laura in the corner by the sink, Gordon a few paces away, and Ponytail standing between two huge crates. Closet guy filled the kitchen entrance. The grand pianos blocked the arch.

"He's referring to a manuscript," Laura told Closet, forgetting to sound British. "But it isn't here yet. We're awaiting delivery. The UPS truck should arrive shortly." Maybe so much action would deter them. Maybe they'd just go.

The Closet shook his huge head. "Nobody uses paper anymore. Manuscripts are digital."

Gordon backed away from the gun Ponytail was swinging around and positioned himself in front of Laura. He lifted his double chin and stared straight back at Closet.

Gordon, thought Laura, I wronged you. I judged you on your starched collar and your boasting. But you are a good man. You have no idea what is happening, but you've seen a gun, a crazy druggie, and the hugest piece of muscle you and I have ever encountered, and you are trying to protect me.

Fear had already filled her eyes with tears, but now she felt the hot prickle of emotional tears. Double crying, as it were.

In his fussiest voice, Gordon Clary said, "It is an historic music manuscript, handwritten long before the advent of the internet. I shall call UPS and confirm the delivery." He took his cell phone from a cute little waist holster.

The Closet simply took the phone away in a hand literally twice the size of Gordon's. They could have been different species. The thug was not a man who could play the organ or piano. His fingers wouldn't fit.

Dropping Gordon's cell phone into his shirt pocket, the Closet tapped his own.

Virginia had run out of the house and left the door ajar. She was now screaming in the front yard, trying to be heard over the whine of leaf blowers. "He killed my husband! Somebody call the police! That man killed my husband!"

Freddy could race out of the living room, run past Virginia, leap into his car, and whip out of here at high speed. Who would stop him? Not the crews with their leaf blowers. Not the neighbor with the flimsy metal rake.

But he'd given his name to Virginia. The rake woman had seen him. Freddy's fingerprints, which were not on file anywhere in the world, were on the statue thing. Very soon, his fingerprints *would* be on file, and he would be too. Filed in a jail.

Br, incarcerated by a vicious woman's vicious joke.

Shawn, incarcerated by a vicious man's vicious plan.

Freddy, incarcerated because he was an idiot, showing up in the wrong place at the wrong time.

He got slowly to his feet, staring down at the pathetic corpse.

Kenneth, he thought, you and me, we're alike. Neither one of us spotted danger, even when we knew there was a murderer around.

Did you refuse to let Virginia replace the furniture? Does she hate your hair? Is she the killer of Maude, and you decided to turn her in, so an innocent med tech wouldn't be blamed? Or are you the killer of Maude, and Virginia didn't take the news very well? Or does she like a different TV channel?

It didn't matter now. Freddy had no way out.

And the dead body in this mustard-colored room also set him up for Maude's murder. The police wouldn't care about motive, because once cops knew you made drug paraphernalia, they didn't care about anything else. You were guilty. Period.

Freddy had always known the risks of glass crime. But he would not go down for that. He would be accused of two murders.

Maude and Kenneth, dead by his hand.

People would think that?

Would his sisters stand by him? He wanted to believe that all three would charter planes, screaming, *Our brother would never do that!*

But he wasn't sure. It was incredibly painful, not to be sure of his sisters.

He took out his cell phone, a lifelong reaction to everything: when in doubt, check your phone. Yet more messages had arrived, but where Freddy was going, messages wouldn't matter.

Might as well be proactive.

He called 911.

Gordon looked into Laura's eyes, but she could send him no message, give him no information, and worse, no hope. They both looked at Ponytail, who obligingly waved the gun again.

Closet caught the motion, saw the gun for the first time, and glared. "Where did you get that?" he snapped. "What do you think you're doing? Put that down!"

Ponytail gave a silly apologetic grin and slid the gun back into his pocket.

From the other end of the house, Laura heard a tiny woof and a faint click. Somebody had come in the *front* door, which of course Laura had failed to lock. She felt almost cheerful. I'm not going deaf after all! I just get distracted. I still have excellent hearing.

It couldn't be Kemmy at the door. She was shopping or else dragging her husband to the doctor.

It wouldn't be Freddy, who had never been here and would surely recognize the car of danger, the car of Closet and Ponytail. There must be three cars here now: the red SRX, the white whatever model these two came in, and blocking their retreat would be Gordon's car, whatever he drove.

The front-door person could be the junk-run guys, but she was fairly sure they'd come to the same back door by which they had taken out the piano. Besides, they had knocked before. They wouldn't just walk in.

Whoever had come inside was advancing. She heard footsteps.

If it was reinforcements for these home invaders, there was nothing she could do about it. But what if it was a concerned neighbor? "Don't come in!" she screamed. "Get out, get out!"

Closet glared at Laura, glared at the hall, glared at the cell phone still in his hand. Even his glare was huge.

A uniformed police officer walked into the kitchen.

They were all astonished: the officer, Laura, Gordon Clary, Ponytail Guy, the Closet.

There was a moment of nothing: no breathing, no speech.

The policeman was much smaller than Closet Guy, but his uniform lent him weight and power. He was loaded with equipment, as if next he planned to climb Mount Everest.

Laura could practically read the chapters flipping through Closet Guy's mind: caught, arrested, imprisoned. Time to roll.

But Ponytail's whole face came apart, like a jigsaw falling on the floor, a mouth here, an eye there. He yanked out his little gun and aimed.

Laura stared at its little black hole. He would pull that trigger until the weapon was empty, he would empty it into all of them; their whole little row—Laura, Gordon, the policeman. She would die from a hole in her heart. *I already have a hole in my heart.*

The policeman was also young; the whole world was young but Laura. Shoot *me!* she tried to say, elbowing to the front, but Gordon Clary pinned her to the cabinets with his back.

Oh, Gordon, don't die for me. I want you to have life.

"No!" said Closet forcefully, dropping his cell, raising his huge flat hand to stop Ponytail. He stepped forward. "NO!"

The gun went off.

THIRTY-EIGHT

Freddy was still just standing there in the mustard-colored room. They had cuffed him. It was not frightening to have his hands fastened behind his back. It was more like the expected end of the road. I'm twenty-six, he thought, and it's over.

He felt bleary and only half-present.

He had that lawyer's number in his cell phone, although the cops had taken his cell; they had taken everything in his pockets, sickeningly satisfied to find a knife there. Of course it was a penknife and it was closed, but they were so smug it was like they'd found DNA.

The place was noisy: engines and sirens and crew, policemen on radios and phones. Outside, he could hear sobbing and yelling.

He remembered a line or maybe a title from some book or play he was supposed to have read in high school English and of course hadn't. *Full of sound and fury, signifying nothing.*

But the sound and fury in this room signified the end of Freddy's freedom. Like Br and Shawn, he was going to be behind a lot of bars for a lot of years with a lot of scary people. I'll be able to remember freedom, he thought, but I won't have it. Shoulda gone to Alaska while I had the chance.

A plaid recliner separated Freddy from the techs and the ambulance guys, who were hanging out until they could move Kenneth. Two uniformed women were taking crime-scene photos and videos.

He thought of Shawn's body camera. If Freddy'd been wearing one when he walked into this house, he could just play his little video and the cops would have said, "Wow, Freddy, Virginia's a piece of work, isn't she? Handing you the murder weapon and all? Gosh, Freddy, how about you go home and rest up while we carry on here?"

Home. His shop. The beads not finished, the pipes not shipped. The Box of Pain. His Instagram account and the followers who would never see another post. That guy who wanted a Freddy would never get one.

Then they were walking him outside, and he thought, This is my last outside. Smell the autumn leaves, Freddy Bell, because this is it.

He hadn't worried enough; that was his problem. There had been so many worries that they had diluted each other. And he had worried about the wrong people.

He thought of his grandmother. He couldn't visit now, let alone bring her home. *Grandma, I'm letting you down. I never meant to let you down. I'm sorry.*

The rake lady with her rake was jumping up and down, waving her cell phone. "I photographed him," she yelled, blocking Freddy's police escort. "Cell phones record the exact moment of the photo. Just before he knocked on the door, we waved at each other. And when Virginia raced out screaming, I photographed her too. She came outside less than a minute after this guy went in. Listen to me! He didn't have time to kill Mr. Lansing."

Freddy tried to process this, but the handcuffs seemed to have cut off circulation to his brain. Plus he was having a yawn attack from nerves or exhaustion.

"Why did you video this man?" the cop asked her sternly, as if photography of neighbors was against the rules in Farmington.

"Because he's cute," said the rake lady, and she grinned, and Freddy saw that she was very young. Probably the teenage daughter. The baggy blue jeans and the old sweatshirt had misled him. She held his eyes, wanting him to smile back, but Freddy's repertoire of smiles was gone.

The cops did not believe her, or they figured one minute was tons of time for Virginia to witness him bashing Kenneth and still get out of the house to scream for help.

———————

Freddy had never sat in the back of a cop car. It wasn't a privilege. He stumbled walking into the police station, maybe because it was the last threshold he had ever wanted to cross.

Everybody stood around, milling here and there, saying stuff.

Freddy felt so detached, his soul could have fallen off. He didn't listen. He kept yawning. You didn't think during a yawn; you were an animal.

They removed the cuffs. Probably you didn't need handcuffs once you were behind bars, although there weren't any bars yet. They were in some large room full of desks and computers and stuff. Bars were the next step. Everything would be a step. Roll your finger pads here, Freddy. Make your statement now, Freddy. Walk into this cell, Freddy.

"Freddy," they kept saying.

He wasn't choosing to exercise his right to remain silent. He was a man one wall away from a jail cell. He couldn't form words.

A cop got right in his face. Wayne Ames. What was he doing in Farmington? Didn't these guys keep to their own territory, like wolverines?

"Hey, Freddy. It's cool," said Wayne Ames, grinning and bouncing on his toes. "You didn't do Robert Lansing. His wife, Virginia, did. The poor guy's been dead for hours, and you couldn't have done it, just like your rake-lady friend said. Anyway, Virginia came apart pretty quick. She told us all about it. She even waved her bloody garden gloves at us. She's quite proud."

Kenneth had been dead for hours? The cops and ambulance guys must have realized that right off. So why the cuffs? Why the little trip to a police station?

Because they're cops, he thought. It entertains them.

He wondered if they gathered around when the shift changed and watched their little body-cam videos together, laughing at the people they arrested, the way Jade laughed at residents on her videos.

Chill, he told himself. Stand still, stay silent, show nothing. He massaged his wrists, although they didn't hurt. He had no cuts or bruises, not even tissue memory from those cuffs. It was just an occupation so he could look somewhere other than at cop eyes.

"And before we even asked," said Ames cheerfully, "she admitted killing Maude!"

Fat, frazzled, weird old Virginia had suffocated Maude?

"See, Maude just wouldn't die," said Wayne Ames, "even with Robert Lansing spooning his own medication into her. Virginia was tired of it. She wanted to inherit, sell their houses, and live large. She went into MMC that evening and nobody noticed her. She capitalized on it. Picked up a hand towel, suffocated Maude, walked back out, wasn't seen leaving either. She feels pretty crafty."

Freddy wanted a cigarette. And he never had gotten breakfast. Or lunch. Plus no sleep.

He wondered if Virginia was also in this building. Sadder, more frazzled, and beginning to realize what her future was.

"You and Laura Maple already figured out that Kenneth was really Robert Lansing, didn't you?" asked Wayne Ames.

I'm not participating in this reveal, thought Freddy. Old Wayne will keep talking regardless. I'm literally his captive audience.

Somebody held out a can of Coke, which wouldn't be as good as a cigarette or a joint, although cold and sparkly sounded great. But if they could get him to drink from the can and then leave it behind, they could lift his prints. He shook his head no, even though his tongue was so dry it hurt against the ceiling of his mouth.

He was suddenly intensely aware that he had not been fingerprinted. These guys knew who had killed Kenneth/Bobby and they knew who had killed Maude and they knew Philip's death was from their own negligence. They didn't need prints to rule Freddy out. He might actually leave this building without his fingerprints on file in a police department.

"The problem Robert and Virginia Lansing faced was that the real Kenneth wrote a will leaving all his money and his million-dollar house in Old Greenwich to charity. It would be nice to know how the real Kenneth died," said Wayne Ames, "but he was cremated so we never will. Robert Lansing cremated the real Kenneth under his own father's name. Then Robert took over as Kenneth. He wrote a new will, as Kenneth, and left the money to himself: Robert."

That kind of complexity was way beyond Freddy, who couldn't even manage to get Grandpa's vehicles insured. Would Kenneth/Bobby's plan even have worked?

Maybe.

Will—husband of Irene—was a lawyer. Freddy could picture Kenneth/Bobby visiting MMC to establish himself in a friendly down-home way with an attorney—Will or somebody else—ensuring that his identity as Kenneth would never be questioned. The considerate lawyer, moved by Kenneth/Bobby's loyalty and love for Maude, would have done whatever Kenneth/Bobby needed.

It was pretty sick to cremate your cousin and pretend he was your dad. Freddy thought of the thing Virginia had handed him, that she killed her husband with. Could it have been a tall, heavy urn? Was the real Kenneth actually *inside* the murder weapon that took the fake Kenneth down?

Whoa.

"Turns out when Maude was first brought to MMC, she even said this man wasn't her husband. Robert Lansing laughed right along with the staff. Apparently most memory-care residents, if they live that long, don't recognize their own family. So nobody paid any attention to Maude."

Maude had had to sit there while people said her "husband" was kind and thoughtful, visiting so often, caring so much. She would have tried to explain. *No, no, he's somebody else! Save me!*

Poor, poor Maude, surrounded by the indulgent smiles of strangers who controlled her. How many months of despair had she suffered before she drowned in dementia and no longer remembered her own complaint?

Freddy didn't want to know this stuff, think about this stuff, or follow up on this stuff. He wanted glass, which was pure. He wanted the degenerate art of pipes. Nothing Freddy ever made was going to be as degenerate as Virginia and Bobby.

"Your grandmother usually sat with Maude for meals. Maybe Kenneth didn't even bother to hide the pill he was crushing and adding to Maude's food. Maybe that's what she saw and that's why she said he was a meany beany. Anyway, Maude was a tough old bird. She didn't die and Virginia got sick of waiting."

Was Virginia really that crafty? It was possible. After all, she had gotten Freddy to hold the murder weapon. Maybe she was evil. It was equally possible that Virginia had slipped way too far down the dementia slope.

But whatever the truth about Virginia's soul, Maude had known the woman who pressed that cloth down over her face and closed strong fingers on her throat.

Not enough that her beloved husband died.

Not enough that she sank into dementia.

Not enough that she failed to convince anybody that "Kenneth" was a fake.

Her own cousin tried to kill her, and her cousin's wife pulled it off, and she knew.

"I drove your car over," said somebody, handing Freddy his own keys. "So you can leave whenever you want."

It was Shawn.

THIRTY-NINE

But it was not Gordon Clary who was hurt, nor the policeman, nor Laura.

Blood spurted out of Closet Guy. He pawed at himself, and his knees gave way. He tried and failed to grip the kitchen counter. His huge body went down slowly, like some great tree.

"Hey!" said Ponytail urgently. "Hey, not *you*. It wasn't supposed to be *you*." The pieces of his face came back together, and he was just a scared kid who needed protein instead of drugs.

This is what drugs are, thought Laura. Crazy awful things with crazy awful endings.

The policeman, who was probably just a local constable and whose experience probably consisted of shoplifters, speeders, and high school graffiti vandals, pressed his hand on the kitchen counter for leverage, vaulted over the Closet, landed on Ponytail, knocked away the weapon, and flipped Ponytail like a hamburger on a grill to cuff him.

Gordon Clary whipped out a real handkerchief and pressed it down on the gushing hole in Closet Guy. Shock had changed Closet's face. He looked far younger and rather handsome. Laura gave Gordon some dish towels because the handkerchief was already drenched. *I wronged you, Gordon. Your tempos are excellent.*

"Sorry," whispered the Closet. "My sister's kid. I'm supposed to straighten him out. Guess I didn't."

All the world is caring for family, thought Laura. Even the bad guys. Except if you're taking care of your family and saving lives, aren't you a good guy?

A second officer sprinted into the kitchen and called for backup and an ambulance. "You're not gonna die," he comforted Closet Guy. "It's in your side, probably missed vital organs. Ambulance barn is only two blocks away. They'll be here right away, and we'll get you fixed up."

"You saved us," she said to Closet Guy. "You saved all three of us."

The second constable didn't agree or didn't care. "Let's us go in the front room," he said to Laura and Gordon. "They're gonna need all this kitchen space to get a stretcher in, and it isn't going to be easy getting a guy this big on a stretcher at all, let alone maneuver it out of here. You got some tight spaces going on." He took Laura's arm.

Laura felt weirdly like a hostess, as if she should say goodbye to Closet Guy, maybe add, "I'll tell Freddy you called." Again she said, so that it would be on record, "He stepped up so we wouldn't get shot. He saved us." She picked up her cell phone, knowing they wouldn't let her back in the kitchen and she would need her phone, need its company and maybe even have to read a digital book instead of a real one if this went on for hours.

In the parlor, Laura sank down on the little sofa. Gordon sat beside her. Laura looked at the phone in her hand. It was Closet Guy's.

"So what happened here anyway?" asked the constable. He looked sixteen to Laura. "This sure isn't what we expected."

"What *did* you expect?" asked Gordon severely. "Were you following those two men? Shouldn't you have been more careful about traipsing in?"

"We sure should've. But that's not why we were here."

Everything the police need is in this phone, thought Laura. Closet Guy's name. Whether he's good at Candy Crush or reads the *Wall Street Journal*. His sister's name, the one worried about her druggie kid. And definitely, everything about Freddy.

"See, Mrs. Maple's daughter, Lindsay, called the station and asked us to do a house check. She'd had an upsetting call from her mother, couldn't reach her mother after trying for a while, and was afraid Mrs. Maple was going to hurt herself. A relative worries about suicide, the police come right over. It's routine." He smiled at Laura. "We were picturing some sad, lonely old lady, and I hadn't finished my coffee yet so I stayed in the car while my partner went in to talk to her, and when I heard gunfire, I figured it was *her*, trying to kill herself. I sure wasn't thinking that she was a tough little broad holding off home invaders."

Laura was no tough little broad. She had cowered. It was Gordon Clary who had been brave, and Closet Guy who had been bravest.

What would Closet have done if she had continued to say nothing about Freddy?

Or was that moot? Maybe all that mattered was what really happened. And what really happened was Closet saved Laura, Gordon, and a policeman. He offered himself.

Greater love hath no man than this: that he lay down his life for his friends.

Laura was weeping again.

"It's the shock," said the constable comfortingly. "Don't be scared. They're both in custody and we're here. It's over now."

When there was no time to think, consider, or plan for the future, Closet Guy did the right thing, thought Laura. It will always count. And back when I had time to think, when I had *years* to think, I did the wrong thing. That will always count too.

"You must have seen that there were three vehicles in the drive," said Gordon disapprovingly.

The young constable shrugged. "I guess we figured that the daughter also called relatives, friends, neighbors, whatever, to check on the mom, and they got here before us."

It sank in. *Lindsay had called.*

I've had my cell turned off, thought Laura. She couldn't reach me. She cared enough to call the police. Closet saved our lives, but Lindsay also saved our lives.

"She's on her way, your daughter," the cop said. "I guess she was right to worry."

Lights flashed everywhere as the cars of volunteer firemen and ambulance crew filled the rest of the drive and pulled up on the grass. People poured in, calling instructions. Crew trotted through the front door pushing a big metal gurney down to the kitchen.

Lindsay is on her way. I needed her. And she's coming.

Laura's fingers were wrapped around a cell phone, but it wasn't hers. I can't use this one instead, she thought. I don't even know Lindsay's number; I just press the contact. "If you could do something for me," she said, "I would be so grateful. My handbag is on the kitchen counter."

"I'll get it," said Gordon immediately.

"No. You two stay out of the kitchen," said the constable. "I'll get it for you, Mrs. Maple." He jogged out, jogged back, handed her the large sagging bag, and said, "Do you know who those two men are? And why they chose your house?"

It was puzzling. Laura had found Freddy easily enough. Why hadn't these guys?

Maybe they were stupid. Or they'd already been to Freddy's grandmother's house and he wasn't home. Maybe Laura was a last resort. Or maybe, she thought, it's all about leverage. They need him for something. Maybe thought he'd obey them in order to save me.

And Freddy would. He was that kind of person.

This shooting, this home invasion, would become a long-term event. There would be a trial, unless these two pled guilty to whatever charges there were. But whatever happened to Closet and Ponytail, Laura would be asked many questions by many officials.

Laura's handbag was on her lap. Its many zippered divisions were unzipped because she could never remember what she stashed where. She slid the Closet's phone inside a pocket and closed it up. She dried her cheeks on her sleeve, took out her own cell phone, turned it on, and called Lindsay.

"Mom!" shrieked Lindsay. "Are you all right? How could you do that to me? You scared me to pieces! I'm still an hour away. Is somebody with you? I need to know somebody is with you."

"My friend Gordon is with me. But I need *you*." Her voice broke. "Lindsay, I need you so."

"What's going on?" Lindsay demanded.

"A home invasion. You foiled it. One person was shot but the ambulance is here and he'll probably be all right. I'm safe."

"What? Mother, be serious!"

"I am. Lindsay, I love you. Now talk to the police officer, okay? Because I'm still shaky. And drive carefully. Don't speed."

FORTY

Shawn was wearing a suit. His pale-blue shirt had an oxford collar with stiff points and buttonholes, and he was wearing a tie. Freddy had never seen Shawn dressed like that. Wouldn't have thought Shawn owned spiffy clothes like that.

Shawn was standing with the cops. He was not their prisoner. He was their colleague. Freddy knew absolutely that Shawn was sending him a message through those bright, eager cop eyes. But what was the message? Freddy was forced to break his silence. "I thought you were in jail in Norwich."

"Sort of. I was in uniform when Auburn cornered me. Do you know her? She's got a dress shop in Middletown. I let down my guard, and next thing I know, she's got a knife the size of a city block she's going to use on my dog if I don't do what she says. So I tell her I'll do anything, just let Snap go. Snap doesn't even try to bite, the one time it would be useful. It turns out that Auburn's a dealer, and she wants me on her team, because—well, I think this is it; the whole thing's a little muddy—I think they needed a dirty cop."

Gary Leperov had been telling the truth? He and Doc hadn't threatened Snap? It was Auburn all along? *I'm your goddamn friend*, Gary had said irritably. Could that be true?

How had Shawn ended up with Auburn at all, let alone in Norwich? Norwich was nowhere near Middletown. It was across the Connecticut River and north, where it felt like another state.

"But I was in uniform, see, and I have a body camera. So everything that happens in front of me is on video."

Auburn was cooked. She hadn't just made a mistake; she'd made it with a cop, when she knew he was a cop. Dealing must be like anything else: you needed to learn step by step or you'd get your fingers caught in the lathe.

Would Auburn really have sliced the dog's paws off? Freddy doubted it, if only because she seemed too fastidious for all that blood. On the other hand, she'd been holding a machete.

But why take Snap from the Way Back? Maybe Auburn figured if it worked with Shawn, it would work with Freddy. She was probably right, but what could she need Freddy for?

Maybe nothing. Auburn was a carnivore. She liked victims.

Why had she driven to his house that night? Had she come to accomplish something and then decided against it? Had she been reconnoitering? Did he even have Snap yet when she and her Cube drove on the grass?

He needed to cut back on his weed intake. His short-term memory was going. He was dizzy from facts and guesses spinning like hot glass out of control. He put a hand out to steady himself on the edge of a desk and remembered just in time not to touch anything. When he looked at Shawn again, the bright message was still there, still impossible to read.

And then Freddy thought, Auburn didn't need to look for a dirty cop. Shawn's already dirty. He buys herb for me and maybe for other guys. I bet he buys from her.

If the cops had arrested Auburn, she was probably out again, because she would have a serious criminal lawyer, not an old jowly dude who was friends with George Burnworth. Would she give Shawn up? Probably not. Auburn would muscle through without yielding. And she'd still have her dirty cop.

The room where they were standing had no windows, but it faced another room that did have a window to the parking lot and the road beyond. It was getting dark out. Streetlamps had come on.

It's still the same day, thought Freddy, even though I can't remember which one.

Another cop, very casual, like it didn't matter, said, "How do you and Shawn here know each other, Freddy?"

Shawn needs me out of here. He handed me my car keys so I'll drive away. He wants to stay a cop and wear a uniform and have a body camera so he can entrap everybody. Or maybe he wants his suit and tie so he can be a detective. Then he'd be a super useful dirty cop.

Freddy shrugged like the simple-minded stoner he was. "He went to high school with my sisters. Small towns. You kind of know everybody." Except I don't know them at all, he thought. I am the worst judge of character there is.

He wondered about Shawn's character. How long had Shawn let his mother suffer before he told her he wasn't in jail, hadn't been in trouble to start with, because the video of him in Norwich had cleared him, not convicted him?

"Let me fill you in," said Wayne Ames, "on what's happening to your friend Laura Maple. Home invasion. Couple of thugs attacked Mrs. Maple."

Thugs? Doc and Skinny? No!

Freddy held his car keys so tightly they imprinted on his palm. "What do you mean—attacked? Is she hurt?"

"My understanding is that she'll be fine."

Who could be fine after Doc and Skinny slapped you around? Who could be fine, knowing your friend Freddy started it and could have prevented it and didn't bother? "What hospital is she in? I have to go see her."

"I just told you she didn't get hurt. One of the mutts got shot by his own partner. He's headed for the hospital; the other one's at the state trooper barracks in Westbrook."

They *were* armed, he thought. Doc shot Skinny. How could that happen? Doc wouldn't shoot. It's like the whole point of martial arts. You use your body.

"We thought you could identify them for us," said Wayne Ames.

You have Doc and Skinny in custody. Doc is a felon. You identified him already. This is just more cop lying to get me talking.

Wayne Ames held out a tablet with a photograph of Doc lying on a stretcher looking so defeated and young that Freddy almost didn't recognize him. *Doc* was the one who'd been shot?

Ames slid his finger across the screen and brought up a photograph of Skinny, looking frightened and even thinner and about sixteen.

Freddy shook his head, meaning, Can't help with the photographs. "You're sure Mrs. Maple is okay?"

Ames nodded.

"And the guy who got shot? How bad is it?"

"Actually, it was kind of heroic," said Shawn. "The big guy jumped in front of Mrs. Maple and some other people to protect them. So he's a mutt, but he saved lives."

Making Doc a good bad guy. Or maybe a good good guy, because once you saved a life, wasn't that your category?

Freddy felt like a dementia patient. Everything was foggy and nothing added up. He was completely sure of only one thing. He had to get out of here. "You guys seem to have everything under control. I gotta check on my grandmother and Mrs. Maple."

He could still visit his grandmother! He was not going to jail! He was free.

And Shawn—he wasn't in jail. But he wasn't free either if Auburn ended up owning him.

Freddy's stuff lay on a table. Nobody stopped him, so Freddy dropped his penknife and change into his pockets. When he held his phone in his hand again, it was as comforting as a friend.

"We'll talk in the morning," said Wayne Ames. "Your house? That good for you?"

Freddy had a lawyer now, in a cool brick building, and if he had to talk with cops, it would be in his lawyer's office. Freddy couldn't remember the guy's name. He looked it up on his phone. "We'll meet there," he said to the detective. "That good for you?"

Ames was irritated, which was nice; anything Freddy could do to annoy a cop was nice. He removed the kennel receipt from his wallet, handed it to Shawn, and walked out.

Nobody stopped him.

Nobody followed him.

Totally amazing.

It was the worst kind of fall weather. Bleak, raw, cold. The half-bare trees were ugly and the street was scruffy. But Freddy was free, which meant that all weather, all trees, and all sidewalks were beautiful. He spotted the Avalon and walked over, his thoughts breaking like glass on pavement.

God, he prayed, *take care of Mapes. Take care of Doc. Be easy on Kenneth. He did visit Maude all the time. Although I guess he actually visited in order to shorten her life. Well, I don't really know that, and I don't know about Virginia either. And what they did to Maude won't ever be okay. So whatever. Use your judgment.*

Freddy sucked in damp, cold air, glad not to be a judge on earth or in heaven and sick thinking about the judgment Mapes rightly would pass on him.

He hunted around the front seat and didn't turn up any cigarettes.

Where was he right now? He brought up the GPS to see how to get on the interstate. Which interstate did he want? The north/south or the east/west? Was it time to head for the horizon?

No. It was time for food. He was starving. He wanted grease and salt.

GPS kindly supplied him with a nearby McDonald's. Freddy pulled into the drive-through lane, ordered, moved up a window, paid, moved up a window, and took his bag of burgers and fries on his lap along with his very large Coke and chocolate shake. He slid into a parking space, drank deep of the Coke, slurped some chocolate shake, and had his first satisfying chomp of burger.

Then he looked at his contacts list, took a deep breath, and called Mapes.

"Freddy?"

"Mapes, I'm sorry. It was all my fault. Are you okay? I mean, I know you can't be okay, but—"

"I am, actually, Freddy. My daughter is here with me. And that huge man? I don't know his real name. He saved my life."

"I heard," said Freddy. "I'm glad. Really glad. Mapes, I'm very sorry they were there at all. I think what happened is, when I got in your car that day, they got your plate number. I was a jerk."

"Jerkdom can be solved," she said softly. "Death, not so much. I'm alive and my daughter is here and I'm happy." Her voice adjusted to its usual bustling self. "We'll discuss things when we're at MMC. Will I see you tomorrow?"

Freddy was amazed he even *had* a tomorrow. "Tomorrow," he agreed. What a great word. Full of hope and choice.

"Good." She hung up.

Freddy salted his fries, opened a ketchup pack, had two bites, and made his next call.

"Dude," said the Leper.

"Heads up, Gary. Bad stuff is going to trickle down. Doc got shot by his little sidekick. He's in police custody. They both are."

"*Doc was shot?* Doc doesn't carry a gun. What sidekick?"

"I don't have any details. But they think he'll be okay. But they'll have Doc's cell phone so pretty soon they'll have your name."

"Freddy. Seriously? My name isn't Gary Leperov. I'm two layers away from that. The question is, are you safe?"

Freddy had been amazed so many times today that finding out Gary Leperov wasn't even Gary Leperov had less impact that it might have. "I guess so."

"Good. What hospital would Doc be in? I gotta get on that."

"I think Middletown. But maybe New Haven."

"Thanks. I'll see you at BABE." He disconnected before Freddy could argue.

Freddy dipped a french fry in ketchup and his cell rang. There were *more* people out there he had to talk to?

It was Kara.

He vaguely remembered not bothering with her messages. How remote her world was, all those kids and horses and the great husband and the carpool line. He was surprised to hear himself say softly, maybe even affectionately, "Hey, Karrie Darrie." He braced himself for a lecture on how feckless he was, not responding to her previous messages. And he *was* feckless, but if he'd had a camera taping him right now, he'd lift his chin, like those guys who lived above the Arctic Circle, and proclaim, *I'm free.*

Not just free of cops.

Free of guilt.

Freddy, who had done everything wrong, felt no nonvisit guilt and not even any Mapes guilt.

"I'm here, Freddy!" cried Kara.

"Here?" he repeated.

"We landed. Are you in the cell-phone lot? Tell me you're in the cell-phone lot, Freddy."

Uh-oh. Something to feel guilty about after all. "Something came up, Kara. I'm about half an hour away."

"Oh, half an hour, that's not bad," said Kara.

She came, thought Freddy. It's all about actually doing something. You can't walk on by. You gotta stop and help.

Doc, of all people. He did the most. Knowing he'll pay the biggest price.

And Kara. She got on a plane and came. She thinks Grandma and I need her, and you know what? I think so too.

"Karrie Darrie?" he said. "I'm really glad you're here."

Reading Group Guide

1. Freddy doesn't mind being "Arthur" on occasion, because at least then his grandma still knows he's family. How would you feel in his place? Are there any other circumstances where you might set aside your identity to preserve someone else's comfort or happiness?

2. Freddy considers his own biggest flaw to be "failing to think." Do you think he's right? How is this failure present throughout the story?

3. Laura struggles to consider herself worthy of forgiveness or trust. Do you think she's too hard on herself? If she were your friend, what advice would you give her?

4. Many of Freddy's problems come from selling pipes to make more money than he could with beads or other glass projects. How do we value art as consumers? How do artists know the value of their work?

5. Do you ever feel like you're trying to please someone who isn't there? Are your experiences similar to Freddy's ongoing quest to make his mother proud?

6. Laura's natural nosiness leads her to take pictures of Maude's records at MMC. How does she justify her actions to herself? Do you think that justification is good enough? Where do you draw the line between privacy and safety?

7. None of the characters are who they seem to be at first. Which characters were you most surprised by? Who did you find most sympathetic?

8. Freddy's sisters constantly assume that he doesn't have any responsibilities because they don't take his career seriously. What are the consequences of that assumption? If you've been in a similar situation, how did you handle it?

A Conversation
with the Author

Why did you decide to write Freddy's story?

When my own mother was in dementia care, I was struck by
the deep goodness of the staff and the constant, loving attendance
of so many families. Dementia is horrifying for the patient and for
the people who love her, but it's a privilege to be able to visit and
comfort and hug and read to her. My mother's courage and constant
good cheer were beautiful. I wanted to tell the rough and cruel story
of dementia.

If you are the family of a dementia patient, you face sacrifice,
sorrow, and above all, a decision: the decision not to abandon somebody just because that person's mind abandoned her. Not everybody
visits or cares. I wanted to write about somebody very unlikely,
somebody you would never expect to do his best and make the hard-
est sacrifices: Freddy. I wanted love, because it's love that keeps
families close in these really lousy circumstances.

Which character do you most relate to?

I'm very similar to Laura in many ways. I have owned smashed
brass, had a parlor pump organ and three pianos, and did indeed
live on Magna Lane where the extended Ives family summered. As
a church organist and member of quite a few concert choirs over
the years, I created a woman I knew well. But Laura *did* abandon
her mother, a decision I came across only once in real life, and it
was wrenching. I wondered how that family dealt with it later—
whether it bothered them or whether they shrugged, as they did
over their person.

You include some pretty specific details about Freddy's lamp-work process. How did you research glasswork? Have you ever tried it yourself?

I have a Freddy, of course, or I could never have written this book. My Freddy is a lampworker who talked to me for days about what he does, where he does it, and why he does it. This is his vocabulary, his attitude, his studio. That was yet another privilege—getting close to an existence so removed from my own.

What's on your reading list these days?

For my own reading, I like high action mysteries and I like history. I read mysteries by the armload. If there's no action, I set it down. Stuff has to happen. I am working my way through the Louise Penny, the Sarah Shaber (both series), and the Daniel Silva books, in order. History for me is a slow read, a completely different occupation from mystery reading. My two histories at the moment are Erik Larson's *The Splendid and the Vile* and Valerie Hansen's *The Year 1000*. I like to have a few books open to the next page in every room of the house, so I can start in immediately, slouching down on the nearest comfy chair or sofa. I like reading several books at a time. You savor an exciting chapter, but instead of racing on, you switch to history.

About the Author

Photo by Greg Douglas

Caroline B. Cooney is the bestselling author of more than ninety suspense, mystery, and romance novels for teenagers, which have sold over fifteen million copies and are published in several languages. *The Face on the Milk Carton* has sold over three million copies and was made into a television movie. Her books have won many state library awards and are on many book lists, such as the New York Public Library's annual teen picks. Caroline grew up in Old Greenwich, Connecticut, and spent most of her life on the shoreline of that state but is now in South Carolina near her family. She has three children and four grandchildren. She was a church organist for many years and accompanied the choirs at her children's schools.

DON'T MISS
BEFORE SHE WAS HELEN,

another quirky mystery from international bestselling author Caroline B. Cooney!

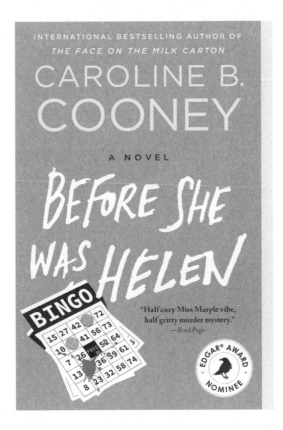